PRAISE FOR
"THE WILLOW WEEPS FOR US"
SUZEY INGOLD

PUBLISHED IN *SUMMER LOVE: AN LGBTQ COLLECTION*
BY DUET, AN IMPRINT OF INTERLUDE PRESS

"Suzey Ingold's "The Willow Weeps for Us," about two English young men who fall in love on the brink of WWII, is a particularly tender tale with many dreamy scenes"

—*Publishers Weekly*

"This gentle romance has the depth and grandness of the era imbued in the glorious scenery and decadent descriptions. With a river punt, pallets of strawberries and piano song, this is a gay Little Love Song and a step out of time."

—*CharlieInABook blog*

D0167125

SPEAKEASY

SPEAKEASY

Suzey Ingold

interlude press • new york

interlude press • new york

"It was an age of miracles, it was an age of art, it was an age of excess, and it was an age of satire."

—*F. Scott Fitzgerald*

CH. 1

"Son," his father says as he leaves the townhouse that morning. "Son, a man is not defined by the school he attends or the merits he earns. A man is defined by the choices he makes."

His father smiles, then. His fingernails dig into Heath's shoulder, making him wince. "I know you'll make the right one," he finishes, and dismisses him after Heath's assurance that he will be back in time for lunch.

Heath lets out a breath. June 29, 1927: a week since his twenty-first birthday. The sun is warm on the back of his neck as the soles of his shoes smack gently against the sidewalk. He slows his pace; he had all but dashed from the house, keen to get out from under the microscopic gaze of his father and mother that has lingered since he returned to the city.

A graduate now, he twists the ring on his finger, stamped with the Yale seal. As his father wore, too, and his father before him. The Johnson men have been attending Yale since the middle of the last century. Economics or law are the only acceptable choices of study for people like them—according to his father, anyway. Heath chose to major in the former, if only because he couldn't bear the idea of becoming a goddamn *lawyer*. A minor in philosophy because what his father didn't know wouldn't kill him.

Heath idles down Fifth Avenue, breathing in the cocktail of fresh-cut grass and motor oil from the busier Madison one block over. He's missed the city. New Haven is quaint and small, and he scarcely had to worry about having his toes run over by a speeding taxicab driver. But New York, Manhattan—it's his home. It's been four long years since he spent more than just the summer or a Christmas break in the city where he grew up.

He steps into the park, though the sun is steadily moving higher into the sky and he knows the air will be more stifling beneath the trees. July is just around the corner, and he can feel it. July in the city means his shirt sticking to his spine, his hair slicked back as much with sweat as with pomade by mid-afternoon. He already longs for fall and the cooler months to come.

His family's standard reaction to the heat is to pack their bags and go to Long Island, where a pleasant, steady breeze will blow through the big house with its wide windows: a different world from this, where the heat gets stuck between ever-taller buildings and settles, thick and oppressive, from July until early September.

His mother, Agnes, complains of headaches and sickness from the heat already; his father, William, makes no comment himself. He takes to spending some of his afternoons at home rather than at the office, however. He stands by the open window with a glass of whiskey, blotting his red forehead with a handkerchief, sweat beading at his temples.

William and Agnes are fondly known as the Duke and Duchess within their social circle and the household: titles earned from a summer's game of Murder Mystery when Heath was just a child which have stuck fast ever since. If the city of Manhattan were host to its own nobility, William and Agnes Johnson would be it—so William's late brother, Ted, used to tell Heath.

William wears his age like a medal of honor. Heath has never known his father without the lines etched into his forehead and the thick curl of his mustache over his upper lip. His shoulders have begun to stoop a little in recent years, however and his waistline is a bit plumper since he turned fifty.

Agnes, for all that she ages, hides it behind a mask of face powders and expensive perfumes. She is younger than William by several years—something she likes to tell to anyone who will listen. It's her darker hair that Heath has inherited, but the green of his eyes is from his father; his mother's are a light shade of blue.

The Duke and Duchess stayed in the city in part to welcome Heath home after his graduation ceremony but mostly for his sister, Amelia, who is younger by three years. Amelia is adamant that she spend her summer finding herself a suitable gentleman to be courted by with the Duchess helping to ensure the emphasis on *suitable*. Stubborn to a fault, Amelia refuses to leave for Long Island until such a man has been found, and neither the Duke nor the Duchess feel comfortable leaving her in Manhattan to fend for herself.

"I won't be by myself," she protested flippantly when their parents expressed their concerns. "Heath will be here."

"Heath has his own future to think about, Amelia," William replied. "We'll stay here until you've sorted out all this nonsense."

"Now, William, it's hardly nonsense. Amelia's future is just as important as Heath's."

"I didn't say it wasn't, my dear, simply that I can't take one more afternoon in this house listening to you bicker over the merits of a boy from the East Coast against a boy from the West Coast. God forbid you forget the middle states!" He threw his hands up in exasperation. "I'm going to see a man about a dog," he muttered and promptly left, to return later into the day in far better spirits—and smelling of them, too.

Heath doesn't mind Long Island, although it never seems quite like New York to him. In Manhattan, he sees friends; he attends dinners and sits in Midtown clubs until closing. On Long Island, he reads and usually has to be woken where he's dozed off on the couch before dinner with his family.

If there is one thing Heath can't stand about passing time at their house in Cove Neck, it's the Duchess's persistent attempts to have him court Mr. and Mrs. Porter's daughter, Louise. The Porters join them for almost every dinner by mid-season, whether at their house or at the Johnsons'. "Isn't it funny," the Duchess preens. "Isn't it funny that the table is always laid for Louise and Heath to sit next to one another? Isn't it sweet?"

Louise is a lovely girl, with fair hair and a rather endearing crooked tooth that Heath knows her to be awfully ashamed of. But she's dull as dust and laughs as though she has something stuck up her nose. Heath just doesn't have the heart to tell either her or his mother that he's not at all interested in courting her, let alone going as far as marriage.

So he sits through the dinners and lets her curl her ankle around his when they move to the porch for dessert, all the while hoping silently that some other man might take a liking to her and take her off his hands once and for all.

Heath stops when he finds a patch of grass shaded by an overhanging tree. He'll get quite the row if he comes back with dirt on his trousers, but he'll take the chance. Carefully seating himself on the grass, he tucks his ankles one over the other and leans back on the flats of his palms. He wishes he'd thought to bring a book. He thinks about the Nietzsche volume sitting on his nightstand.

A couple of girls walk past his shaded spot on the grass with their arms linked as they stroll leisurely. They glance at him from beneath the brims of their sisal cloche hats; they nod at him politely as they pass. He sends them a smile that dimples his cheeks in return.

"Good morning, ladies," he calls to them, for he is nothing if not a gentleman. Although Amelia would probably protest, were she there, that she prefers not to be greeted by every egg sitting in Central Park.

But these women's smiles widen. They exchange a look that he's clearly not meant to see. "Morning, mister," the shorter of them replies. "I do hope you're not going get grass stains on those Oxford Bags, or heaven help your wife!"

Heath chooses not to correct her. "I'll be careful. I didn't plan to linger, anyhow."

They bid him a good day and continue on the path toward the ponds. It's getting steadily hotter, and the humidity increases with the temperature. The heat can make some hot-headed—Amelia and the Duke share that tendency—but it never affects Heath in that way. It can make him lethargic, or uncomfortable, but it doesn't make his temper rise. Little does, he supposes; his demeanor is naturally calmer than that of his father and sister.

He rises from the grass after a few moments pass; his forearms are stiff from leaning his weight against them at an odd angle. He walks back with a little more purpose than before and stops only to buy a newspaper from a street vendor near the house. He thanks the man and slips the paper under one arm as he takes the steps two at a time up to the front door.

Martha, the housekeeper, lets him in and promises him with a warm wink that there's fresh, cool lemonade in the living room. "You'd best wash the dirt from your hands first, though," she chastises in an affectionate fashion. He sets the paper down in the hall and promptly heeds her advice before he joins his family. The Duchess would never react quite so warmly.

They're not alone, however; a fourth figure is silhouetted where the bright sun streams through the window.

"Heath, it's about time. You didn't mention Francis would be calling." The Duchess raises an eyebrow pointedly.

"He didn't know." Frankie turns and grins before he marches forward to hug Heath tightly.

"Good old Frankie David," Heath laughs. "I thought you were in the South with your parents?"

Frankie makes a face, discreetly enough that Heath's family doesn't see. "You know how I feel about the South, Heathcliff," he mutters. The familiar nickname makes Heath's grin widen. Frankie majored in economics with him at Yale, graduating alongside him, class of 1927. "I'm sorry I missed your birthday last week."

Heath shakes his head and pours himself a glass of lemonade. "Don't be. It's good to see you." It was a quiet affair, twenty-one ushered in without unnecessary pomp or circumstance. His parents bought him a gold-plated pocket watch with his initials, HMJ, carved into the back, and Amelia gave him a leather-bound notebook that, she whispered over dinner, was meant for his own philosophical musings. Heath wouldn't claim that he brimmed with profound ideas, but it seemed personal and thoughtful when Amelia could as often be careless and brash.

"I wanted to take you out later, as a belated birthday gift." Frankie looks over to the Duke and Duchess. "As long as I'm not interrupting anything, of course."

"You're not." The Duchess fans herself as she looks out of the far windows. "I'll likely to take to my bed after lunch to avoid the worst of this heat. You'll stay to eat with us, Francis." It's decidedly more a command than an offer.

"Of course." Frankie is effortlessly polite, when need be.

Heath thinks of the boy he first met four years ago this coming fall. Younger, of course, rounder than he is now where he stands before Heath, his hands resting in the pockets of his pants. Frankie started running track in sophomore year and it did a world of good for his focus and drive at Yale as much as for his physique. And for Frankie—Francis—the fact that it wasn't what his parents pictured for him made it all the more appealing. They'd far rather he spent his free hours on more studious activities: fewer tennis shoes, more textbooks.

Frankie was Heath's first friend at college and certainly his closest. Heath made a promise to the Duke to work hardest the first fortnight of his freshman year, to not get distracted by parties or girls or campus life, and he kept that promise. He sat in the library night after night, blocking out the sounds of merriment that passed by under the window.

On the night they met, Frankie was not there to study. Frankie was there because he had been dared by Mark Tanner—a snarly-faced freshman whom Heath had the displeasure of encountering almost every day for four years thanks to their adjacent dorms—to take a whizz in the stacks of the Greek philosophers.

Heath, lifting his nose from the book and blinking his eyes, which were weary from reading so late, heard what could only be the popping of buttons, obvious in the otherwise quiet library. Ignoring his instinct to sit put and stay quiet, he allowed curiosity to get the better of him. Stepping silently to the end of the stack, he peered around the edge in time to catch Frankie having some difficulty producing, and fixed him with such an appalled stare that Frankie buttoned himself back up.

Rather than point out the obvious about what he'd been about to do, Heath handed Frankie a copy of Plato's Socratic dialogues and returned to his table. Frankie took the seat next to him without invitation and propped it open.

"I'm an economics major," he told him, opening the book all the same. "Francis David. You can call me Frankie."

"Heath." He smiled but didn't take his eyes off the volume propped in front of him. "Coincidentally, I am, too—an economics major. But you look as though you could do with a lesson or two on morality."

Frankie rose, then. He walked over to the literature section and skimmed the titles until he selected one from a lower shelf and brought it back with him. *Wuthering Heights*. "'If he loved with all the powers of his puny being, he couldn't love as much in eighty years as I could in day,'" he quoted. He pushed the book over to Heath with a sheepish smile before he turned back to the Plato. "I'd like to minor in English literature, if I can."

Although Heath's name had nothing at all to do with Brontë's tortured hero, the nickname stuck. Later, Heath became accustomed to being greeted by a booming cry of "Heathcliff!" across the main quad in the brisk New Haven mornings.

They sat together for the rest of the night. When they eventually emerged from the library, an irritated Mark Tanner sat alone on the bottom step of the entrance, shivering in the cool, dark air.

"Must have been a mighty long piss," Mark sneered, lighting a cigarette with shaking fingertips.

Heath did not relate such a story to the Duke and Duchess; rather, he allowed them the sweeter, albeit blind, belief that the two met in a study group for their first economics project of the fall. They've met Frankie only once or twice, and Heath's never met Frankie's parents. Frankie paints a picture of them, in their big Savannah house, that sounds too elaborate to be true: liquor and barn dances and his father being foul-mouthed to his neighbors. Heath has told him, more than once, that he should write a novel of it all, which makes Frankie guffaw and protest that, in their narcissism, they would enjoy that far too much.

"Heath." The Duchess's eyebrows are pinched into a frown, the one she wears when she's frustrated with him. "Darling, please. Go and wash for lunch. I can still see dirt on your palms, Heath Maximilian."

Frankie slips out with him and ducks to whisper into his ear as they take the hallway to the right. "Now, Heathcliff, whatever have you been doing to get so downright filthy?"

Heath huffs out a breath and flicks Frankie's ear with his finger. "Don't you start, now. This house is bad enough without you taking on the role of a third parent."

"Come away with me." Frankie says it casually, reminiscent of late night conversations in the dorms. They had talked of travel to Europe, to explore England's rolling pastures and the French Riviera, to drink wine in Venice and see the Acropolis in Athens. It is a fantasy, better left in one's imagination than spilled over into reality.

"You make it sound so easy," Heath mourns, scrubbing his palms together beneath the stream of water. "Why not the whole world?

Someone call Phileas Fogg, fire up the steamer!" He shakes his head and shuts off the tap.

Heath looks into the mirror above the sink and observes the two of them where they stand side by side. Frankie is taller and broader than he, with his fair hair swept back across his head. His blue eyes are narrowed. Heath fiddles with the collar of his shirt and then sweeps a hand over his jet-black hair.

"Don't futz around." Frankie's reflection turns to him.

Heath purses his thin lips.

"We could do it. You said it yourself, you don't know what you want to do, and your father's only given you until fall to decide. Decide to come away and you have six months—a year? Maybe longer."

"Life isn't fiction, Frankie. At least, not for most of us." Heath hears the tinkling of the bell being rung for lunch at the other end of the hall. "Not a word of Europe over lunch, that's all I ask."

Frankie's mouth tightens into a thin line. He doesn't consent, but he doesn't say he won't oblige, either, so Heath has to make do with that and hope for the best. He doesn't doubt that if Frankie wants to go, Frankie will go. Heath himself certainly has the means to, the motivation to put an entire ocean between him and his family and his home life, and little concern for his father's wishes for his future career as a stockbroker. Perhaps he'd do well to be a little more like Frankie David.

Heath holds out his hands for the Duchess to inspect when he walks into the dining room. She nods her approval and touches Heath's wrist in a gesture of affection. He sits to Amelia's right, across from Frankie, with the Duke and Duchess at either end of the table.

"How was your walk this morning, son?" The Duke breaks off a chunk of bread and pops it into his mouth, then chews on it slowly; crumbs stick in his mustache.

"Satisfying, thank you, sir."

The Duke looks somewhat displeased. Perhaps he hoped for something akin to "enlightening" rather than "satisfying." Enlightening enough that Heath may have made his decision for the fall. "And you, Francis? Have you made your arrangements for after the summer? Or are you as indecisive as our Heath here?" The Duke titters. "Although why he's so torn up on a decision like this escapes me. A job, a future career laid out and waiting, and he can't quite *decide* how to say yes. Is that it, Heath?"

Heath clears his throat and fiddles with the silverware. "Something like that, sir," he replies lightly, although it doesn't seem as though his father is in a joking mood.

The Duchess touches her fingers to his wrist again, but this time with less fondness. "Those serve a purpose other than to be played with, Heath, please." He draws his hands into his lap and twists his fingers together tightly.

When Heath looks up and catches Frankie's eye, he sees a hardened gaze. If his stories are anything to go by, Frankie would have overturned a table before he'd let his parents chastise and scold him.

"I can't say I've quite made up my mind yet either, sir." Frankie splays his hands with a carefree grin. "There's a whole world out there. More possibilities than one could imagine. I want to be sure I've considered as many as my mind can handle." He taps a finger to his temple before he takes a swig from his water glass.

The Duke, scratching beneath his nose, looks perturbed by this idea. "Not so taken by the South? There are plenty of opportunities here in Manhattan for a man in your position."

"Oh, sir, don't get me wrong, I love this city as if it were my own, but I may cast my net farther than just New York."

Heath kicks the toe of his shoe into Frankie's ankle. To his credit, Frankie barely flinches and smiles tightly in Heath's direction.

"Young men and their ideals." The Duke's smile has disappeared, but fortunately for both Heath's nerves and Frankie's ankles, the food is served and acts as a distraction.

A silence settles as they begin to eat. The taxicabs roar and stutter their way down Fifth; the sound reaches them from the street. It is like a lullaby to Heath, the heartbeat of a city he knows as well as he knows himself. His mother clearly doesn't agree; she twitches as someone whistles out on the street. Perhaps she misses the quiet of Elizabethtown, where she grew up, even if she's been in New York for as long as she's known the Duke.

Theirs is a story he thinks of as a fairy tale, perhaps because she used to tell it to him as a bedtime story when he was a child. "Please, Mama!" he would beg, little hands tugging at her larger one with exactly the kind of energy he was not supposed to have at bedtime. "Mama, tell me the story of you and Papa when you were young and in love."

"We're still young and in love, baby. We'll always be young and in love." She smiled and laid her hand over his dark hair, wild and similar to her own. "Once upon a time, there was a girl called Agnes, and for her eighteenth birthday her parents took her to New York City for the very first time. She'd never been to a city like New York before, loud and dirty!" His mother gasped, as though it were the most outrageous thing one could imagine. Her fingers tickled Heath's ribs until he was giggling and breathless, squealing for her to "Stop, Mama, stop!"

"So, Agnes. Agnes wasn't allowed to go out in the city by herself; her Mama *and* her Papa forbid it! But what did she do?"

"She went out by herself," Heath whispered, blankets tugged up to his nose, wide eyes peeking up over the top.

"She *did*. She went out by herself and walked through Midtown Manhattan, but she was too busy looking around her to think where she was going, and she got her shoe caught in a crack on the sidewalk. And she would have toppled down to the dirty, dirty ground if it hadn't been for someone breaking her fall."

Heath beamed, voice muffled beneath the blanket. "Papa."

"Her knight in shining armor," she agreed, stroking the curve of Heath's cheek with her thumb. "He saved her from stumbling once; but he saved her in so many other ways, too. That's love, baby. You be good and remember that when you're a big boy. Someone's going to need you to save them one day, too. You'll make such a good knight, I just know it. You've got your Papa's strength."

"Mama." Heath pouted. "Finish the *story*."

Laughing, she consented. "Well, I think you could finish the story, Heath. You know how it goes."

Heath puffed out his chest, making the blankets balloon before they deflated again. "They got married and became Mama and Papa to one beautiful little boy. And an Amelia." He hid his giggles as his Mama tut-tutted at him.

"Now, don't be mean to your sister. You've got to be a good big brother."

A good big brother to the little, red-cheeked, screaming bundle who was brought to the house, who dribbled on him and bit his fingers. Heath scrunched up his nose in distaste, but agreed nonetheless. "Promise." He crossed his finger over his chest, eyelids drooping.

It's been a long time since the Duchess told him that story—or any story, he supposes. Sometimes, it seems as though his parents pick and choose when they want him to play grown-up and when they want him to play baby, expecting him to follow along with a game whose rules he doesn't know. An adult, graduated from Yale with a degree to his name. A child, returned to his parents' house in New York, wandering the streets with no clue to his destination or path from there.

Heath is pulled from his thoughts by his mother's voice.

"It's as though he's a million miles away." The Duchess watches him with fond adoration in her eyes. It's not an expression he sees as much as he used to when he was the little boy who clung to her legs and believed his mama was the most beautiful woman in the entire world. When did she stop being his mama and became the Duchess to him as much as to anyone else?

Amelia nips his forearm with her fingernails. "You're such a goof."

"Amelia, physically assaulting your brother is no way for a young girl to act, especially around guests," the Duchess says.

Amelia sits back and puts her hands in her lap, but her expression is surly. Heath watches her eyes flick to Frankie across the table. "Have you a girl, Francis?" She leans back in her chair and demurely tucks her ankles together. "A Southern belle, maybe?" One eyebrow quirks with the corner of her mouth.

Frankie shakes his head. "Can't say I have. But I much prefer the girls here in New York, anyway. There's hope for me still, I'm sure." He chuckles.

"More hope than for Heath. That Louise Porter is *shameless* in how she flirts with him, acts like quite the little vamp. And yet he's not asked her to go steady with him. It's been years." Amelia scoffs.

Frankie doesn't comment; he knows exactly what Heath thinks of Louise. He also knows just the kind of person Heath might prefer to take out, were that an option.

It was one night in junior year, at the delirious stage of the night when study cards are finally abandoned in favor of a smoke on the front steps of the dorm. The ends of Heath and Frankie's cigarettes burned bright in the darkness. Fallen leaves were picked up on the breeze and settled a few feet farther down the street.

They were joined by Julian, an economics graduate of the year before who was studying for his master's degree and had volunteered to help the boys study for their midterm. Julian spoke like a grown-up; he bummed them cigarettes and spoke about girls as if he actually understood them. Julian had always been friendly with Heath; his father was an old schoolmate of the Duke's. Heath had always thought Julian was the most beautiful person he'd ever seen, with his blond hair swept back in tousled elegance and his penchant for bow ties that matched the color of his suspenders.

Later, Julian bid them goodnight and hopped off the steps, heading back to the little room he was renting in a house off-campus, whistling to himself as he went. Heath watched him go as the cigarette burnt to a stub between his fingers and cursed when the burn pinched his skin.

He stubbed it out properly and then looked over at Frankie, who was studying him carefully.

"It'd be all right with me. I know all the things you hear, but I wouldn't say a word. And it wouldn't change you. Not for me."

Heath wasn't sure he ever admitted to himself how, sometimes, he dreamed of pretty men with tan skin and bright eyes, of strong hands and coarse jaws rather than the dainty women he should fantasize about.

But he let Frankie wrap an arm around his shoulders and squeeze him tight, until he stopped shaking quite so violently. "Is there something wrong with me, Frankie?"

"There ain't a goddamn thing wrong with you, Heathcliff. You're as perfect as pie." Frankie gave Heath's cheek an affectionate pinch. His grin was clownish. "Sometimes the world just don't make sense, that's all."

"It's as if he's got cotton wool stuffed up right where his brains should be," Amelia continues now, at the table, reaching up to rap her knuckles against Heath's skull. She imitates a hollow sound with her tongue, clicking it off the backs of her teeth.

"Heath's got a mind for bigger things than girls, Amelia," the Duke comments. He tips his glass to his son. "A Yale graduate in our midst. Two, in fact." He toasts Frankie, too, before taking a sip. "Not everyone's as dead set as you are on finding someone to settle down with."

"So you're saying you'd be satisfied if I were a spinster for the rest of my days?" Amelia has always been more inclined to challenge the Duke than Heath ever is.

"That's not what I said, and you know it." The Duke looks at the Duchess in exasperation. "Sometimes, I wish Amelia could be a little more like Heath, and him a little more like her," he mourns, as if both of his children aren't sitting at the same table.

"Do you have siblings, Francis?" The Duchess asks, with just a bat of her hand in response to her husband.

"No, ma'am, not—not really. A younger brother, but he passed away as a babe. Influenza." It's the only time he ever sounds anything but cynical about his home life and his family, when he talks of the baby brother he once had.

"How awful, Francis. I can't begin to imagine how your mother must have felt."

The table sinks into silence as the plates are cleared. The Duchess excuses herself to rest; the Duke gets up only to light a cigarette, which he smokes by the sideboard. He doesn't offer one to Heath, nor to Frankie.

"Will you be passing the summer in the city, Francis?" Amelia taps her fingers on the arm of her chair.

"Perhaps." He leaves it at that.

Amelia stands to excuse herself. Her chestnut brown hair falls just shy of her shoulders in carefully constructed waves. Her body is slim and lean, elongated by the cut of her dress and the low heels on her shoes. Her smile is almost wicked as she walks around the table. She lays a hand on Frankie's shoulder for half a second. "Don't be a stranger."

Frankie raises an eyebrow at Heath across the now-empty table and Heath bites back a laugh, disguised as a cough into the back of his hand. He would much rather not have Amelia take to Frankie. There are plenty of eligible bachelors in New York City without Heath having to lose to his sister the one who is like a brother to him.

"Have you plans for the afternoon, boys?" The Duke asks from the sideboard.

Heath opens his mouth, but Frankie beats him to the punch. "Yessir, we do! We should be going, in fact. If that's all right with you."

The Duke chuckles and stubs out his cigarette. "Go on, get out of here. Just bring him back in a reasonable state. I know what you young boys get up to these days."

Heath stands and straightens his pants.

Frankie steps into his side as they walk toward the door. "Gosh, I hope he doesn't, not where I'm taking you," Frankie whispers into his ear, and Heath shakes his head.

"Don't be getting us arrested now, Frankie. Respectable Yale graduates, we are, have to represent our alma mater with an air of elegance and grace." Heath puffs out his chest and puts a hand to his breast. Frankie turns to him and mirrors the action, the two of them by the door, staring directly at one another as they chant "*Lux et veritas,* light and truth!" in perfect unison.

They collapse into snorts, shooting elbows at each other's ribs as they tumble out into the hot air of the afternoon. Heath gets his breath back as they walk a few paces down Fifth. He slips his hands into his pockets. "Wherever it is you're taking me, it better have a nice cool one on the rocks waiting for me."

"There'll be far better than just a little moonshine where we're going."

Heath raises an eyebrow. "You found some Indian Hop?" He mimes smoking. Cigarettes are habitual, but a little extra something is reserved for truly special occasions.

But Frankie shakes his head. "Stop playing detective; you'll ruin all my fun." He knocks their shoulders together companionably.

Slicking a hand through his hair, Heath turns his face up to the sky, relishing the rays of the sun against his cheeks. He resolves to take the afternoon without thinking of his parents, of what they want—or, God forbid, what *he* wants. He's young, and it's a summer's day, and for right now, that is all that matters. "Better be a good surprise." Heath grins at the indignant expression on Frankie's face.

"Must you be so obvious in your complete lack of faith in me? It wounds, Heathcliff."

They turn right down Fifty-seventh Street. Heath gives Frankie a silent promise not to ask any more questions, sealed with him miming buttoning his lip. The street isn't very busy at this time of day, mid-afternoon; most people are inside to escape the heat. Music spills from apartments above, windows are thrown open and people sit on fire escapes to smoke. The scratch of a gramophone is accompanied by live piano from a restaurant on the corner, where a group of middle-aged women sits, sharing gossip as they fight the heat with delicate fans splayed over the lower portions of their faces.

Frankie stops short outside a barbershop on the corner of Fifty-seventh and Seventh Avenue and catches Heath's arm. Heath squints at the unassuming location, at the red and white barber's pole that twirls and reflects the sunlight. The flaking lettering painted on the window reads "Jerry's." It is quiet inside. One lone figure sits with his head tipped back as his jaw is cleaned off and cologne is patted on the sides of his neck.

Heath runs a hand over his own smooth jaw—he shaved just this morning—and looks at Frankie wordlessly, merely quirking one eyebrow upward.

"Come on." Frankie tugs him inside. The bell over the door chimes as they walk in. "Afternoon, Jerry."

"Frankie!" The elderly barber walks forward to clasp Frankie in a handshake. "Can't say I was expecting you back so soon." He chuckles and it makes his whole face crinkle up. "Sometimes takes weeks before they're back. They always do come back, though."

Frankie curls a hand over Heath's shoulder. "Jerry, I'd like you to meet my friend Heath."

"Of course. Heard all about you last time Frankie was in here. It's good to put a face to the name."

Heath nods and shakes the man's hand, glancing back and forth between his friend and the barber blankly. All this—for a shave?

The customer gets to his feet, digging out a few bills to pass to Jerry. "Art around today?" he asks, not sparing Frankie or Heath so much as a glance. "I've been trying to pin him down to talk investments for a week now."

Jerry puts his hand up in surrender. "Don't expect me to have any control over that one. He does things his way, you should know that by now." He sticks a thumb over his shoulder. "He should be downstairs."

The man nods and walks through the door at the back of the barbershop. Curiosity mounting, Heath watches him go. He knows all about the underground network of bars across the city, has visited some of the illicit establishments more than once. The Duke took him to his club of choice shortly after his graduation: a stuffy, smoky room filled with old men. It smelt like sweat and Heath was wildly uncomfortable there.

Liquor, Prohibition laws or not, is easily found when one knows where to go. New Haven was a breeze; a ready supply of bootleggers was willing to sell to students with cash in their pockets. The Duke and Duchess always have at least one bottle tucked away in the sideboard, which remains locked when the Chief of the New York Police Department is among the company. Then, soda waters with lime are passed on silver trays instead of the mint juleps his mother is partial to.

But he still can't see why Frankie would build such a buzz about another old blind pig—as though Manhattan isn't teeming with them. Every week, there are rumors of another raid and boarded up stores appear on street corners. Where one goes under, another appears. The clubs start as nothing but whispers on the breeze, until jazz once more pulses from beneath the sidewalk.

"A shave, while you're here?" Jerry asks. He wipes his hands on the towel knotted through the ribbon of his apron.

Heath declines, but Frankie drops himself into a chair. "I'll take one." He glances up at Heath. "My friend here is looking rather neater than I am today."

Jerry lathers the soap, twisting the soft bristled brush before tapping the excess off the side neatly. His hands look soft and clean; his appearance is altogether impeccable, down to the sweep of his silvery gray hair. Save for a few flecks of shaving foam, even the cream apron over his clothing is spotless.

Heath perches on the edge of the counter, swinging his legs. He pats his pockets for a cigarette and tucks it between his lips.

"Here." Jerry tosses him a matchbook and throws a wink at Frankie, who looks more and more pleased with himself by the minute. If it weren't Frankie, Heath would be more than a little annoyed by the cloak-and-dagger behavior.

Heath slips a match out of the book and strikes it against the back. He touches the match to the cigarette and waits until it's lit before he shakes the match out. He takes a drag and turns the matchbook over in his hand, rubbing his finger over the gold lettering on the otherwise black card. *TJ*.

"Who's TJ?" He looks up.

Jerry sharpens a razor against his leather strop before he brings it to Frankie's throat. Neither of the men reply straight away; both seem preoccupied with the tasks at hand. Heath continues to smoke, filling his lungs before he releases puffs of cloudy air into the warm interior of the barbershop.

"You'll have to ask Art about that," Jerry says finally, as he rinses the blade in a bowl of warm water.

"I haven't heard the story," Frankie adds, tilting his face to inspect the exposed line of his throat with a clear satisfaction. "Can't say I exchanged more than a word or two with him last time I was here, though."

Heath huffs out a laugh and stubs out his cigarette. "Frankie, if you dragged me out this afternoon to surprise me with nothing but secrets and nonsense, you're certainly succeeding." He rolls his shoulders back and sighs. He tips his head forward, chin touching his chest, and closes his eyes. Memories of the preparatory school he'd attended as a teenager come to mind, of the young boys with secrets and stories they wouldn't tell Heath. They giggled about him behind his back, only laughing harder when he asked if they wouldn't be so kind as to let him in on the joke. They didn't dislike him, exactly, and he had no beef with them save for their teasing, but he never thought of them as friends.

Some days he left school sure he was the fool, with a big invisible dunce cap tacked to his head to make the other boys jeer and continue their jests. His mama would tell him he was the smartest boy of them all, but he was so tired of feeling like the idiot. It was different at Yale, where Heath found a solid group of boys from all across the country whom he could call his friends. The only fools were the boys still giggling in groups about things that probably weren't funny at all.

"Have a little patience," Frankie says. He tips his head back to allow Jerry to finish up the last of his shave and wipe down his chin. "I didn't just bring you down here to watch me getting a shave."

Heath grinds his teeth. "I should hope not."

"Even if I do paint an awfully pretty picture, wouldn't you say?"

Heath rolls his eyes and hops down from the counter. He looks young next to Frankie, with his shorter stature and narrow features. He purses his lips; the thin line of his mouth is pink against the golden tone of his skin. He's dressed swankily: his white shirt fits to the lines of his shoulders and is tucked neatly into the waistband of his brown pants. He twists a stray strand of dark hair around his index finger and tucks it back into place.

Shaved and dried, Frankie pays up and wishes Jerry a good day. Frankie starts toward the door at the back of the room and then glances back over his shoulder at Heath. "Well? Aren't you coming?"

Heath hazards a look at Jerry, who smiles and turns back to brushing down the chair. Heath follows Frankie and holds his breath, not at all sure what he may find behind the door, and rocks up onto his tiptoes to peek over Frankie's shoulder.

He sees nothing more than a storage room with a sink on the right-hand side and a closet with hooks on its side, where a couple more aprons are hung up. A few boxes are stacked up in the far corner, along with two chairs that are each missing a leg. Frankie shuts the door to the barbershop before he walks up to the closet, opens the door and steps inside.

An excited laugh bubbles up from Heath's stomach as he bounds to follow him; it seems his initial idea may hold true. And even if it isn't quite such a novel thing as Frankie has made it seem, he can't rein in the adrenalin that pumps into his veins as he steps through the door of the closet.

The back of the closet swings to the side and Frankie holds it for Heath to step through. He shuts the closet door behind him and steps out to the top of a winding wooden staircase. The soles of their Oxfords tap against the wood. Heath is nearly dizzy from watching his feet as they wind down the narrow staircase, finally coming to another door. He can hear the low sound of voices and a gramophone playing.

Frankie hesitates with his hand on the door, turning to Heath. He shakes his head and opens the door. The sound crescendoes as they step inside one low-ceilinged, large room. At one end is a long bar of polished oak with stools around its perimeter. Behind the bar is a young man drying glasses that he stacks on the shelves. He tips his head as they enter and his gaze flickers straight from Frankie to Heath in obvious interest. He has long, slicked-back blond hair; the white sleeves of his shirt are rolled up to his elbows, and the shirt is paired with black pants and suspenders.

"Quiet this afternoon," the man comments and gestures to the chairs by the bar. "Should pick up within the hour, I would say."

Frankie pushes Heath forward with a hand at the middle of his back, and they take two seats. While Frankie orders for both of them, Heath takes the opportunity to look at the rest of the space. The setup is nothing remarkable: small tables with chairs, a baby grand in the corner and the scratchy gramophone. A few other men sit at the tables, drinking and talking. The man who was receiving a shave when they arrived sits alone at one table with some papers spread out before him. A half-empty glass lolls in his left hand. Heath's gaze lingers on a pair sitting at the table nearest the gramophone with their heads tipped close together. His vision is obscured where he sits, but if he didn't know any better, he'd think they were holding hands.

He frowns and swings himself around on the stool. The bartender sets a whiskey sour down in front of him. He puts a second napkin on the bar and sets upon it a pale yellow drink with a sprig of mint garnishing the top. "And a Southside for our returning Frankie." He winks.

"You've been here before." Heath props his chin on his hand and looks at Frankie. "Recently?" He picks up a matchbook from the bowl on the bar. Black, with gold lettering. *TJ*. Just like the one on the counter upstairs. He slips this one into the pocket of his pants.

Frankie nods and takes a sip of his drink; the crushed ice clinks against the glass. "Yesterday."

"You know, I wasn't so sure that there really *was* a Heath." The bartender is back. He eyes them as he rests his weight on his forearms, against the bar. "You wouldn't be the first to come in here under the pretense of just, having a *look*. For a *friend*."

Frankie gestures to Heath. "In the flesh. Heath, meet Alfie."

"Charmed." Alfie's eyes bore into Heath's.

Heath has to look away. "Nice to meet you," he mumbles. He buries his nose in his glass as he takes a long sip.

"Don't be shy," Alfie coos. "Nothing to be shy of here." Alfie moves down the bar to go back to his glasses. "I like him already," he tells Frankie in a theatrically loud whisper.

Heath rubs the back of his neck and looks up at Frankie. "What are we doing here?" he mutters, taking another sip of his drink. The initial excitement has waned, and now Heath feels as though he's being made fun of. "Can't we go? It's a perfectly nice day; we could go sit in the park." He tries not to sound as though he's pleading.

Frankie snorts. "You hate the humidity at this time of the day. Just relax, will you?" He trails a thumb through the condensation on the side of his glass. "We can leave soon, if you really want to."

"I do," Heath retorts, his shoulders hunched as he leans over his glass.

The back door behind the bar swings open and a man walks out shouldering a crate, which he sets down on the bar. He's tall and broad; his cream shirt contrasts with the tan skin stretching over his arms. A pencil is tucked behind one ear; strands of hair fall into his eyes.

The crinkles at their corners suggest that he is a little older than them, perhaps in his late twenties.

The man catches Heath staring, but where Heath expects him to glare or tell him to cut it out, he gives him a polite nod. A hint of a smile sits at the corner of his mouth, but doesn't stretch any wider. "Afternoon, Frankie."

"New kid's very shy," Alfie comments from the other end of the bar, where he shines the side of a glass with a dishcloth. This causes the man to turn, and he leans back against the counter behind the bar as he fixes his gaze on Heath.

"I apologize if he's been giving you grief." The smile does break now. His teeth are a little crooked.

Alfie gasps indignantly. "I've been a saint!"

The man sighs and widens his eyes in Heath's direction. "The devil, more like." He pushes up from the bar and offers a hand to Heath. "Arthur Houston. But call me Art."

Heath matches the face to the name he heard earlier and takes him to probably be the owner of the establishment.

"Heath Maximilian Johnson." He nearly flushes with how pretentious it sounds.

"Quite a mouthful you've got there. I'll stick to Heath, if that's all right with you."

"I suppose it'll suffice," Heath consents teasingly.

Frankie nudges him with his elbow. "Still so eager to leave?" he asks in a murmur as Art turns back to his crate; the muscles in his bared forearms shift as he pries it open with a knife.

Heath stutters over getting caught staring and knocks his fist gently into Frankie's arm. "Next round is on you, too, just for that."

"No complaints from me." Frankie whistles to Alfie, who moves down to make them another round. "Let's take this one over to a table," Frankie suggests. They move to a couple of upholstered armchairs that have seen better days.

They clink their glasses; Heath savors the cool kiss of his against his palm. "I think there's something you're not telling me about this place." He looks around again.

Behind the bar, Alfie playfully juggles three glasses until Art smacks him with the dishcloth and tells him to cut it out before he breaks something.

Frankie leans forward and sets his glass down on the small round table. "You're right, there is." He looks up. "I know it might not look like all that much right now, but you should see this place come dinnertime and beyond. But the popularity of it isn't what I wanted you to see, either. Not really." He pauses for a beat. "Heath, everyone who frequents this place, more or less, is like you."

Heath frowns. "Like me how?"

When Frankie doesn't respond, Heath sighs. He leans back in the armchair, and his gaze flickers to the gentlemen he noticed earlier, a few tables over. He blinks a few times, and his breath catches in his throat as he watches the taller of the two press his lips to the corner of the other man's mouth. Over the music, he can hear their soft chuckles. But louder is how they look at one another. Heath's never seen anyone gaze the way these two men are, at each other. Not even his parents.

Heath tears his eyes away from the men, concerned he is intruding on their private moment, and looks back to Frankie. Frankie takes a sip of his drink and says nothing, but tilts his glass in the direction of the two men.

"Oh." Heath understands now. "How did you—" He snaps his mouth shut and laughs in disbelief, running a hand through his hair. "Is there something else you're not telling me?"

Frankie snorts and reaches over to smack Heath's knee. "Honestly, Heathcliff. If I were even slightly interested in playing that side of the field, I'd be head over heels in love with you by now."

Heath rolls his eyes, but he can't help the smile that he hides in the rim of his glass. Frankie is a handsome young man; he'll surely take that as a compliment.

"Actually, I crossed paths with Julian last night."

"*Julian?*" Heath's drink nearly ends up on his lap.

Frankie nods. "Tall, lanky, perpetual need to match his bow tie to his suspenders?"

Heath scowls. "Hush up, I know who Julian is."

"You make it too easy to tease."

"Julian," Heath prompts, his fingers tapping the arm of the chair. He didn't know Julian was in New York for the summer, let alone that he is—if he is. Which, he supposes, he might not be. Frankie's in this bar—has been here before; and *he* has no interest in any of its appeal, beyond the alcohol and convenient location.

"Julian." Frankie nods. "I was having dinner with some friends over on Madison late last night. Julian was there with his parents." Heath smiles. He's always liked Mr. and Mrs. Thorne. "My friends were due to drive back to Oyster Bay; Julian's parents wanted to turn in for the night. He suggested we go for a drink and took me here."

Heath fiddles with his cocktail napkin, curiosity nipping at his nerves. "Why here?"

"That's what I asked, once we were down here. At first, I thought just as you did—that it was just any old blind pig." Frankie clears his throat and nods toward the bar. "Until Alfie propositioned me."

Heath whips his head around so fast that his neck twinges. Alfie catches them staring and pauses in wiping down the bar. He shoots them an exaggerated wink.

"Apparently it's quite normal behavior for him, or so I'm told."

Heath swallows and sets his near-empty glass down on the table. "So, is Julian…? A three-letter man? A homosexual?" He whispers, though he needn't here. It's probably the first time he's said that word aloud.

"I don't know if it's quite so one-or-the-other for him, but he's certainly interested. In men."

A few moments of silence pass. Heath's mind fumbles to find a grasp on the club itself, let alone Julian.

"He asked about you."

"About me? Asked what?" Heath starts to panic; his hand won't stop twitching against the arm of the chair.

"Relax." Frankie frowns. "He wasn't sure. He just wondered. It's why he took me down here, thought perhaps I could take you sometime." Frankie smiles. "And here we are."

"Here we are," Heath repeats, enunciating each word. He breathes out and then jerks in his seat as the door to the speakeasy bangs open. Loud, raucous laughter enters with five men who look to be in their mid-twenties.

"Art!" One of the men booms and saunters over toward the bar to shake the owner's hand.

His friends are more demure in their greetings, if nothing else. They order a round of drinks before they sit at one of the tables nearest the piano.

"Edward, get up and play for us!" the loudest of the bunch urges, pushing at his friend's shoulder until he obligingly gets up. Having drained the contents of his glass, he makes his way up to the piano, unbuttons his shirtsleeves and rolls them up to his elbows.

The man's fingers stumble over the first few notes as he settles into a tune; his friends let out an enthusiastic chorus of cheers before they quiet down some. The man with the papers snaps his leather-bound folder shut with a sigh and gets up. Art opens the door to a back room to let him slip in there for some peace.

The couple at the next table gets up to dance first; the taller drags the other to his feet, and tugs him close to his chest with a hand settling on the small of his back. Their feet are out of sync, and they laugh as they step on each other's toes. The loud boys join them within a few moments; the four of them twirl each other around. Heath can't tell if they're drunk or just wild.

"I'd never thought about it, really. Until last night, when Julian took me down here."

Heath looks at Frankie. He tilts his head and gestures for him to go on.

"That you wouldn't be able to do things like that. Go dancing with the one you want to dance with. Walk arm in arm through the park or share a quick kiss after dinner unless you were in private somewhere."

Heath looks away. "I don't want your pity, Frankie."

"I'm not *pitying* you, Heath. I'm trying to find a way for you to do all that. And not just with some dame who'll never make you smile the way you ought to be allowed to smile."

Heath doesn't reply. The music from the piano clashes with the quieter gramophone still playing. Combined with the yells of the dancing men, it makes the beginnings of a headache pulse behind his eyes. He bends forward, sticks his head between his knees and forces oxygen in and out of his lungs through gritted teeth. Footsteps approach their table. A pair of shoes is just visible out of the corner of Heath's eye.

"Is he all right?" someone asks in a murmur. Alfie.

"He'll be fine. I think he's just a little overwhelmed."

The feet move out of his line of vision; steps tap back toward the bar.

He is overwhelmed. Overwhelmed and suddenly tired, too. Exhaustion crashes over his bones. He wants to keel over right here and sleep for a week. Perhaps all of this might make a little more sense in a week's time. Even with his head between his knees, Heath can't block out the merriment coming from the other side of the room. They sound so free, and that's what kicks hardest against Heath's ribcage, nearly collapsing it.

Never has Heath felt free. Free to make his own choices beyond what color shirt to put on in the morning, let alone to be himself. He's spent twenty-one years drilling it into himself that he likes things this way, that it's just fine for him. Twenty-one years, and now he's crumbling with the possibility that there might be more that he could want, that he could *have*.

"I'm going home," he announces as he pulls his head from between his knees, blinking as the rush of blood from his head makes him dizzy.

He stands up and straightens his pants. He digs into his pocket for a few bills and shoves them at Frankie. "For the drinks."

Frankie pushes his hand away. "It was supposed to be a birthday gift, remember?" He looks concerned. "Shall I come with you?"

Heath clears his throat and reluctantly pushes the bills back into his pocket. "No. I'd like to be alone. I'll call you tomorrow." He turns to leave.

"Heath," Frankie calls after him. He's on his feet now, looking uncertain. "I'm sorry."

With a stiff smile, Heath shakes his head. "You needn't apologize. I'll talk to you tomorrow, Frankie."

The floor could be ice beneath the soles of his shoes as he skids toward the door, wanting nothing more than to feel the breeze on his face and the touch of the sun. He's halfway up the stairs when his foot catches, and his stomach plummets before he regains his balance using the handrail. He forces himself to calm down.

Heath takes the steps more carefully, rounds up to the top and slips out through the back of the fake closet. He hears voices in the barbershop and peeks around the door, then walks out when he sees it's only Jerry and Art.

"Leaving so soon, kid?"

Heath manages to stammer out an excuse about familial obligations to Jerry and ignores Art entirely as he makes for the door.

He gets out onto the street and sucks in a deep breath of fresh air. Someone bumps into his side and mutters at him. Heath turns to call out an apology when a strong grip takes hold of his elbow.

Art drags him back to the doorway.

"You seemed a bit shaken up back there. Didn't want you walking straight out into the road and getting flattened by the next taxicab driver who thinks he's training for the Indianapolis 500."

"Thank you. I appreciate it, truly." When Art makes no move to let go of him, Heath wriggles pointedly. "I'm sure I'll be fine from here."

Art's grip loosens but he doesn't quite let go. "As I said, you seemed shaken up. Is everything all right?"

Heath sighs and wrenches himself free, taking a step back. "Listen," he says in a low voice. "I'm not going to run off to the next copper and turn your little… establishment in. So you needn't to worry about that."

"I'm not worried about that, I'm worried about you. You look as though you're shivering and it's ninety degrees out."

"You really shouldn't. I can look after myself just fine. It was good to meet you, Art. Thank you for your hospitality." He takes a step back.

"Hope to see you again, soon, Heath Maximilian Johnson." Art doesn't take his eyes off him; Heath can still feel them once he turns his back and starts down Fifty-seventh Street.

And if he goes the entirely wrong direction and ends up looping all the way around the block to get back to Fifth, that's a complete accident.

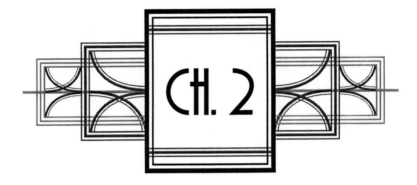

CH. 2

HEATH RETIRES TO HIS ROOM when he arrives home and feigns sickness when the Duchess comes to check on him at dinnertime. His family leaves him in peace, then, which Heath is grateful for. His headache has only worsened, even away from the underground cavern of the bar. He sleeps fitfully at best, for every time he closes his eyes, the scenes he witnessed play out against his eyelids.

Of men, dancing, and talking. And kissing. As though it were the most normal of occurrences. He understands that that's the charm of the place; he can make sense of that. What he can't make sense of is how these men can correlate how they act below ground with how they are above. How they don't go *mad* with it. Heath thinks he might be going mad already, and he was only down for a short pocket of time. Barely exchanged a few words with a man who wasn't Frankie.

He awakes with a start late the following morning: Amelia hammers on his door until he pulls his head from under the blankets. "Come in," he manages, his voice thick and scratched from sleep.

She flounces in, hairpins between her painted lips, her fingers combing through her short hair. "What on earth are you doing still in bed at this hour?" she mumbles with a frown before sitting on the edge of the bed and beginning to fix the pins into her hair.

When Heath doesn't reply, his eyes half-lidded as he remains stationary in the bed, she presses the back of her hand to his forehead. Heath grumbles and swats at her cool wrist. He wriggles away from the touch.

"Are you sick? You feel absolutely fine to me." She twists a lock of hair around her finger and stretches it out before she pins it back. "Are you moping?" She smirks. "*Darling*, did someone break your heart?" She pouts. "Do tell."

"I'm not moping." Heath sighs and pushes the blankets back. He sits upright and fixes his sister with a look. *Satisfied?*

She preens and tugs playfully at the collar of his cotton bedclothes. "If you're not moping, then why the melodramatics?" She gasps and throws her hand to her forehead, tipping her head back. "Oh, I can't possibly have dinner, I must go immediately to bed. Do not disturb me. Oh, is it morning? I hadn't noticed in my lair of darkness and despair!" She sucks in a lungful of air and collapses against the bed as if she's been impaled.

Heath watches the show with the corner of his mouth turned down and his arms folded over his chest. "You needn't tease." He kicks her, and she scowls, rubbing at her leg as she sits up.

"That's no way to act toward your only sister, who merely came to ensure you weren't dead or incapacitated." She stands and moves to the closet. She picks out a shirt and a pair of pants.

Heath wants to protest that he's perfectly capable of dressing himself, but watching her there, with his clothes in her hands, reminds him of summers long past. The two of them always liked to play dress-up, stealing into the large dressing room that the Duke and Duchess shared. Amelia would pull their father's pants onto her small, five-year-old legs, tuck her dress inside and drag her legs around while gripping the waistband so she didn't go toppling to the floor. Heath would loop a string of pearls around her neck to finish the outfit, with one of their mother's summer hats perched on his own head and slipping over his eyes.

The game would go on as long as they were allowed, before either Martha or the Duchess herself found the two of them, still giggling as they were dragged out of the room by their ears and reminded, not for the first time, that Mama's and Papa's clothes were *not* for playing with. Heath would be told to set a good example for his younger sister; Amelia, would be reminded to not always follow her elder brother's ideas so blindly. Neither would listen. Instead, they would link hands and run to the living room with someone chasing them in exasperation.

But Amelia doesn't start putting the pants on herself now, just lays the clothes she has chosen over the chair. "Where did Frankie and you go yesterday, then?"

Mumbling something incoherent, Heath shrugs and rubs a hand over the back of his neck. Amelia doesn't seem too concerned as she fiddles with the beads of her necklace and twists them between her fingers.

"And Frankie? Did he leave when you did?"

Heath looks at her with his eyes narrowed. "Why do you care so much about what Frankie does?"

Amelia merely hums to herself as she goes to sit by the window. She nudges the drapes open so that sunlight spills into the room, making her but a silhouette by the window. "He's very handsome, I suppose. Smart, too, if he went to Yale. And his family—the Duke says he comes from a very respectable family."

Heath groans and presses the heels of his palms against his eyes until he sees spots. "Absolutely not, Amelia. Don't even think about it."

"Why not?" Her tone is petulant and whiny, the one, Heath recognizes, that she uses on their parents when they won't give her her way. "What's so wrong with me?"

"There's nothing wrong with you. And there's nothing wrong with Frankie, exactly, but I'm still not going to let him anywhere near you."

Heath has watched Frankie take out a string of girls in New Haven, and a few in Manhattan in the past summer or two, besides. He's watched him woo them with his charming smile and baby blue eyes, with compliments and a brush of fingers behind their ears. He's also watched him get bored and restless after a few weeks and conveniently forget to call on them, while Heath becomes the buffer for the heartbroken girls who pound on Frankie's door at all times of the day asking if he might spare them just a moment or two.

"Not Frankie, Amelia. There are far better men in this city than Frankie David." He sighs, remembering his promise to call his friend. He doesn't know quite what he'll say to him. He's not upset with him and he doesn't want to lead Frankie to believe that he is. He lifts his head and looks at Amelia. She's stopped playing with her necklace; her forehead rests against the window, and her eyes are closed. "I want the best for you. You deserve the very best. He's out there somewhere, I promise."

Amelia stands slowly and smooths her hands over her pale green dress, which is a few shades lighter than her eyes. The light from the window shines like a halo around her brown hair, but the illusion shatters as she crosses the room to the bed. "That's all I want for you, too," she says, before her gentle expression cracks and she cackles. "And the only person I worry about finding anyone is you, you hopeless goof." She ruffles his hair and bounds toward the door, with a final yell to tell him to get dressed.

Heath thinks of the club as he slides out of the bed. He's sure that isn't what Amelia has in mind, in wanting the best for him, but maybe he could find someone who brought that color to his cheeks and flutter to his heart, who felt the same for him, too.

The Duchess fusses over him when he finally emerges downstairs with his jaw freshly shaved and his dark hair slicked back. Satisfied that he is perfectly well, she pushes him right back in the direction of his room. "We're leaving for Long Island in an hour; put together something respectable to wear for dinner with the Thornes this evening."

Heath freezes with his palm pressed to the wall to keep his balance. "Julian's family?" As if he doesn't know.

She looks at him. "Yes, dear. Julian's been a good friend to you at Yale, hasn't he?"

Heath nods but says nothing.

"Come on now, Heath." She shoos him toward the stairs and sighs. "Honestly, what has gotten into you today?"

"Of course. I'm sorry, Mama."

"Mr. Heath?" Martha steps in front of him as the Duchess retires to her own room to get her things. "Francis David is on the phone for you."

"Thank you, Martha." He walks to the hallway and picks up the phone. "Hey, Frankie."

"Jesus, Heath. It's after midday, I was starting to get worried."

"Did you call already? No one told me."

"Martha said you were in bed and she didn't want to disturb you. Are you all right?"

Heath leans back against the hallway table and folds one ankle over the other. "I'm all right. I'm sorry for running out yesterday."

"You needn't apologize. I didn't think of how much it might be for you."

"It was a lot at once," Heath agrees in a murmur.

"Are you… are you going to go back? I can come with you, if you'd like me to. If you'd like to go, at all."

Heath hesitates. "Maybe." *Probably.* "We're going out to Long Island this evening."

"When will you be back?"

"Tomorrow, I think. We're only having dinner with Julian's family, tonight."

"You should talk to him, Heath. About TJ. About—all of it. He might understand better than I can."

"You've always understood me just fine, Frankie. You're like a brother to me." He thinks briefly of Amelia and how much he knows he could never tell her. "More than."

"Well, I'm not going anywhere, and neither is TJ. Whenever you're ready, Heath."

Heath hangs up with a promise to call the next day, when they're back in the city, and hurries to pack his things before the Duchess has a chance to worry over him again.

THEIR HOUSE AT COVE NECK is open and awaiting them when they arrive; the scent of fresh freesias in vases floats in the air coming through the porch windows. Amelia and the Duchess take a turn around the gardens and soak in the afternoon sun. The air is so much less muggy out here than in the center of Manhattan. The Duke, meanwhile, takes to his study to tend to some business. Heath is left alone on the front drive, toeing at the gravel path.

Heath walks down to the shore, no more than a few yards away. He slips off his shoes and socks where the sand begins. He leaves them there to collect on his way back and rolls up the bottoms of his pant legs. The sand is burning hot beneath his soles, so he strides quickly to the edge of the bay and lets out a contented sigh as the water tickles his toes. People from the houses across the bay dot the far shore; the distant shrieks of children playing and roughhousing carries across the water to Heath's ears.

The Thornes are their neighbors here; Julian's car is parked in the driveway. Heath takes a few steps into the water so he can peer around the overhanging trees that hide part of the Thornes' beach from the Johnsons'. Someone is in the water—sure enough, Julian's head pops up near the end of the Thornes' wooden jetty. He shakes his hair out and it smacks back wet over his head.

"Heath!" Julian waves, pushes off from the jetty and swims around toward him.

Heath walks to the Johnsons' own jetty to meet him and reaches the end of the wooden platform as Julian hauls himself up the ladder. His black bathing shorts cling to his thighs; drops of water shine against his tan skin. Heath desperately hopes that his cheeks don't appear as hot as they feel and is grateful that he's wearing sunglasses, so Julian can't see how hard he's trying not to look at him and to focus instead on an indistinct point over Julian's shoulder.

It's been no more than a few weeks since he last saw Julian—he had come to Heath's graduation, to cheer for him, Frankie and the other students in Heath's class that he knew. He'd sat wedged between Heath's parents on one side and on the other, Amelia, who spent most of the ceremony making eyes at him.

He's clearly spent time outside, soaking up the sun. His blond hair is fairer than usual, golden now even when it's wet; his long limbs are a little leaner than Heath remembers from last summer.

"Hi, Julian."

Julian hurtles down the jetty toward him and wraps him in a hug, with little concern for his own state of undress or the fact that he's dripping wet. Heath tries to push him off, but Julian is taller and stronger than he is.

"You're a nuisance," Heath mutters into his bare shoulder and wraps his arms around Julian's back briefly before they break apart. The sun will dry his clothes quickly enough.

"And it's wonderful to see you, too." Julian winks. "Goodness, Heath, better change this shirt before dinner. You don't look very presentable." He tugs at the damp material that clings to Heath's skin.

Heath snorts and bats at his hand. "And whose fault is that? The Duchess will have a fit if she sees me like this. I shall have to tell her it was all your doing."

Julian flutters his eyelashes. "I am the picture of innocence."

Heath bites back a comment about how he looks absolutely anything but innocent, standing under the sun with water drying fast on his skin. "Sinful, perhaps," he mumbles under his breath with a glance toward the house.

His conversation with Frankie comes to mind—ought he to say something to him? About TJ, and to ask why he didn't come to him earlier. To *him*—not to Frankie.

"Penny for your thoughts?"

Heath looks at him and decides to say nothing. Perhaps later. When he's wearing more clothes. "I should bathe before dinner. It's hot out." He runs a hand through his hair and wrinkles his nose at the feel of the sweat sticking to the back of his neck.

"Why bathe, when you could just go swimming?" Julian tugs him toward the end of the jetty.

"Julian, I'm fully clothed, stop playing." He pushes at Julian's fingers, which are locked tight around his forearm. "Julian," he says again, in warning.

Julian just grins, and before he knows it, Heath topples face forward into the water. He emerges spluttering. His clothes are heavy from the water that drags him. Julian jumps in after him. The splash sends a tidal wave crashing over Heath's head.

"*Heath?*" It's the Duchess, with Amelia on her arm, on the beach. They shield their eyes from the sun as they look out toward the two heads in the water. "What on earth are you doing in there with your clothes on? Have you got heatstroke?"

"I'm fine!" Heath calls, swimming back toward the jetty.

The Duchess sighs. "Then stop acting like such a child. And don't be trailing water into the house. The floors were freshly washed this morning, they don't need another!" She pauses and raises a hand to Julian. "Good afternoon, Julian."

Heath gets a hand on the railing of the ladder and yelps as another wave hits his back. He looks over his shoulder. Julian looks far too smug as he paddles back to his own beach.

"I'll see you tonight; I hope in a more orderly state." Julian disappears below the surface, leaving Heath to drag himself to the house while the Duchess follows behind him and tut-tuts and Amelia sniggers into her shoulder.

HEATH BATHES, WASHING THE SMELL of the bay from his skin and out with the soapsuds. He slicks his hair back neatly, just as the Duchess approves, and ties his bow tie at a perfect level at the hollow of his throat. He walks down the hall to Amelia's room to accompany her downstairs to join their parents. She is just fixing a pair of emerald earrings into her ears when he knocks on the door and enters with her permission. Her white dress is striking against her skin. He joins her by the mirror, he in a classic black and white ensemble, with a green pocket square tucked into the breast pocket of his jacket. It hadn't been intentional, but they make a striking pair. Their matching green eyes meet each other's gazes in the mirror. Amelia's eyes have flecks of brown that blaze out like solar flares from her pupils.

"You always did clean up rather nice." It's as close to a compliment as his sister is apt to grant, when it comes to him. Amelia slips her hand through the crook of his elbow; the Duke and Duchess await them near the front door. The Duchess makes a noise of approval at their attire. Her dress swirls in a flash of silver as she turns toward the front door; the Duke stands by her side with a hand placed on the center of her back.

The Thornes' house is bathed in light, and sounds of conversation and laughter come from within. As they take the stairs to the front door, Heath picks out one laugh in particular—shrill and grating. His arm tightens in Amelia's. The Duchess goes ahead. They find the Porters in the hallway in conversation with Delilah, Julian's mother.

"Louise!" The Duchess beams and glances over her shoulder to make sure Heath is quite aware of this addition to the dinner party. "What a lovely surprise!"

Heath resists the urge to roll his eyes; he can tell full well from her tone that it is no surprise at all.

"Charming, isn't she?" Amelia whispers into his ear.

"Louise? She's fine, I suppose."

Amelia chuckles now, one eyebrow arched. "Our *mother* and her scheming ways."

She moves ahead to greet the Porters with kisses on cheeks, and then accepts a glass of champagne from the butler. Heath sees Julian in the dining room with his father and rocks up on his toes to try to catch his attention, but Louise steps into his line of vision.

"Heath! I haven't seen you all summer," she purrs. The smell of her floral perfume is overpoweringly sweet as she presses a lingering kiss to his cheek.

Julian looks over, then; his lips curl in surprise as Heath politely returns Louise's gesture of affection.

Heath mouths a hopeful "Save me?" in his direction, but Julian doesn't move.

They take their seats for dinner, all present save for Julian's older brother, who lives in the city with his wife of one year and claims he is far too busy to visit for dinner, as Delilah mournfully tells them over the first course. Louise has claimed the seat at Heath's side and has not so subtly dragged her chair a touch closer to his so their elbows may brush as they eat. Julian is across from him, with his legs stretched out under the table. His face remains passive while his toes nudge at Heath's ankles every now and again.

"So, Heath. What's next now that you've graduated?" The question comes from Mr. Porter, no doubt concerned for his daughter's future should Heath begin courting her as Louise so clearly hopes he will.

The food goes stale in Heath's mouth, and he swallows dryly before he washes it down with a swig of water. One blissful effect of the day's surprises had been that they had, for a time, taken his mind from other worries. "I can't say I've come to a decision yet, sir. I'm hoping to take the time this summer to decide what's the best option for me."

No one says anything until the Duke clears his throat and takes over, as he is wont to do. "Of course, Heath has a position ready and awaiting him at my firm. With his bright mind and talent, he'd make an excellent addition. I'm sure he'll make the right choice."

"Perhaps the right choice need not always be the obvious one," Julian offers. He looks at Heath as though he means more than what he says aloud.

"Certainly, Julian's choice to continue studying wasn't what I'd hoped for him," Mr. Thorne adds. "These young men—sometimes they just need their time to spread their wings before they're clipped for good." He winks at Louise, who giggles.

"Well, Heath's so smart, he could do anything he chooses." Louise preens.

"I'll drink to that." Julian tips his glass to him.

The dishes are cleared, and Heath excuses himself to the porch. Down at the shore, the water rocks against the end of the jetty; the breeze picks up the strands of Heath's neatly styled hair and washes cool air down the back of his neck. Footsteps approach him.

"Everything all right?" Julian's touch is light against his back.

Heath nods and breathes out steadily, slipping his hands into his pockets. "Seems every time I go anywhere these days it becomes a discussion of my future. It's a little oppressive."

Julian shuts the door and leads him to sit at the top of the stairs that lead from the porch down to the garden. He pulls a monogrammed cigarette case from his pocket, opens it with a click and offers one to Heath, who declines, before taking one for himself.

"I'm afraid that doesn't go away," Julian admits, striking a match to light his cigarette, his hand cupped so the breeze won't get to it. "There is one place where, I'm sure, you could go and be free from that kind of talk."

Heath hums. He props his elbows up on his knees and rests his face in his hands. "You mean TJ."

"Frankie tells me you didn't quite take to it as we had expected."

"It was a lot. I think I'd like to go back, though. When I get back to the city." Heath glances around. Julian looks pleased by this admittance.

"Did you meet Art?"

"Briefly. He seemed concerned about me." Heath laughs.

"Of course. Art is concerned about anyone who comes to his sanctuary. I think he feels an obligation to any man who crosses the threshold."

Heath remembers how he retorted the day before, accused Art of only being concerned about keeping his club a secret. His stomach curls in guilt. He looks up to the night sky, picking out faint stars behind the clouds. "Why didn't you tell me sooner?"

"Why do you think, Heath?"

Heath licks his lips. "You didn't know how I'd react." The same reason he's never thought to talk to anyone about it; Frankie is the exception and he all but figured it out for himself. "But you knew? About me?"

"Suspected. And when Frankie took a look around TJ and didn't smack his fist into my face at my suggestion to take you there, I became sure."

Julian stubs out the last of his cigarette; when Heath looks up, Julian's eyes are fixed on his. The others' voices, albeit muffled by the closed door, can be heard in the dining room. The drapes obscure Heath and Julian where they sit on the porch steps. Julian joins their lips. He tastes of cigarette smoke and champagne. This isn't unfamiliar to Heath, who has kissed a few girls. What is new is the slightly rough texture of Julian's lips and the smell of his cologne, and the hand that comes up to firmly cup the back of Heath's neck.

Heath pulls back as Julian's fingers curl against the nape of his neck. He purses his lips and blinks a few times.

"Should I be apologizing?" Julian murmurs. He looks very much as though he'd far rather kiss him again than apologize.

Heath shakes his head and places a hand on Julian's wrist. "You needn't apologize. But I think I'm going to go back inside. If that's all right."

"Of course, Heath." Julian lays one further kiss on his cheek, then rises and offers a hand to Heath.

They reenter the house side by side, the backs of their hands brushing, those inside none the wiser. Heath lets Louise hang onto his side for the rest of the evening with the memory of Julian's lips fresh in his mind.

Y

IT'S RAINING WHEN HEATH AWAKES. Water splatters against the windowpanes; thick clouds block the sun. The outside world is glum, and Heath has half a mind to bury his head under the blankets. But he thinks of the city, of TJ waiting under Jerry's barbershop. Beneath his skin is an itch to get back to the city and its hubbub, and part of that itch is for a place that, just the day before yesterday, he wasn't sure he would ever return to.

He dresses quickly and goes down for breakfast to find his father regarding the tempest. "I had plans to play golf this afternoon." He grunts at the weather once again and returns to the morning paper; his bushy eyebrows are knitted in a frown.

"Perhaps it'll pass," Heath suggests. He settles into a seat and helps himself to coffee.

The Duchess regards him coolly over the top of her own cup before she sets it down. "Someone's chipper this morning." She smiles. "It's good to see you back to your usual self, sweetheart. Couldn't be anything to do with a certain someone, now, could it?"

Amelia lifts her head from where she's sprawled out over an armchair in the corner of the room with an unread magazine in her lap. She fixes Heath with a look of clear amusement, knowing full well how he feels about Louise and her penchant for clinging to him like a limpet. Of course, she doesn't know of Julian and their kiss shared on the porch under the night sky; although Heath doesn't think he'd pin his good mood on that, either.

"Louise is…" He trails off, stumbling for a word that might once and for all deter his mother's matchmaking with this particular young woman. "Charming. But I'm just not sure she's quite the girl for me."

The Duke tut-tuts. "Nonsense. Louise would make a fine wife, Heath. You ought to take these things a little more seriously and not fool around with her heart." He sets down his newspaper and toys with the end of his mustache. "Now, it wouldn't do to propose until you have decided on your future. You need to be able to offer a suitable promise of stability. But once that's decided, I do think it would be about time."

Heath gapes. After all he has grown up to believe of his parents' romantic and heartfelt relationship, he'd never have expected them to think of marriage as such an institution, a means to an end in making Heath into a proper gentleman. "I don't love her."

"What's that got to do with anything?" The Duke frowns at him, as though he must be mad to think in such a way.

The Duchess sighs and reaches across the table for his hand. "What your father means, is you can *learn* to love her. In time."

There's a sour taste on Heath's tongue; his appetite and good mood shatter with the clap of thunder overhead. "If you'll excuse me, I think I will go put my things together for the trip back to the city."

"Oh, we're going to stay another day, didn't Amelia tell you?" The Duchess clicks her tongue in her daughter's direction.

Amelia yawns. "Slipped my mind. Heath, we're staying another day." She closes her eyes.

"I'd like to leave. Please." Heath looks out of the window at the Thornes' house. The trunk of Julian's car is propped open as their butler hastily fits his bags into the back. "In fact, I shall ask Julian if he can take me back."

The Duke sighs. "If you must." He excuses him with a wave of his hand, and Heath speeds from the room and out into the storm so he can catch Julian before he leaves.

"Julian!" Rain is lashing into his eyes and he can't see a damned thing. His shirt sticks to his skin as the water soaks right through it.

"Heath?" Julian grabs his wrist and tugs him up the steps so they are under the awning at the front of the house and out of the way of the worst of the weather. "What are you doing running around like a madman in this storm? What's wrong?"

Heath laughs, feeling somewhat empowered and high from his jaunt through the rain, away from his parents even while the heat of their disapproval lingers on his back. "Can you give me a ride back to the city? My family is staying another day, but I'll go mad if I'm stuck in that house any longer."

Julian claps a hand over his shoulder. "Of course, I understand. Go get your things, and I'll bring the car around to the front of your house in a few minutes."

He does exactly that, not paying the slightest attention to his mother's cries of protest at how he rushes through the house: soaking wet, spraying water every which way. He calls out his goodbyes and joins Julian in the car. A shiver ripples down his spine now that he's out of the rain and sitting in his wet clothes.

Julian rolls his eyes and reaches to the back seat, where he has a blanket. He shakes it out and tosses it over Heath's body. "No sense in you catching a chill, now."

Julian pulls out of the driveway and drives toward Manhattan. The thunder has stopped, but the rain still rushes down; the wipers on the windscreen squeak as they fight the onslaught of the water. "What has gotten into you today?" Julian asks, when Heath falls silent with the blanket tucked under his chin. "In all the time I've known you, I've never seen you so much as say no to your parents, let alone run out of their house into the pouring rain."

Heath shakes his head. He has no idea where the spurt of rebellion has come from, but now he wonders why he hasn't done it sooner. It feels good to make a choice for himself, even if it is so simple as to leave for Manhattan a day early.

"When did you decide to keep studying? Rather than go work for your father?" It was a point of contention in the Thorne household—still is—but Julian went ahead with it nonetheless, with no lasting damage done to his relationship with his parents.

Julian cracks a grin. "I'd decided by the end of my freshman year at Yale. I just chose not to tell my father until I had to start making applications, lest he spend three years of my life trying to convince me otherwise. It would have been a fruitless effort on his part, but it would have grated on my nerves."

Heath chews on the skin at the edge of his thumb in silence.

"What would you like to do, Heath? No restrictions, the world an open book. What would you do?"

"I don't know," Heath admits in a murmur. "There's so much I don't know about, I don't know how I *could* know." It would be so easy to follow his father's plans for him, as he always has, when he can't provide a decent counteroffer of anything he'd rather do—even though he's sure there is little he wouldn't rather do than work in stocks and shares. He says as much to Julian, who hums empathetically, drumming his fingers on the steering wheel as he hits the gas on the main road. The rain is easing off. The sun peeks through the clouds and illuminates the city skyline Heath can just make out in the distance.

"This summer, then. You've already been given it as a grace period, so make the most of it. Figure out what you do want, truly. Find your options."

Heath rests his head against the window and lets the thrum of the engine, which reverberates through the entire body of the car, rattle his bones pleasantly. "I wouldn't know where to start."

"Frankie mentioned he's thinking about traveling. I'm sure he'd welcome your company."

Heath lifts his head and frowns. "I think that might be a little too far afield for me." He smiles wryly. "I'm not quite at a Frankie David level in my aspirations."

"Who is?" Julian shoots him a smile. "You should talk to Art. He has a good grasp on figuring out what people need. Does it without even realizing sometimes, I should think. Take TJ—poured his passion into a little club that's become a haven for so many."

"Have you known him long?"

"A year." Julian slows down a notch as they approach Roslyn. "I found the club almost by accident last summer. I was strolling down Fifty-seventh and Alfie was sitting on the doorstep of Jerry's with his jacket draped over his shoulders like a cape. He called out to me and asked if I wanted a nightcap. Completely ossified. Thought he might upchuck on my shoes right there and then when I stepped over to make sure he was all right. He insisted on taking me downstairs and Art took him from there. He didn't seem too surprised. I stayed for the nightcap I'd been promised and, well. I suppose it was fortunate that Alfie called out to me rather than any other man in the street. Art says he has a sense for people but I think it was just dumb luck."

"You went back," Heath fills in, moving the blanket to tuck it under his arms now that he's warmed up some and the blanket is just trapping his damp clothes closer to his skin.

"Every day for two weeks. Until my parents started getting suspicious about just who I was spending all my time with, so I had to be a little more selective in my visits."

Heath bites into his lower lip, worrying the flesh with his teeth. "Do you ever fear that someone might find out?" he asks quietly. He glances at Julian out of the corner of his eye.

"Of course." Julian lets out a breath. "But I think it might be worth it, for the time I've been able to pass being unapologetically myself."

"Unapologetically yourself." Heath smiles. "I like that."

"Well, you should try it sometime then. The door is always open to you, Heath. Alfie called this morning, in fact. Art's been asking after you. Apparently he is all kinds of concerned after the way you ran out that night."

Heath tries to clamp down on the way his stomach flips at that revelation. "I ought to apologize to him. I think I was rude when I left."

Julian reaches across the dash and squeezes Heath's forearm. "I'm sure he understands."

They fall into a companionable silence as Heath looks out of the window. The road, still wet, glistens in the emerging sunlight. He wonders if it's still raining in Cove Neck and hopes that the sun will follow them all the way to Manhattan.

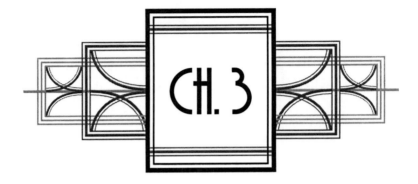

CH. 3

HEATH CAN'T SAY HE'S HAD many opportunities to be at home by himself. Martha is there, of course, and when he goes downstairs that evening, he can hear Louis in the kitchen, whistling to himself as he bangs pots and pans around. It seems a far less pressurized environment without the Duke and Duchess around, as though the rooms have expanded and breathe easily. He ducks into the kitchen, for which his mother would chastise him were she here. Martha fusses and says he ought to eat before he goes out, but Louis takes him at his word when he says he's not hungry and wishes him a good night.

He foregoes a jacket for the evening, comfortable as he is in chestnut-brown pants paired with a cream shirt. He knows that he has no airs and graces to uphold in the space beneath the floorboards of Jerry's, and takes comfort in that knowledge when it settles over his shoulders as he starts his short walk over to TJ, a little more than ten blocks south. The nerves don't kick in until he's turning down Fifty-seventh. His feet begin to slow; his palms are clammy where his hands rest in his pockets.

Heath tries to calm his mind, but all he can think of is TJ, and Art, and a world he has no more than dipped a toe into. And he is alone—no Frankie by his side to act as a buffer tonight, nor Julian, who had offered to accompany him several times, each suggestion declined politely by Heath.

He drags his feet to the corner of Seventh Avenue. Spying Jerry through the window relaxes him somewhat. The bell over the door tinkles when he walks in.

Jerry cracks a grin and walks over to shake his hand. "Good to see you again, Mister Heath. Care for a shave, or shall I send you straight on your way?"

Heath rubs a hand over his jaw; a day's stubble lines his chin. "Sure. I'll take a shave this time."

He's biding his time, giving himself the opportunity to pause before he goes downstairs. But he really could use a shave, and it's soothing to listen to Jerry stir the lather before the cool brush touches the underside of his jaw. Heath lets Jerry shave him in silence; nods in approval at the cologne he is offered: a dusky scent that makes him feel fresh after his walk. He pays and tips generously before he steps through the back door of the barbershop toward the closet. He swings its loose back to the side and steps through.

It's far louder and busier than before—Friday night in full swing. The first of the new month. The live band has extended beyond a sole, coerced piano player to include a man with a trumpet, who accompanies two men at the piano as they fumble out a tune. Every table is full; more people hang around the edges of the room. The bar is packed, and Heath has half a mind to run right back up the steps and try again on Monday.

But he doesn't. It helps, he supposes, that he spots a familiar face at the end of the bar, nursing a Gin Rickey in one hand, with the other tapping out the rhythm on his thigh.

"You seem to have migrated to the other side of the bar." Heath smiles and touches Alfie's shoulder lightly, to catch his attention.

"Heath!" Alfie sets down his drink and wraps an arm around his shoulders, squeezing him tightly before he lets go. "Ah, a man can't work all hours of the day. I'm merely another paying customer tonight."

"I don't think you can call yourself a paying customer when you don't pay," Art says as he appears at their end of the bar, setting out the ingredients for a whiskey sour. Heath watches him mix the drink with apt interest—not least because he's impressed that Art has remembered his drink of choice from his first visit. Art's movements are sinuous and perfected: the tilt of his wrist as he separates the egg white from the yolk, the way the muscles in his forearms tense as he shakes the liquid and pours it out over a glass of ice.

"Why should I pay when I'm a valued employee?" Alfie's voice pulls Heath back from his reverie while watching Art work. Alfie flutters his eyelashes at Art. A cheeky grin plays on his lips and Heath looks away. He stares down at the wooden bar and runs his fingers over the dents and marks in the oak.

"Again, I feel as though the modifier is superfluous." Art pushes the finished drink toward Heath. "On the house. Welcome back, Heath."

Heath blinks in surprise. He thanks him and slides onto the recently vacated barstool next to Alfie's. He wants to ask Art so much more, especially since his talk with Julian, but Art moves down the bar to tend to someone else, with a promise to see Heath later. "I hope so," Heath calls out a fraction too late, and catches Art's bemused expression before he turns to an older gentleman clamoring for his attention.

"It's good to see you again." Alfie lays his hand just above Heath's knee, curling his fingers over the inseam of his pants. "Art was beginning to worry you wouldn't come back. I knew you would, though." His eyes twinkle as he squeezes Heath's leg before he takes his hand back.

"You spoke to Julian."

Alfie nods. "I did. He said you'd be back. And here you are." He tips his glass to Heath's.

Heath turns away from Alfie's intense gaze and studies the club's patrons. He recognizes the group of young men near the wall, whose raucous laughter bounces off the low ceiling; a few older gentlemen sit more demurely at their tables, smoking, their feet tapping on the polished floors. A couple with their arms looped around each other's waists stand near the bar. The shorter tilts his head up to whisper something into the taller man's ear and then settles his head on his shoulder. The taller presses his lips briefly to the crown of the other's head and his eyes flutter closed as he lingers with his nose buried in dark curls. The intimacy makes Heath's chest ache for something he doesn't know, but can still understand is something he wants.

"It's all right to want it." Alfie has moved closer; his breath tickles Heath's ear and skates down his neck. "The trick is to not let it consume you."

Heath turns back to him. "What do you mean?"

Alfie sits back a little, but not so far that Heath can't feel the heat that radiates from his body as their knees bump. "I've seen many a man come down here and watch the others with that same look in their eyes. They know they want to find that, but they're too scared to actually take a step forward. So, they keep watching and they keep drinking, and it can become too much.

"It can eat you up inside, shred your insides to pieces." Alfie clasps a hand to the back of Heath's neck tightly. His breath smells sweet, boozy and hot. "Don't let it," he growls out.

For a split second, Heath thinks Alfie might kiss him. But he doesn't; he sits back and gradually his hand falls away from Heath's neck to settle on his shoulder, a light touch. "So." Heath licks his lips. "Take that step?"

Alfie nods. A catlike grin tugs at the corner of his mouth. "And should you need any assistance, I'm always more than happy to help in any way I can." His hand falls to Heath's knee; his fingers trace the inseam of Heath's pants up his thigh.

Heath stares down at his hand for a moment before he catches on. He scrabbles to bat Alfie's hand away. "That's—that's fine, I should be fine. I'll be fine. But thank you. I suppose."

Alfie doesn't look particularly put out. "Suit yourself." He drains the dregs of his drink and sets the empty glass down on the bar. "If you'll excuse me, then, I believe my services may be required elsewhere." He slicks a hand through his dark blond hair and walks past Heath.

Heath watches him go. He sits in an empty chair at a nearby table with a slightly older gentleman, who gives him a smile that expresses familiarity. A moment later, the two rise and walk toward the back room.

"You're not going to run out again, are you?" Art has appeared at Heath's end of the bar. His hands rest against the bar as he stares at Heath in concern. He studies Heath's expression carefully before he sighs and says, "I keep telling Alfie to go easy on the new ones. It's a lot to take in without him putting his hands everywhere."

"Is he—? I mean, was he suggesting—? Does he do that a lot?" Heath rubs a hand over his face and leans forward, propping his chin up in his hand.

"*I* don't pay him for it. But I let him operate down here to his heart's extent. Better that than he hang around on street corners up there." Art frowns. "Although it has led to a few unfortunate incidents involving smashed bottles, which I don't appreciate."

Heath doesn't reply. Instead, he swallows down his drink and pushes the empty glass back over to Art. "Another, please," he rasps. Art is right about one thing. It's a *lot*, especially with the memory of Alfie's hand pressed against his thigh still burned into his skin.

Art glances at his glass and then back at him, looking displeased. "Wait here a moment, will you?" He slides out from behind the bar. He approaches the group of young men, taps one on the shoulder and leans down to address him individually. The man nods and follows Art, ignoring his friends' protests about leaving their little party.

"Carter is going to take over for the night," Art tells him as the man takes his place behind the bar, tosses a dishcloth over his shoulder, plucks Heath's empty glass away from him and adds it to the stack to be washed. "We're going."

"We?" Heath asks as Art hauls him to his feet.

Art keeps his hand pressed firmly against the center of his back as he guides him toward the exit. "I'd rather you took the time to mull things over without a drink in your hand. And you look as though perhaps you shouldn't be left alone right now." Art lets his arm return to his side when they reach street level.

Heath has no reason to protest, especially when he remembers what Alfie said about not letting it consume him. How many men has Art had to pick up off the bar, hoary-eyed, confused and overwhelmed by it all? He decides not to ask and just follow his lead. Heath shivers as they step out of the barbershop onto the street. It's not cold, but it's a definite contrast to the stagnant heat that settles below with so many bodies crammed into a small space.

They walk in silence for a few blocks, and Heath takes the time to study Art from out of the corner of his eye. He's dressed simply, in a blue shirt buttoned to the top but without a tie to complement it, straight-legged gray pants with suspenders to match, no jacket. His eyes are deep-set, pale blue and framed by dark eyelashes. His hair is long but styled back neatly; only a few stray strands break free and fall into his eyes, loosened, no doubt, by the humidity inside the club. He walks with his hands in his pockets but his shoulders back, as though he has been brought up just as Heath has: to stand up straight and carry himself with pride.

"I apologize for Alfie's behavior," Art says finally. "Really, he—"

Heath cuts him off with a wave of his hand. "It's fine, you needn't—"

"—has *no* sense of boundaries sometimes."

Their gazes meet as they speak over one another; a grin curls over Heath's lips that he sees mirrored on Art's face.

"I'm fine. Feels nice to walk, though, so really I should be thanking you for that."

Art nods. "I needed a break, too. Sometimes it seems as though I spend entire days trapped down there."

"Trapped?" Heath looks at him. "Is that how you feel?"

"Yes and no." Art pushes those stray strands of hair back, tucks them behind his ear. "I'm immensely proud of what TJ has become and what it allows people. That men can feel free, where they feel confined by their everyday lives. But as the man who has to work down there, who doesn't just visit in his spare moments? It can sometimes seem as if the roof is about to cave in over my head. Not often, but sometimes.

"The first month or two, I jumped every time the door opened, sure that it would be the cops coming to smash the whole thing and cart me off. I could be done for the liquor alone, let alone anything else they might discover about the place. The fear eased over time, and it helps that Jerry keeps an eye on the new faces he lets come below. After a while, I started to realize it would all be worth it—even if it does come crashing down one day. It would be worth it for the time that I've been able to give to those who thought they'd never have any."

Heath listens to him, content to walk by his side. He slides his hand into his pocket and touches the matchbook. His thumb glides over the lettering. "And… TJ? Someone special?" Curiosity gets the better of him, makes him more forward than he might otherwise be.

Art chuckles as they cross into the center of Times Square and turn left onto Forty-second Street. "In a manner of speaking, yes—but not in the way I imagine you're suggesting. TJ Houston was my uncle. He raised me."

"Houston, of Houston Mechanics?" Heath recognizes the name from companies the Duke has discussed with him.

"One and the same." No wonder Art holds himself well, being a *Houston*. "My parents passed away in an accident when I was a child, but Uncle TJ loved me like a son. Would have paid to send me to any college of my choosing, but I never wanted to go. He would tell me he didn't care what I chose to do with my life, as long as I put my big heart to good use." Art stares at his feet as they walk.

Heath doesn't push, lets the silence hang between them until Art is ready to speak again.

"He passed away a few years ago. I took my inheritance and set up TJ. I think he'd be proud, if he knew. I'd like to hope so, anyway," he finishes quietly.

"I'm sure he would be," Heath assures him, and Art seems to appreciate it, even if Heath couldn't possibly know. The words may be empty but the sentiment is not.

"And you? No, let me guess: Harvard graduate, a job on Wall Street and a debutante just waiting for you to ask for her hand?"

Heath folds his arms over his chest. "Yale, actually."

Art snorts, but it isn't in an unkind fashion. "My apologies. A *Yale* graduate."

"No job of any kind, yet, although I'm sure my father would love it if I were to take him up on his offer. As for the debutante…" He trails off with a grimace. "It's complicated."

"Isn't it always?"

They've reached the corner of Vanderbilt Avenue; the beady-eyed eagle on the corner of Grand Central Station caws down at them.

"The Yale Club is around here, isn't it?" Art teases.

Heath ignores him and marches ahead. He opens the door to the station and steps inside. He rarely has reason to venture inside; however, the ornate ceiling alone is worth a visit. As a child he had begged Martha to take him inside, pleading with her to the point of tears to let him lie down on the floor. Patches of the floor were warm from being bathed in the sunshine that streams in sheets through the arched windows high up. All he wanted was to look up at the constellations painted on the ceiling, to trace them with his little hand and make up stories about who put them there in the sky. She never allowed it for more than a moment or two and then scolded him for dirtying his clothes on the floor, which a hundred feet had stepped on in the past few seconds alone.

"Planning a trip?" Art catches up to him, keeping close behind his shoulder.

"Hush." Heath walks out into the main atrium and cranes his head up to look at the gilded ceiling. "I haven't been here in years," he admits in a murmur. He turns on his toes as he looks around.

"TJ used to take me here. He'd let me lie on the floor and make sure no one stepped on me."

Heath smiles ruefully. "I was never allowed more than a second."

"By all means." Art gestures to the floor. "Don't let me stop you."

Heath stutters, glancing around them. The station is rarely quiet; even now, with the clock ticking past nine o'clock, people still mill around; trains run out to Long Island late into the night in the summer. "I shouldn't."

Art hums but doesn't comment. Instead, he loops his hand over Heath's elbow and leads him toward one of the other corners of the station. He offers no explanation, but leaves him in one of the arched corners near The Oyster Bar. Its doors are propped open and it's full of patrons.

Swaying on his heels, Heath waits. He doesn't know long he's supposed to stand in this corner or, even why. He gets his answer when Art's footsteps stop somewhere behind him.

"Do you always do what's expected of you, Heath?" It's Art's voice. A glance over his shoulder tells Heath that Art is standing at the opposite corner of the small space created by the arches of the station's architecture.

Heath looks up at how the wall curves, tips his head as far back as he can to see how the smooth arc of the ceiling extends to the opposite corner. He laughs softly, in awe of how the sound carries from one corner to the other over the sheet of ceramic. He clears his throat before he replies. Would Art be able to hear just as clearly as he heard him? "I suppose I always have," he murmurs. "I've had no particular reason not to."

Evidently Art can hear him, for he replies, "That doesn't seem like a very good reason in itself to do it."

Heath stares at the wall in front of him. He wants to protest, to tell Art of how he left the house in Cove Neck that morning.

"What do you want, Heath?"

"That seems to be a popular question today," Heath muses. "I don't know what I want, in all honesty. I'm hoping I might begin to find that out."

Art doesn't reply, but Heath hears his footsteps approaching until he can feel the heat of his chest against his back. "Well, I don't think you'll find your answer by talking to a wall."

ART WALKS HIM BACK TO the townhouse even though Heath insists that he'll be just fine, that he could even pick up a taxicab. They talk a little of Heath's family and of Frankie and Julian, while Art wonders aloud with an amused twinkle in his eye whether there's any particular reason he keeps attracting Yale alumni to his club. Heath invites him inside for a nightcap that Art declines, saying he has to get back to the club to relieve Carter of bartending duties and close up for the night.

"I hope to see you again soon?" Art's voice lifts in a question as he stands looking up at Heath from the bottom of the steps that lead up to the front door.

Heath makes no effort to hold back the beaming smile that tugs at his lips. "I'll be sure to call in the next couple of days," he promises. "And thank you, Art."

Art waves goodbye and walks down the edge of Central Park back toward Fifty-seventh Street.

Heath slips into the house quietly, although he doubts Martha will have waited up for him as the Duchess might. He closes the door and realizes with startling clarity that he has one very special reason to go back to TJ soon. It isn't for the sanctuary of the place, or for the alcohol or the music, or even for the possibility of a kiss like the one he shared with Julian at Cove Neck. It's Art.

The promise of the next visit hangs over him as he makes his way to his room to ready himself for bed. He soon finds his mind is too busy to contemplate sleeping, so he chooses a volume of Aristotle from the small shelf and takes it to sit by the window until his eyelids droop. Dawn is already touching the horizon when his head finally hits the pillow.

Y

IT OCCURS TO HEATH, as he takes his morning coffee in the living room of the quiet house: He's met men like Art before. Confident men, handsome men, men who live as though the whole world were within their grasp. It's a far cry from arrogance, although Heath met plenty of arrogant men at Yale. Arrogance irks him, but the kind of confidence that men like Art exude intimidates him.

Perhaps for that reason he doesn't return to TJ that day, as much as another part of him longs, not so much for the club or its intimate atmosphere, but for Art himself, to spend more time basking in the surety of his words, in the hope that some of it might rub off on him.

His family returns by mid-morning. He makes himself useful and carries his mother's and sister's bags to their rooms. The Duchess lays a white-gloved hand on his cheek and studies his demeanor. "You seem better today," she comments, but adds nothing more before she slips past to exclaim over the dahlias in the hallway that have passed their best.

It is a beautiful day; the air is still hot, but a gentle breeze skims through the trees that line the edge of the park. Heath doesn't let the heat deter him from his plan for the day, and walks south toward the public library near Bryant Park. He finds Frankie exactly where he expects him, seated at a large table in the back of one of the reading rooms, with atlases and maps spread out before him. A stub of a pencil is propped between his teeth, and a frown knits his eyebrows. His suit jacket is draped over the back of one of the empty chairs drawn up beside the table; the sleeves of his pinstripe shirt are folded halfway up his forearms.

Heath slips into one of the chairs opposite him, startling Frankie out of his staring contest with the unresponsive pages. "Do the Australian plains have anything of interest to say today?" He gestures at the book nearest him. Frankie removes the pencil from his mouth and uses it to prod Heath in the arm. Heath grimaces at the trace of spit it leaves against his sleeve.

"One day, they'll talk back," he insists, eyes sparkling in jest.

The library has long been a spot of sanctuary shared between the two friends in the years after their first meeting between the stacks. Heath likes to sit with an impossibly tall pile of books by his side and dip in and out of them as he pleases, while Frankie plans extraordinary journeys across the globe. He's planned significantly more travels than he has ever embarked on, but for all his talk of going to Europe, he has yet to go anywhere farther from home than New Haven.

"How was Cove Neck?"

Heath shrugs. "The same as ever. I left early—Julian drove me back yesterday."

Frankie returns the pencil to his mouth, mumbling around it. "You could have called on me."

"I went to TJ," Heath blurts, loud enough that one of the few other figures in their end of the library shushes him. Heath raises a hand in apology.

"You still could have called on me."

"I didn't need a damn fire extinguisher," Heath grumbles.

Frankie looks up from his book. "Did you have fun, at least?"

Heath switches around to sit beside Frankie and tells him in brief terms about his evening. He doesn't mention the kiss shared with Julian, or how he finds it difficult now to think about Art without his heart seeming to skip a beat.

Frankie listens attentively and doesn't interrupt until Heath is finished. At some time during his story, the man from the next table moves to the other end of the library.

"I'm glad, Heath," Frankie says finally. He wraps an arm around his shoulders and tugs him in for an awkward one-armed hug across the wooden desk chairs. "Now, onto more important matters." He grins. "How do you feel about Mexico?"

"That's south," Heath points out. "I thought you abhorred the idea of going south."

Frankie taps his pencil on the scrap of paper in front of him. It's blank save for one word scrawled in Frankie's handwriting—*Cuba?*—with a deep score through it. "I suppose. I'm somewhat unsure about spending a week cooped up in a boat in the middle of the Atlantic."

Heath can't help but chuckle at Frankie's look of apprehension. "Perhaps Lindbergh could lend you his plane. Only thirty-three hours to Paris from Long Island, hm?"

Frankie pales.

Heath leaves his friend to contend with the dilemmas of travel and selects a few books. His mind is still muddled from too little sleep and dozing off with Aristotle in his hands, so he decides to peruse the fiction aisles and carries a small selection to the recently vacated table next to Frankie's. Frankie scribbles something on his paper, tongue poked between his teeth in concentration. This is the Frankie he knows from dozens of afternoons spent studying in the library at Yale, through late hours of passing books back and forth when one of them hit upon what they needed for their examinations or assignments. Heath looks away, flips open the first book on his pile and settles himself more comfortably into the chair.

He reads slowly that afternoon. The warmth and quiet of the library are incredibly soporific for Heath's already tired bones. His elbow rests on the table, his head is propped in his hand, as he turns the pages and yawns. He feels content. His pleasant haze is broken when Frankie, his expression bordering on manic, drops himself onto the chair by his side.

"Marrakesh!" He whispers so loudly he may well have not bothered whispering at all.

"Marrakesh?" Heath repeats, rubbing the heel of his hand over his eyes.

Frankie looks positively ecstatic. What would Marrakesh hold? Heath can't even begin to think. He looks toward his stack of books and pulls one out from the middle of the pile. That reduces his pile to a spread across the table. "One for you, perhaps." He puts the volume of Jules Verne's *Around the World in 80 Days* into Frankie's hands.

"Well, what exactly constitutes going *around?*" Frankie mumbles as he studies the front and back cover of the book with disdain.

"I believe it's circumnavigational." Suddenly, Art hovers by their table with a hardbound book tucked under one arm.

Warmth creeps up the back of Heath's neck and over his cheeks; his stomach swoops pleasantly. If Frankie notices, he doesn't comment.

Art twirls his finger. "Crossing every time zone, perhaps?" He shrugs. "I haven't read the book, so I couldn't say for sure." He gestures at the empty chair across from them.

"Of course," Heath responds quickly and tidies his books back into a stack.

Frankie hums and puts the book down. "That might be a little ambitious," he concedes, before he reaches over the table to shake Art's hand. "Good to see you again. And in daylight, too!" he adds in a jovial tone.

"Can't spend my entire life underground, as much as there is to be done down there." Art's gaze flickers to Heath before going back to Frankie. "How go the travel plans?"

Frankie sighs and glances back at his disorganized table. "Not well. I should call it a day soon, anyway. I have a date with a wonderful young lady this evening."

Heath pauses and looks at Frankie with narrowed eyes. "*Which* wonderful young lady?"

Frankie, his eyes wide, raises his hands in surrender. "Not your sister. Although she did call me from Cove Neck the other day." He lowers his hands and continues, since Heath hasn't dropped his mutinous stare. "About you. She was concerned, that's all. I assured her you were fine."

Heath softens and sits back, placated for the time being. He might remind Amelia about finding a man that isn't Frankie, however. Just for good measure.

Frankie excuses himself. Heath makes him promise to be nice to the woman of the week. Perhaps one of these days, one of these women will stick. He says as much to Art once Frankie is in the stacks putting away the books, out of earshot.

"I haven't known either of you all that long, but it's clear how much you care about one another," Art comments. He waves to Frankie as he walks toward the exit. "You two are obviously close."

"He's like a brother to me. Sometimes I think he knows me better than I know myself."

They sit in silence. Art studies his book and Heath studies Art. Heath feels privileged, in some sense, to be allowed to get to know Art outside of TJ and the environment of the club. He is the same man above and below, but he is more than just the owner and bartender that Heath imagines many of TJ's frequent customers see. He is more than the man who built the sanctuary below Fifty-seventh Street and welcomed patrons from all corners of New York and beyond.

"What are you doing on the Fourth?" Heath asks, pulling Art's attention from his book. "It's next Monday."

Art closes it, but keeps his thumb between the pages. "The same as every year." He smiles. "I like to watch the fireworks from the water's edge. I thought of having TJ closed for the day but was met with protests, so Alfie's going to take charge for the night."

"You won't be there at all?"

Art looks undecided. "I may call there earlier in the evening, but I'd quite like to enjoy my evening off. It's somewhat of a rarity."

"Perhaps I could join you?" Heath toys with the edge of his cuff as he waits for Art's response. "My family and I would usually spend it on Long Island, but my parents have been invited to a party here in the city."

"You don't wish to attend?"

Heath groans. "More opportunities for my mother to parade me around in her attempts to find me a suitable wife? I'd rather not. Frankie has promised to spend it the day with his godparents, with whom he stays every summer. He can't say no when they've been so generous year after year. So I have no excuse for this damned party unless I find something else to do with the night." He looks up from his sleeve to Art with a hopeful glance.

"I doubt it could rival a night with the upper crust, Manhattan's finest, but you are more than welcome to join me. I'd be grateful for the company, in all honesty." He opens his book again, but his eyes look over the top at Heath. "I'll pick you up at six."

Heath's heart seems to dislodge itself from his chest and shoot up into his throat. "Six it is," he replies. He doesn't get much more read that afternoon—nothing until Art excuses himself to meet an investor back at the club, with a promise in place for Monday.

Y

COME MONDAY, ALL HEATH CAN hope is that punctuality isn't on the list of Art's best attributes, for Heath is running really rather late. Heath isn't at fault, either. Amelia's been in his room for the past hour, telling him about the young man she was set up with this week, who turned out to be, in her words, "the single most dull person on the

East Coast." She sits by the window with her legs curled up beneath her, a cushion at the small of her back.

"And to top it all off, he had the audacity to assume I might want to *kiss* him at the end of the night! After listening to him talk of his family's aptitude for premature balding for close to three *hours.*"

Heath makes a sympathetic noise as he flicks through his wardrobe. He's not even changed his shirt yet, let alone fixed his hair, and it's awfully close to six. "Amelia, I really ought to be getting—"

Amelia pays him absolutely no attention. "Why are men such awful, self-centered pigs? He wasn't handsome, not really, and Mother insisted that he was quite the catch." She makes a noise of disgust from the back of her throat. "The only thing about him that might make him a catch is his worth." She sniffs. "But I won't choose a husband based on that alone. It's not becoming."

She finally looks over at him. "Aren't you going to change? I thought your friend was coming at six. And your hair looks dreadful; you really ought to put something in it before you go out, especially when it's so humid."

Heath sighs. "Yes. I know. If you wouldn't mind." He gestures to the door with a tight smile just as the bell downstairs jingles. Heath frantically checks the time: the second hand is just skipping onto six o'clock.

"I'll leave you to it." Amelia glides to the door. "Do hurry up, Heath." She tut-tuts and slips out, closing the door behind her.

Heath quickly pulls a shirt from the closet and changes, clicks his suspenders into place and selects a light suit jacket. His hands shake as he slicks pomade through his hair. Art converses with the Duchess downstairs, and that worries him, as if he couldn't trust Art to be anything but charming and subtle. "It isn't as though this is a date, anyway," he tells his reflection firmly as he knots a crimson bow tie around his neck before he strides toward the door.

Amelia is on the landing, peering down at Art and the Duchess in the hallway.

"You didn't tell me this friend of yours is so *dapper*," she hisses with the corner of her mouth turned down.

Heath glances over the railing and has to admit, she's right. Art's white shirt is buttoned all the way up to the collar and he's wearing a simple black tie under a white jacket. "Well, he's—I mean, I can't say I'd really *noticed*—all I'm saying is that he's—" Heath sighs. "Yes, I suppose he's rather well put together," he finishes and fiddles with his hair.

Amelia glances at him out of the corner of her eye and then bats his hand away from his hair. "Oh, stop, you look wonderful too, my dear brother." She kisses his cheek. "Now, your friend—does he have a girl?"

Heath holds back a giggle. "No. No, he doesn't have a girl. But I'm not sure you'd quite be his type."

Amelia looks outraged. "I'm starting to think you just don't want me to go out with any of your friends," she huffs and then pushes at his shoulder. "Go on, already, you've kept him waiting with only the Duchess for company for long enough now."

Heath makes his way downstairs and is met with a wide grin from Art. "Don't you look charmingly patriotic," he comments, taking in Heath's appearance.

Heath chuckles and shifts under his gaze, touching his red bow tie self-consciously. It's complimented by a white suit and blue shirt. He'd barely noticed the color combination in his haste.

"It was lovely to meet you, Arthur. Do come round again, won't you?" The Duchess clasps his arm in an affectionate gesture before giving Heath her cheek to kiss. "Have a good evening. Be sensible."

Heath guides Art to the door before Amelia can make any attempt to have herself introduced. Fifth Avenue teems with people; they spill out of Central Park as the gentle warmth of the evening settles over the merry revelers. They have parties to attend, picnics to enjoy, fireworks to watch. The fireworks over the bay at Cove Neck are always beautiful, but Heath always longed to see a display from the city, his home. "Thank you for inviting me." He smiles up at Art, who bumps his shoulder into Heath's in response.

"Of course. You needn't thank me. Is it still all right if we detour past TJ before going down to the water's edge? I want to be sure Alfie has things at least somewhat under control." Art sighs and shakes his head, but not without a smile on his lips.

"Absolutely. We have plenty of time."

The summer has been a spirited one, but tonight it is tenfold. Men tip their hats as they pass; women shoot them polite smiles and greetings. The atmosphere puts a spring into Heath's step as they walk toward the club. Art tells him stories of previous Fourths of July spent in Manhattan with his uncle.

"When I was eight years old, he took me up to the rooftop of our building to watch the fireworks. I'm sure it can't have been strictly legal—he opened the door at the top by bashing through it and then propped it open with a brick while we sat up there."

Heath chuckles, trying to imagine someone like his father, of the same class and stature, doing something like that. He finds he can't, not even a younger version of his father with less purpose to his step.

"We sat on the edge of the rooftop with our legs over the side, and I swear my heart never beat so hard." Art pounds his hand against his chest to demonstrate his point. "I had one hand around Uncle's wrist the entire time—not because I was worried *I* might slip, for I knew he would catch me if I did. No, I worried he might, and I wouldn't be strong enough to help him."

"But if he had, you would have fallen with him."

Art nods. "I know. But I was sure that if I held on, he wouldn't fall. After that year, we began to go down to the water instead. I think he was concerned that I was more traumatized by the entire incident than I let on."

"He might have been right," Heath comments.

"Perhaps."

Art opens the door to Jerry's as they reach the corner of Fifty-seventh and Seventh and allows Heath to step in before him. Jerry doesn't look up: He's busy shaving the man Heath recognizes as one and the same customer from the first day he'd visited the establishment with Frankie. Art sees him too and sighs, lifting a hand. "Not today, Mr. Peters. It's a national holiday and I have taken the day off."

"Consider my presence just food for thought then, Art," the man responds as he closes his eyes and tips his head back to let Jerry at his neck. "I'll return on Wednesday to hear your answer."

Heath carries on to the back room as he eyes Art, whose mouth is tightly drawn and whose forehead is creased by a worry line. He doesn't ask until they're on the staircase and winding down into TJ, the music and talk loud from within. But Art simply shakes his head and places a hand at the center of Heath's back. "Just a little business. I'll deal with it later in the week. Tonight, my focus is on you and you alone."

"I shan't object to that." Heath hides a smile and tries to compose his expression before he opens the door into the club.

He hears Art curse behind him as they step inside. The room is packed almost wall to wall. Three men fight to play piano all at once, hands criss-crossing; another leans against the back of the piano and sings along to one out of the three tunes. Art guides Heath to the bar, where Alfie's voice can now be heard over the din. For someone with half a dozen boisterous men yelling drink orders at him, he appears to be in remarkably good spirits, laughing with one as he pours a drink for another. He has a dishcloth wrapped around his neck like a scarf and a rose tucked behind one ear.

"Everything all right?" Art calls out. He slots Heath into a space by the end of the bar and steps behind him.

Heath can feel the heat of his chest against his back; Art's hands rest on the bar at either side of his body. He catches the wink Alfie shoots at him and laughs as heat rises to his cheeks.

"Everything's Jake! Now, really—I thought this was supposed to be your day off. It's almost as though you don't trust me at all." He shoos the two of them away. "Unless you want a drink, move along, the both of you. I have customers to attend to."

Heath feels more than hears Art huff. "I suppose that's us told, then," he murmurs. He slips his hand into Heath's. "Come on. Let's enjoy the last of the daylight."

Heath slides his fingers between Art's, interlocking their hands tightly, with their palms pressed together. He enjoys it for what it is, with the knowledge that they will have to part once they reach the street. He almost wants to protest, to tell Art to forget the daylight or even the fireworks and just stay below, where they can share this touch for as long as they please.

But he doesn't. He allows himself to be guided up the stairs and ignores how empty his hand feels when Art slides his hand free and lets it hang by his side again. The man, Mr. Peters, has left. Jerry is cleaning his supplies.

"I'll be going home now," he tells Art.

Art nods. "That's fine. Alfie's organized a few of the boys downstairs to take rotations watching the door. I wouldn't expect any trouble on a night such as this, though."

They bid him goodnight and step onto the street. Rather than start south, as Heath expected, Art starts across the road.

"Hold up, where are we going?" Heath frowns. "You're not taking me up onto any rooftops, are you? Art, I'm really not sure I—"

"Hush," Art tut-tuts at him and gestures to the entrance to the subway. "It's an awfully long walk, even if it's a little cooler at this time of the night."

Heath hesitates. He looks at Art and then at the entrance, where people filter to and from street level.

"What's wrong?" Art pauses at the top of the stairs and looks at Heath with his head tilted in question. When Heath doesn't reply straightaway, Art fits the pieces together. But rather than laugh at him or chastise him for being so snobbish, he just walks back and rests a hand against his arm. "It's perfectly safe, I promise. You might even enjoy it."

Heath stutters. "I'm not scared. I've just never had any particular reason to take the subway, that's all."

"Well, now you do."

Art digs a few quarters out of his jacket pocket as they step toward the entrance. Heath quietly wishes that Art's hand were still in his to guide him. He contents himself with keeping close to his side as they take the steps down and blinks as his eyes adjust to the artificial light below ground. The turnstiles clink as people pass through them; from within the station a train moves off with a roar and a clank. Art presses the required coins into Heath's palm. Heath watches how he passes through and copies his motions exactly.

It seems like an event in itself to Heath, as they make their way onto the southbound platform; the concrete strip is crowded with other bodies down its entire length. Bright lights flood the tracks from the tunnel ahead as the train trundles, creaking, to a halt. The doors are flung open, many pour out and impossibly more crush inside, Heath and Art among them. It's hot and stuffy inside the subway car, and from somewhere farther down the train comes the sound of a trumpet.

"All right?" Art murmurs into Heath's ear, and he nods. But he's unprepared for the jerk as the train starts again, and he would lose his footing completely if not for Art's arm, which circles his waist to keep him steady. It's crowded enough in the car that no one notices. The other riders are too wrapped up in their own circles of friends as gossip is shared and last-minute plans for the evening are made. Art doesn't move his arm the entire ride, keeping Heath steady between the hand on his lower back and Art's chest. Heath curls his fingers into the lapel of Art's jacket and holds on. He breathes in the scent of his cologne and listens to the clack of the wheels on the tracks as they hurtle toward the end of the island.

Heath is a little lightheaded by the time they push out onto the platform again along with dozens of other patrons. The heat from the train presses along his hairline; his skin is hot and clammy until it meets the welcome, cooler air outside and above ground. He whirls to face Art as they separate from the crush of bodies and starts to laugh. Erratic and wild, he must look mad, but he doesn't care. "I did it!" Heath twirls on his toes and marches off toward the water's edge with Art jogging after him.

"You did," Art assures him. "Didn't I tell you there was nothing to be scared of?"

"I wasn't scared!" Heath reminds him. He catches Art's eye and sees that he is only teasing anyway.

There's still daylight left—time until fireworks begin to decorate the sky. Art buys a couple of sodas from a vendor hawking his wares up and down the busy promenade, and they choose a bench by the water's edge. Children run up and down the path crying out in glee and trailing ribbons. They are followed by harassed-looking nannies and parents, whose expressions show that they hope all this will be over with sooner rather than later so they may get them home and into bed.

Heath watches with a fond smile before his gaze moves past the people to the water. Brooklyn sits across the river; people are lined up along the railings there, too. He breathes in the scent of cotton candy and lets the breeze brush through his hair. "I don't know quite how you do it." He turns to look at Art. "But I seem to feel infinitely calmer whenever I'm around you. As though my brain isn't quite such a twisted-up mesh of thoughts that I can't make head or tail of."

Art looks contented as he turns back toward the water. "If nothing else, I'm glad I can do that for you," he replies quietly.

If he could, Heath thinks, this would be when he kissed Art. Alfie's words from the week before ring in his head. He would give his thanks with a press of lips, because perhaps that might communicate more than his words could ever truly say. As if sensing Heath's eyes on him,

Art turns back. His own eyes flicker down to Heath's lips before he meets his gaze once more.

"Perhaps I might cash in that look later," Art murmurs, his smile more flirtatious than it had been before.

"Perhaps," Heath agrees.

They stand and crowd close to the railing once the light has faded, two bodies among many as the fireworks begin. The sparks shoot up, arcing over the Statue of Liberty and twinkling above her flaming torch. Heath feels the back of Art's hand bump against his own and they stand like that for the whole display, with the backs of their hands pressed together where they stand side by side.

IT'S NOT TOO LATE WHEN Art delivers Heath to the doorstep of the townhouse. The park is still full of people chattering late into the night, and parties in full swing can still be heard on their walk back from the subway station near TJ. Heath imagines his family will still be out—the house looks too still for them to have returned. He considers inviting Art in as they stand together on the top step. He knows Art has no place to go, save for back to the club, should he wish to. Heath imagines he won't.

They're somewhat secluded beneath the awning of the house; no one is passing by. Art's hand cups Heath's jaw; his thumb brushes over the curve of his cheekbone. Heath tilts his face up to meet Art's gaze. The blue of Art's eyes is darker in the low light.

"I had a wonderful time tonight," Art says finally. His breath ghosts over Heath's lips. They stand so close.

"I did, too." Heath swallows.

"Cash or check?" Art whispers, and it takes Heath a moment to understand what he is asking. The promise of a kiss lingers in the air between them.

A holler comes from the park, startling Heath, but Art doesn't move his hand.

"Check," Heath replies, and lays a hand on Art's chest. "Another time," he adds. It is not a rebuff but a promise, and he hopes Art realizes that.

It seems he does, for when his hand does fall back, it isn't without a lingering press to Heath's cheek, which tingles in its wake.

"Goodnight, Heath." Art walks a few steps and then turns. With a lopsided grin, he blows him a kiss.

Heath catches the kiss in his hand and tucks it into his breast pocket. "Goodnight, Art. Get home safe."

CH. 4

HEATH IS THE FIRST ONE in bed and the last awake. Amelia is chattering animatedly when he starts downstairs, still rubbing sleep from the corners of his eyes even as he makes his way into the dining room. "Good morning." He takes his seat and blinks against the strong morning sunlight flooding in through the windows. They're cracked open a notch, but the city seems to be far quieter than it was yesterday.

"How was your evening, darling?" The Duchess doesn't wait for an answer before she continues. "It really is an awful shame that you made other plans at the last minute. Not that your friend Arthur wasn't charming and polite but, you see, Louise was there last night and she asked after you. Goodness, I felt so bad I lied and told her you were feeling under the weather rather than say you made other plans."

Heath makes a noise of protest. "You needn't *lie* on my behalf. I'm sure she'd have understood the truth just as well."

"That is as it may be. She's coming to dinner this evening. I expect you to be both present and displaying your sweetest self."

"But I had other plans for this evening."

The Duchess eyes him coolly. "And what plans are those?"

Heath snaps his mouth shut. He thinks of the club, of how he woke up thinking of going there to surprise Art. Of perhaps stealing him away somewhere to follow up on their promise, if he still wanted to. Heath hoped he did.

The Duchess sighs, pulling Heath from his thoughts. "You've been acting very strangely this past week or so, Heath. You're barely in this house at all. Do you mean to tell me that you spend all of this time with Francis or Arthur? They'll surely have other things they can attend to without you for one evening. Francis's godmother stopped by last night and she told me he's found some new girl."

"Arthur hasn't got a girl," Amelia chips in, unhelpfully.

"Well, he might if Heath weren't taking up all of his time. You'll be here for dinner. And I won't hear of you sneaking off after dessert, either."

"Don't argue with your mother, Heath." The Duke appears in the doorway, in full business dress. "That's quite unlike you—and entirely unbecoming." He straightens his suit and collects his briefcase from a chair. "Son, I'd like you to meet me for lunch today. I'm going to introduce you to some of my colleagues." He sinks his hand down over Heath's shoulder; his fingers bite into Heath's collarbone. "I know I permitted you the summer to make your decision, but it seems you could do with a little help in thinking more seriously about the matter. One o'clock, please."

Heath stares at his lap. "Yes, sir. One o'clock."

He eats his breakfast in silence while Amelia returns to her tale of an old school friend who eloped with a piano player from the South. Amelia is sure it meant she was in a family way. He tunes her out as a weight that he'd managed to shed returns to his shoulders. He is good at slipping back into his role of perfect son: polite, demure, suggestible. When he glances up as he finishes eating, it's to find his mother looking at him not with any hint of concern at his sudden quiet, but rather with satisfaction and pride.

"Excuse me," he murmurs and stands. He wipes his mouth with a napkin before he tosses it down onto the table and starts back toward the stairs.

"Please put on a suit to meet your father, Heath."

"Of course, Mama."

Footsteps clatter after him but he doesn't turn until Amelia's hand tugs at the sleeve of his shirt.

"Heath, wait, won't you?" A strand of her dark brown hair falls into her eyes and she pushes it back, peering up at him. "What's wrong?"

"Nothing." He forces a smile. "What is it? I need to dress or I'll be late." It's a lie, and they both know it. It's not quite ten; he has plenty of time.

"Heath. I met someone. Someone *amazing*. Someone special." Her smile is giddy, and Heath has to stop himself from blurting out, "Me too."

"Oh? Come." He slips his hand into hers and tugs her toward his room. "Tell me everything."

His name is Edward. Amelia can't seem to tell Heath exactly what he does, but gets wrapped up in her description of his charming appearance and wide smile. Of his carefully tamed curls and sharp jawline and the hazel eyes she got so lost in. Of how he was unfashionably late to the party but apologized for it not just to the hosts but to every individual guest, too. Of how he was breathless and exhausted by the time he reached Amelia, only to spend the rest of the evening by her side, recounting his college days at Columbia and teaching her how to fold a paper napkin into a small bird. Amelia has the bird tucked into the pocket of her dress, and she sets the little crumpled being on her palm and shows it to Heath.

Heath has seen Amelia squired by a variety of men. Young, handsome men, well read and traveled, versed in the arts and yet primed to take over their family enterprises. Men who drive Dusenbergs. *Wealthy* men, all of them. He doesn't doubt that Edward is wealthy, too, given the circles he's running in, but for Amelia to lack a precise understanding of what Edward does for a living and the size of his bank balance is unusual. Heath hasn't seen anything like this light in her eyes, or the way she stares at the paper bird as though it were a diamond ring on her finger.

"I'm happy for you," he tells her honestly, if with a hint of envy, as he sets out a pair of cream pants and turns back to the closet to find the matching jacket.

"He's coming to dinner tonight, too. So you'll get to meet him." Amelia swings her legs off the window ledge; the heels of her shoes tip-tap against the wood. "Just think. Before the summer's out, both of us could be set to be married."

Heath whirls around so fast that he knocks a book from the top of the dresser. It crashes onto the floor. Amelia laughs, her head thrown back as she coos with glee.

"Oh, you are far too easy to tease. I know you'll never propose to Louise, no matter how much Mama puts her hands together and prays for it. You ought to be careful of her puppeteering skills." She takes a breath and leans back against the window. She hums as her back connects with the warm glass. "There'd be a far easier way to deter her, you realize."

"To find a woman I would actually like to marry?"

Amelia nods.

Not for the first time, Heath wonders if such a woman could exist. He adores women—they can be sweet and pleasant, beautiful and wonderful companions. But he has never met one that made his heart race in his chest as it has done recently around Art, or back at Yale when he admired Julian from afar. He will have no choice but to marry eventually, though. Louise his mother may eventually relent on, but the question of marriage altogether? He thinks not. If he won't find it in him to love any woman the way he's expected, what difference should it make whom he proposes to?

Heath sighs and sinks onto the end of the bed. "I can as much imagine a future with Louise as I can with any woman," he says quietly.

"That's because you haven't found the right one yet. When you do, you'll know. Edward walked into the room last night, and it was as though I'd known him my entire life. You'll understand what I mean someday."

Heath does understand, and that's entirely the problem.

He leaves early for lunch so he can call on Frankie on the way and ask his advice about the coming evening. The world is gold-tinted through the lenses of his sunshades; sun filters through the trees on Fifth and casts shadows onto the street below. Frankie is closing the door behind him when he approaches, and looks surprised to see Heath hovering at the bottom of the front porch steps.

"Heathcliff!" He jogs down to him and pulls him into a hug. "You know how I adore any visit, planned or not, from you, but I'm late for a social engagement, I'm afraid."

"Of course, I should have called." Heath touches his fingers to the delicate blue material tucked artfully into Frankie's breast pocket. "Lunch with your girl?" Frankie nods. His expression reminds Heath of Amelia's from that morning. "Well, if love isn't in the air today!"

"Shall we have a drink tonight? I can tell you all about her; and I believe you might have something to tell me too, perhaps?" He raises an eyebrow.

Heath waves him on as Frankie turns to go in the opposite direction. "I have a family dinner this evening, no excuses or exceptions. Tomorrow?"

"Tomorrow." Frankie waves back and strides at double speed down the avenue.

Since his time with Frankie was cut short, he would have the time to walk to his father's office. But it's hot under the midday sun, and he can only imagine the reprimand he'll get if he's sweaty beneath his neat suit. His feet take him, on autopilot, to the corner of Fifty-seventh and Seventh Avenue; the bell above the door of Jerry's announces his entrance as he steps inside. Jerry is alone, reading the newspaper at the counter.

"Quiet downstairs," Jerry warns when he sees Heath.

"Art?"

Jerry shakes his head. "Out this morning. Try later in the afternoon, kid."

Heath swallows his disappointment and steps back out onto the street. He's disgruntled and tired now, and time is marching on. He could take the subway and be a few blocks from Wall Street within ten minutes. But he doesn't, rather whistles for a taxicab and then proceeds to curse the traffic along with the driver for the entire ride.

His father isn't angry, however, when he sees him step out of the taxicab, dressed appropriately as he is. Perhaps he thought Heath mightn't come. He introduces Heath to a group of middle-aged men. Some he knows; some he doesn't. He isn't introduced as a Yale graduate, as a smart young man, or even simply as Heath. "This is my son," the Duke says with a hint of pride, as if that alone conveyed all that anyone might wish to know about him.

He follows the men blindly through a maze of streets in an area of the city he barely knows. Heath voices his confusion when they reach a small bookstore with books stacked up so high at the windows that barely any light filters inside.

The Duke wraps an arm around Heath's shoulders as he leads him through the small store and toward the back. "I don't think of you as a child, Heath, and I apologize if I have given you that impression. You're a man now. And this world? This is one you will soon be a part of, too. Should you choose to take up my offer, that is."

Pushing at a wooden panel on the wall, his father's colleagues press ahead into a back room. Heath smells cigarette smoke and whiskey and has to bite down on his lower lip to keep from laughing aloud. "A speakeasy?"

"The best in Manhattan, son."

The corner of Heath's mouth twitches. "Debatable," he mumbles and follows the other men down the staircase into the establishment.

It is grandiose in comparison to TJ—three times the size and decorated far more extravagantly. A bar at one side has people pressed up against its edge, but as many sit at circular tables scattered across the floor, served by girls in short dresses, strings of pearls and heavily made-up faces. If TJ is inconspicuous, this club is a blaring siren. It seems neither subtle nor discreet, but simply *loud*. But the clientele says it all—the club owners need not be careful, really, when they have some of the wealthiest and most powerful men under their low roof.

The party is led to a table near the back, one of the few available. Heath swipes a matchbook from the middle of the table, turning it over in his hand. "Eden" seems to be a popular choice for lunch on Wall Street. He slips the matchbook into his pocket as a token for Art.

Heath quickly comes to see that he is merely an accessory at this lunch. None of the men pay him much attention; his father, too, only utters a word or two to him during the course of their meal. The girls flit around, and disgust churns in his gut as the men fondle them as though they were nothing but playthings. Heath is wildly uncomfortable. He wants no part of this world. He barely touches his food, sits in silence and keeps his eyes off the girls even when they lean past his shoulder to try to garner his attention.

"I hope this has given you some food for thought," the Duke says to him when they finally reach street level once more. The men are to return to the office, although in Heath's opinion a good many of them are far too drunk to do any such thing. "I know you'll make the right choice."

Heath nods stiffly, turns from them and strides past the line of taxicabs toward the subway. The right choice. The right choice isn't to be found anywhere on Wall Street, least of all in the world into which his father is trying to lure him.

He considers calling at TJ once more, in the hope that Art might have returned. But he decides to return home instead, and takes to his room to rest until he has to dress for dinner and confront not only his sister's new beau, but also Louise. Amelia has gone to the salon to have her hair freshly bobbed, he is told when he returns, and the Duchess is in her room. Heath pauses outside his mother's door before he raps lightly and enters when she calls out permission.

She's lying on the bed with her shoes slipped off and her head propped up on a stack of pillows. In her lap is a book that she doesn't appear to be reading. Her expression is a little drowsy as she beckons him over. "Come here, baby."

"Can I join you for a little while?" Heath feels like a child again, crawling in next to his mother after a bad dream.

The Duchess smiles and pats the space beside her on the bed. He shrugs off his jacket and unlaces his shoes, leaving them by the chaise longue before he settles beside her.

She works her fingers through his hair, rubbing her thumb against the back of his ear. "How was lunch with your father? I hope his colleagues were civilized with you."

Heath scoffs. He closes his eyes as he curls into his mother's touch and breathes in the familiar scent of her perfume. "They didn't pay me much attention. I just observed." He pauses. "I didn't like it, Mama," he whispers.

"Oh, Heath. We just want the best for you, that's all. You know that."

"What if what father wants isn't what's best for me? Perhaps something else might be better."

"Such as? I know you're not thrilled about the idea of going into investment banking like your father, but so far you haven't been able to suggest an alternative. You can't just sit around reading books for the rest of your life."

"I know that." Heath sighs. "I don't know yet. But there will be something, something that isn't going to work at Harvey & Taylor."

His mother hushes him in a gentle tone and tilts her head down to kiss his forehead. "Let's not fight over it, sweetheart. Let's rest now."

Heath breathes out and rests his hand on his mother's arm. "All right. Just a little while."

THE DUCHESS SELECTS HIS CLOTHES for that evening: a pink and white candy-striped shirt and white pants. She tweaks his collar and fixes him with the same look of pride that he knows from first days of school, graduations and the like. Heath doesn't doubt that she expects more from him tonight than to be on his best behavior. She expects him to at least suggest to Louise the possibility of a future together, for the two of them. As much as he likes to earn that look upon her face, it is an expectation he will not be able to meet.

Amelia flutters between the dining room and the hallway, turning a chair here, straightening a painting there, as though she cannot possibly stay still for even a moment. Heath watches her doing this for some time before she catches him staring. "So silly, for me to be nervous." She chews at the end of her thumb, and he catches her wrist and tugs it away.

"The only thing silly is that you'll smudge your lipstick if you keep that up." He winks and wraps an arm around her to ground her. "Amelia? What do you think I ought to do about Louise?"

She tilts her head and taps her painted fingernails on the end of her chin. "Act like a total ass all night until she realizes you aren't quite such a catch after all, and goes off you of her own accord." She catches Heath's incredulous look and cackles, pulling him into a proper hug. "I think perhaps you ought to just tell her you'd rather remain friends. Tell her the *truth*."

Heath doesn't comment that these two statements are not entirely the same thing.

Louise arrives almost simultaneously with Edward, which causes quite a stir in the hallway as Martha ushers everyone in. Heath sees just a flash of the top of Edward's head before he has his arms full with Louise. He guides her into the day room and seats her next to his mother, then accepts a drink from Martha when she comes round to them.

Amelia giggles as she tugs Edward toward their little group, proudly presenting him. Heath looks away from Louise as he takes a sip of his drink. He starts when he recognizes the man before him and promptly chokes on the fruity liquid.

"Darling, are you all right?" Louise thumps him on the back with her handbag until he regains his breath enough to beg her to stop.

"I'm fine. Apologies." He clears his throat and offers a hand to Edward, whose eyes give away that he, too, recognizes their connection. Edward, Heath happens to know, is rather skilled at the piano, if his renditions at TJ are anything to go by.

"Pleasure to meet you, Edward. I've heard so many wonderful things." Heath squeezes his hand as they shake. *I won't tell if you don't.*

"Likewise, Heath. Amelia talks very fondly of you." Edward wraps an arm around Amelia's waist.

"Are you sure you're all right?" Amelia asks, frowning at him. "Your cheeks are awfully red."

"Are you still feeling as poorly as you were yesterday?" Louise fusses, pressing a hand to his forehead and coddling him.

"I'm quite all right. If you'll just excuse me while I find some water."

Heath steals from the room, not going in search of water, but simply taking a moment to settle himself. Footsteps come up behind him; his head snaps up and he finds Edward a few steps away.

"Heath, I know that—"

Heath raises a hand. "I don't want them finding out any more than I imagine you do."

Edward nods slowly and steps closer. He lowers his voice to a murmur. "I do honestly care about her. I've never met anyone like Amelia."

He glances past Edward's shoulder to where he can see Amelia, with her head tipped back in laughter as she stands with Louise and the Duchess; the Duke stands to one side and observes the group. He turns his attention back to Edward. "All I ask is that you don't hurt her. She deserves to be happy. If you can make her happy, then I have no objections—no matter which way your feelings may lie."

Edward claps a hand to Heath's elbow and squeezes tightly. "Thank you." He smiles, one eyebrow raised. "And I have to ask—how did your evening with Art go? You two are the talk of the club."

Heath stutters and bats his hand away. "Oh, hush up," he mumbles. His cheeks are hot now for a different reason as he returns to the dining room.

Enough conversation flows around the dinner table when they sit to eat that Heath can keep to his thoughts. The weight of Louise's hand against his arm barely strays throughout the entire meal. He has to say something, just as Amelia told him. He's let this go on long enough and, as much as he finds her exhausting, Louise deserves just as much happiness as he wants for Amelia.

He reaches for Louise's hand once the dessert plates have been cleared and laces their fingers together. It is nothing like holding Art's hand; hers is so dainty in his, and a little clammy, too. "Would you care to take a walk? I'd like to talk to you in private."

Louise's eyes light up, and he thinks he should clarify right away, lest she get any ideas about him dropping to one knee on Fifth Avenue. "I'd love to," she gushes and wraps her fingers around his hand. Her nails dig into his skin.

"If you'll excuse us."

The Duchess beams and waves them off. Amelia gives him an encouraging nod. "The truth," she mouths at him.

A version of the truth is what he gives her as they walk one of the quiet lengths of the park with her arm through the crook of his elbow. "I'm sorry for ever making you believe we would be more. I know I should have spoken to you sooner, but I was afraid to hurt you."

Louise looks as though she may cry at any moment. But she doesn't run from him, or hit him, or scream at him. "I understand," she says finally. She straightens her back with an air of maturity. "And while I wish you had told me sooner, I'm glad I finally know. I had wondered, but…" She trails off, laughing, and turns her head away. "The Duchess kept insisting you were merely a little shy."

"Of course she did," he mutters with a roll of his eyes. "The woman's a tyrant."

She tut-tuts. "You shouldn't be rude about your mother."

Taking back her arm, she steps away from him as they turn to walk back toward the house. "I'd like us to be friends. We've known each other so long, Heath."

"Friends," he agrees and slips his hands into his pockets. "I think that sounds like a wonderful idea."

Louise leaves shortly after they return to the house. The Duchess doesn't so much as ask; the slump in her shoulders as she sits in the corner of the living room with a glass of water pressed to her temple is enough for Heath to understand that she knows. He goes to her and kisses her cheek. "I'm sorry," he whispers, and she shakes her head.

"There will be other girls."

Heath swallows and nods, then sits by Amelia and Edward. Edward offers him a cigarette, which he accepts despite his mother's noise of distaste.

"Will you go tonight, still?" Edward asks quietly when Amelia turns to speak to the Duke.

Heath shakes his head. "No, not tonight. I think I've given my mother enough of a headache for one evening, without sneaking off. And you?"

Edward glances over at Amelia. "No, I think not. I'd like to remember this evening exactly as it is, with no other embellishments." He cracks a grin. "Someone else can tinkle the ivories for the night."

Heath chuckles. "You're rather good, you know? I was impressed."

Edward mimes a bow before Amelia steals his attention and suggests she show him the view from the upstairs balcony. It's an indication of how she feels that the Duchess doesn't bat an eyelid as the pair rises from the couch.

Heath clears his throat. "I'd like to decide on my future, first. Before I choose a girl to settle down with. So I may provide her with stable ground beneath my feet. You understand, don't you?" He looks at his parents, who seem both surprised and pleased. It isn't a permanent solution; it will only serve to buy him some time. But he can't stand to see them so obviously disappointed with him. At least this may appease them while he makes sense of what he is going to do with all aspects of his future.

"I think that's a very sensible decision, son." The Duke tips his glass to him. "We have every faith in you."

Heath excuses himself to retire to his room. He pauses at the top of the stairs to look through to where Amelia and Edward stand on the balcony, entwined in one another's arms.

Y

HIS PARENTS SEEM CONTENT TO leave him to his own devices again the next day. Part of him—a very large part—nearly hurtles straight out the door to TJ. However, he promised Frankie he'd see him, and it isn't a promise he intends to break for the sake of turning up on Art's doorstep first thing in the morning. Besides, he no doubt has other matters to attend to during the day—business, as the day before, when he'd called at Jerry's. But if there is one thing Heath is sure of today, it's that he has a kiss waiting that he fully intends to cash in, come hell or high water.

Frankie phones first and suggests a restaurant that's on the other side of the park and boasts the best Italian cuisine in the city. It's a little cloudy out, a smattering of gray over the usually clear and bright sky. Amelia left a little before him to have lunch with Edward and his parents a few blocks away at their townhouse. Heath takes a winding route through the park, to while away the extra time he has allowed and enjoy the cooler breeze that ripples through his shirt. He passes many a couple taking a turn through the park, arms or hands linked, heads tilted toward one another. It makes his heart ache; but now it aches for one person, and one alone, rather than a general wistfulness for something he doesn't have, or doesn't truly know.

Frankie awaits him outside the restaurant with a fedora perched on his head and a cigarette between his fingers. He stubs it out when he sees Heath, and greets him with one of his customary, bone-crushing hugs. "I feel as though I am once again complete." He lightly cuffs Heath's head in an affectionate, brotherly way, and they step into the restaurant. "Good to have you back, Heathcliff."

"I wasn't aware I'd left." He squeezes Frankie's shoulder. "I'm sorry if I've been caught up in other things this past week."

"You don't need to apologize. I just missed having you around, that's all."

The server leads them to a table, and Frankie rattles off an order for both of them before he can so much as produce menus, startling him before he retreats.

Heath snorts. "Frankie knows best?"

"When it comes to food, yes. Yes, he does." Frankie toes Heath's ankle beneath the table. "How are things? Above *and* below ground, that is."

Heath kicks him back with a little more force. "How's your girl?"

Frankie pulls a face. "I think that's over," he mumbles into the back of his hand.

Heath fixes him with a look. "What was that? An entire four days you managed this time?" He groans and buries his face in his hands. How glad he is that he managed to deter Amelia from wanting a date with his fickle-minded friend!

Frankie raises his hand in surrender. "In my defense, this time it was entirely *her* doing, not mine. She's the one who called it quits."

Heath isn't convinced. "And why was that, Frankie?" With a sweet smile, he gestures for him to continue.

"She *claims* I was flirting with a cigarette girl as I ordered our drinks last night. I maintain I was doing nothing of the sort."

"You're a cad, Frankie David. A regular old drugstore cowboy." This time it's Heath who reaches out to whack a hand on Frankie's head. "Here's a novel idea, my friend. Try treating the one you're with with a touch more respect. It might go down rather well."

Frankie scowls and rubs at the crown of his head. "What would you know about it?"

Heath shrugs. "I have a sister, don't I? Girls these days, they won't take any nonsense from men like you."

"How insightful, thank you," Frankie replies. This kick goes sharply into Heath's shin.

THE TWO FRIENDS SIT LONG into the afternoon, whiling away the time over tonic water and nursing the strain on their stomachs from the pasta dishes they'd devoured. Frankie has tomato sauce spattered on the front of his shirt; Heath is in no way smug as he removes his napkin.

The clouds have cleared, and the low afternoon sunlight streams in through the wide windows. Heath tilts his head back to watch as it glints on the silverware at a neighboring, unoccupied table, before he looks back to Frankie. "Would you be horribly offended if I left your most delightful company now?" he asks, with a hopeful smile.

Frankie's expression is a knowing one. "To go see your fella."

"Something like that." There's little Heath can do anymore to control the expression he gets whenever Art is brought to mind. "I have something that needs to be cashed in."

Frankie clinks their nearly empty glasses together. "And I really don't need to know more than that. Off you go, young Heathcliff. Fulfill your great namesake's legacy. Perhaps a little less on the tortured side, if possible."

Heath sighs as he stands up and stretches. "No matter how many times you try, Frankie, Heathcliff will never be my namesake. I doubt either of my parents have even read *Wuthering Heights*."

"Maybe you were adopted," Frankie suggests with a cheerful grin as Heath goes toward the door.

The walk seems long on such a heavy stomach in the heat, but he keeps on, feeling his body relax from the large lunch as the sun warms the back of his neck. His pace picks up as he gets nearer; his heart flutters as though there is a bird trapped in his ribcage, struggling to get free. He wonders if Art has thought of him at all over the past few days, as Heath has thought of him. He wonders if he spent yesterday wondering when he'd see him again, glancing at the door every time it opened, hoping the next person through it would be him.

These thoughts have him practically tripping into Jerry's parlor. Jerry starts when he sees Heath, then bellows with laughter and gestures him on. "He'll be pleased to see you," Jerry grins, clapping Heath on the back as he starts into the back room. The bar is quiet; the dregs of the afternoon are easing into evening. There's no sign of Art, however, which makes Heath's feet grind to a halt on the stone floor.

Alfie looks up from the bar and whacks his hand against the door to the back room of the club. "Art! You have a visitor. You'll like this one," he adds and shoots Heath a wink before he turns back to the bottles he's putting on the shelf.

Art slams into the bar with a grunt. "What part of don't bother me unless—" He catches sight of Heath, and a grin splits over his previously grumpy expression.

"Unless Heath comes by," Alfie finishes for him. "I did exactly as I was told, thank you very much."

"Hey." Heath practically bounces on his toes; one word is hardly enough for him to convey any of his feelings. He gives up on holding back and shoots across the bar to hug Art, nearly knocking him backward.

Art's shoulders shake with laughter as he wraps his arms around Heath's smaller frame and tucks him close. "Hi, you. I was starting to think you were staying away on purpose."

Heath shakes his head. "Never. I had a few family things to attend to. I'm sorry. I should have called."

"Yes." Art's eyes twinkle. "You should have."

Art's gaze flickers down to Heath's lips, and Heath inhales sharply; his eyelids droop as he tilts his head up. But rather than kiss him, Art clears his throat and disentangles their bodies. "I'm afraid I do have some work I need to finish before tonight." He squeezes Heath's waist. "Sit. Have a drink. Give me an hour, at the most, and I'll be all yours for the evening."

"Yes, of course, Art. I don't mind taking care of the bar again tonight, not at all," Alfie chirrups from behind them.

Art pays him no attention. "There's somewhere I want to show you tonight. No objections." He kisses his hairline and leaves him in the bar with Alfie.

Heath turns on Alfie the moment the door has swung shut behind Art. "Where's he taking me?" he probes. He hops onto a barstool and lets Alfie mix him a drink.

"How should I know? It's not as though he takes every emerald-eyed college graduate on little mystery trips around Manhattan." Alfie sets a drink down. "Although I do know that it's one of the most beautiful spots in the city."

"So you *do* know!"

"You'll get nothing out of me, so don't waste your breath."

That doesn't stop Heath from trying. He drives Alfie progressively crazier for the next hour while he picks at clues and tries to stumble upon exactly what Art's plans are for them. By the time Art emerges from the back room again, Alfie looks fraught, with his elbows on the bar and his head in his hands. "Take him away, please," he begs Art. "He's reminds me of my cousin the one time he messed around with dope." He makes a face of distaste.

Art slips a hand around Heath's elbow and hauls him up. "Come on, then."

As they did before, they hold hands as far as street level before they let their arms fall to their sides. Heath shows Art the matchbook from Eden as they walk out. The silver lettering on the white case looks gaudy in the daylight. Art shakes his head in amusement, takes it from him and tosses it into the nearest trashcan on the street. "I'm sure many would like to call TJ seedy, but it is nothing of the sort compared to places like that, if you ask me."

Heath nods in agreement. "I felt so uncomfortable there. And not just because of the women. The whole atmosphere." He shudders.

Art's hand ghosts over the curve of his spine. "That doesn't surprise me at all." He takes him down to the subway, but they don't go nearly so far south. Art leads him above ground at the Brooklyn Bridge stop.

Heath looks toward the water, admiring the frame of the bridge against the horizon. "The bridge? Are we going onto the bridge?"

Art doesn't reply but tugs him by the wrist away from the bridge and walks down the block to City Hall and a locked subway entrance.

Heath glances at the entrance and then up at Art. "It's closed." He gestures at the gate. "I'm confused."

Art looks at him. "Yes, it is. But that doesn't mean we can't go inside."

"Actually, I think that's exactly what it means." Heath frowns. He watches as Art fiddles with the lock, jamming what looks like a penknife he has pulled from his pocket into the clasp. "Art," he hisses. He glances around them, but the street is quiet. "Art, you can't just *break in* to a subway station! Are you trying to get us arrested?" *Because I can think of plenty more creative ways we could do that*, he adds silently.

Art turns, a patient smile on his lips. "Heath. Will you please breathe and trust me? If only for one evening."

Heath drags a breath into his lungs and looks around, keeping an eye on anyone walking past who might spot what they are doing. The sun is beginning to set. Art's back is curved where he's bent over the lock, and muscles shift beneath his shirt.

The lock clicks, loud on the quiet street. Art lets out a noise of triumph and guides Heath in as he slips the gate open a bit. Art grabs

Heath's hand and they hurtle down the steps into the subway station, laughing as they stumble over the bottom step. Art catches him with an arm around his waist. Heath blinks as his eyes adjust to the dim light; his eyes turn to the ceiling. A circular stained glass window is set into the ceiling. It has a delicate blue pattern that lets in a dim stream of light. The tiles are deep green; the whole station is far more of an artwork than the others he has seen.

"Why is it closed?" Heath asks as he admires the way the light falls to the floor, tinted blue from the window.

"They close it overnight. The train goes straight through to the next stop. They claim it's not used enough once the commuters have come through but really, I think they want to preserve this as long as they possibly can." Art trails his fingers over the grooves between the tiles.

Art walks up behind Heath. He wraps his arms around his waist and tucks his chin over his shoulder. "Hi," he whispers, nosing behind his ear.

Heath shivers and slides his hands over the arms around his waist. "Hi," he repeats in a murmur. He tips his head back so he can meet Art's gaze.

Art turns Heath until his hands rest at the small of his back as he pulls him into his chest. "Cash," he whispers, the tip of his nose nudging against Heath's. "Or check?"

"Cash," Heath replies without a moment's hesitation. He stands on his toes as he joins their lips with his heart beating so loudly he's sure that Art must be able to hear it in the quiet of the subway station.

Even in surroundings so beautiful, the rest of the world seems to fall away at the edges, pale in comparison to the touch of Art's lips against his. Heath feels Art's hand on his neck, pressing against a pulse point; Heath's heartbeat pounds into Art's palm. The light scratch of Art's evening stubble catches on his chin, and Heath sinks onto his chest. Heath's hands cling to Art's biceps as they kiss.

A rumble sounds; light bursts into the atrium as a subway train rattles its way past City Hall station and on to the next stop. Heath starts and nearly smacks their heads together, but Art catches him and holds him fast.

"You all right?" Art sounds breathless. His eyes are a darker blue than Heath has seen them.

Heath nods shakily and glances at the tracks, which are now empty once more. "Bit of a surprise, that's all. I suppose I'd forgotten where we were."

"Well," Art says slowly. He licks his lips as he dips his head and tilts Heath's chin up. "Allow me to cloud your memory some more, then."

HEATH LOSES TRACK OF TIME in the deserted subway station, and it's Art who eventually pulls them apart and suggests they go back to the surface. Heath knows Art's right, but he still protests before being led back up the stairs. They pause at the gate and peer through it into the dark night before Art pushes it open. They sneak back onto the street. Heath feels giddy; so giddy that he nearly forgets himself completely. He swings their hands where they're still laced together between them as they walk for a moment before he lets go.

"I hoped to broaden your horizons, but it seems as though I may have truly corrupted you," Art teases. "Sneaking out of closed subway stations—"

"Only because you snuck me *in* in the first place!"

"—holding my hand for all the world to see."

Heath sighs and his gaze drops to watch his footsteps. "That was more by accident than anything else," he mumbles and slips his hands into his pockets to prevent any more accidents of that nature. He looks up at Art. "But I wish I could."

"I know." Art brushes his fingers against the back of Heath's neck. "I do, too."

They travel back to Midtown in a taxicab—Art doesn't object when Heath says he thinks he's seen enough of the subway for one day. The backs of their hands touch where they rest on the leather of the backseat, and Heath watches the lights of the city flicker past: Times Square, where theater patrons huddle together beneath brightly lit awnings; the still-busy restaurants and eerily-lit barber salons and bookstores, with their secrets stored beneath the floorboards.

"The worst-kept secrets in Manhattan," Art murmurs as he looks past Heath out of his window. He, too, notices the establishments that line the street. "One of our regulars is in training with the NYPD. He says that for every bar they shut down, another three appear in its place. They're nothing more than dogs chasing their tails, and it takes time from other things that require their attention."

"Why not stop trying altogether, then?" Heath frowns.

"While the law is in place, they can't simply ignore it. Especially not when they receive tips from the public."

Heath looks at Art in surprise. "People do that? To what end?"

"Personal vendettas, usually," Art replies drily. "It's a fickle business; people know how much money there is to be made. They often don't think of how much there is to lose."

Heath thinks of TJ, compared to the few other speakeasies he's visited in Manhattan. "Yes," he murmurs. They have a lot to lose, if caught selling alcohol. But none so much as TJ, and Art, were they to be seized.

Art appears to have sensed how Heath has tensed beside him, for his hand slips into Heath's in the dark of the taxicab. "It doesn't bear thinking about," he says in a whisper. "We must just keep on. Day at a time." He smiles against Heath's ear. "And do our best not to make too many enemies along the way."

Heath's lips curl into a grin. "I can't imagine you having any enemies, at all."

Art doesn't reply, but lets go of Heath's hand and sits forward to address the driver. "Just here is fine, thank you."

Walking into TJ with Art by his side is akin to walking into a party on the arm of the most famous man in the world. An almighty cheer goes up the moment they open the door, so loud that Heath worries someone on the street might hear it. He keeps close to Art's side as he weaves through the crowds to greet friends and acquaintances. Art introduces him to Toms and Johns and Peters and Marks. All are perfectly polite, in their drunken states, but they eye Heath with interest, curious about this man whom Art has clearly taken to.

Have there have been others for Art, like him? Others that Heath doesn't know about, other men whom Art has kissed in broken-into subway stations, other men whom he has walked around his club with his arm tucked around their waists? Heath excuses himself after a short while, slips from Art's grip and gives him a peck on the cheek in reassurance before he makes his way to the bar.

"Heath!" Julian pulls him to his chest and hugs him tight. "I'd hoped I might stumble upon you down here sooner or later. How are you?"

"Julian." Heath smiles. "I'm well. It's been a lovely week, actually. And you?"

Julian's smile fades slightly. "All right, I suppose." He steps back and slides onto a barstool, regarding Heath coolly. "I thought perhaps you'd call this week. Especially after what happened in Cove Neck."

Alfie, with wonderful timing as always, puts a drink down in front of Heath. "Glad to see you've calmed down some." He winks and offers Julian a refill, which he refuses.

Heath takes a sip before he looks back at Julian. "I'm sorry," he says finally. "I had a few things to take care of, and…" He trails off. His excuses are threadbare, at best. "I'm sorry," he repeats.

"Heath, I—" Julian snaps his mouth closed when Art slides in next to where Heath stands at the bar and wraps an arm tightly around his waist. Heath can smell traces of alcohol on his breath when he tips his head up to smile at him. "Art. Good to see you again."

"Likewise." Art looks between the two of them. "I wasn't aware you two were acquainted."

"Oh, Heath and I go back years." Julian looks less and less amicable toward Art by the second.

"Old family friends," Heath adds and quickly reaches for his glass.

In truth, he'd forgotten all about Julian; his mind was too filled with Art, who was seeping into every crevice of his conscious. He hadn't thought Julian's kiss meant anything, just reassurance shared between old friends. Julian, the fantasy Heath had created and clung to for years, had become Julian, the very real man who had kissed him on the back steps of the house at Cove Neck. He longed for the former, but the latter was simply a reality that didn't inspire Heath into action. Not like Art.

"And you? Of course, I was aware you'd met, but this I hadn't heard about." Julian laughs sharply as he gestures at them. "I suppose I shouldn't be surprised. Little more than a week, is it, Heath? That you've been coming here?"

Heath doesn't say anything; he's somewhat ashamed as Julian's eyes bore into him. Julian is hurt, that much is clear, and it was never Heath's intention to do that.

"Perhaps it is time for you to make your way home, Julian." Art's tone is firm and his grip around Heath's waist tightens.

"Perhaps." Julian shrugs. "Or perhaps I will take another drink, after all. If it's all the same to you."

Heath feels Art about to move and he grabs his arm. "I'll take him home." He turns to Julian. "I'll take you home, Julian. We can talk. The air could do me some good, at any rate. It's awfully stuffy down here."

"Fine," Julian growls. He stands up and reaches for his jacket where it's draped over the bar. "Art. Always a pleasure."

Art snorts under his breath. "Likewise." He presses his lips to just behind Heath's ear. "Are you sure about this?"

Heath nods. "Don't worry. Just give me some time with him. I owe him an explanation."

Art looks confused but lets him go with a promise to call at the house tomorrow.

Julian has pressed ahead and waits by the door to the staircase, lighting a cigarette with a hand cupped protectively around the burning end of the match.

"Come on." Running a hand through his hair, Heath sighs and leads him up the stairs. He doesn't say anything else until they are out on the street, walking uptown toward Julian's parents' house on Park Avenue.

"I'm sorry."

Julian scoffs and takes a drag on his cigarette. "You said that already." He puffs out another lungful of smoke, which floats in the air before it dissipates. "Frankie let slip about the feelings you have—or, *had*, I suppose—about me. That night that I took him to TJ. I thought kissing you would encourage them rather than extinguish them altogether."

Heath lays a hand on Julian's arm. "You mean a lot to me, Julian. You're one of my oldest and closest friends. The best way I can explain it is that the feelings I had for you were only ever part of a fantasy. Something I knew I couldn't have. It took kissing you to realize that. Does that make sense?" He looks at Julian, whose profile is sharp against the streetlights that line the avenue.

Julian nods. "It does." He pauses to stub out his cigarette and toss it away. "In my sophomore year at Yale, I developed quite a thing for Professor Jenson."

Heath bites his tongue to stop himself from laughing. "The one with the mustache?" he asks, one eyebrow raised.

Julian bumps their shoulders together and scowls. "Yes, the one with the mustache. I used to pay so little attention in the class that by the end my buddies would have to kick me in the shins just to get me to move. But it was all a fantasy." Julian pauses. "He insinuated to me, at the end of that year, that should I come back to his house, he would give me a higher grade on my paper. Needless to say, I did *not* take that offer, and the fantasy crumbled into reality."

Heath winces. "Julian, that's awful. You're not at all as bad as all that," he jokes feebly. "It was a nice kiss, really."

"It just wasn't what you actually wanted. It was what you *thought* you wanted."

Heath nods. "Exactly."

They walk in silence past lit-up houses whose windows are thrown open to let in the night air. "Art's a wonderful man," Julian says. "I can understand what you see in him. And he in you."

They stop at Julian's house, and Heath pulls his friend into an embrace. "You are, too, you know," he whispers. "Wonderful."

Julian hums. "Thank you, Heath." He pulls back. "Is your family returning to Cove Neck later this week, too? My parents drive out tomorrow, I think."

Heath nods. "I believe so. They were making plans over breakfast." He rubs at the back of his neck. "I'm not sure yet that I'll go with them, though. I might stay here."

Julian's expression is impassive. "Well, I'm sure I'll see you in one place or another soon enough."

Heath raises a hand as Julian turns and takes the stairs up to the front door and drops it to his side only when the door closes.

He hopes to spend the next few weeks with Art; he still has some summer to while away with at least a little less pressure about his future. Whether his parents would let him stay in Manhattan alone while they went to Long Island, he isn't sure—they aren't apt to without protest, at least. Heath crosses to Fifth and finds the house dark and quiet.

"An argument to have in the morning, then," Heath says to the empty hallway, before he climbs the stairs to his bedroom.

CH. 5

HEATH'S FAMILY LEAVES FOR COVE Neck at the weekend, planning to spend the better part of the next two weeks on the water and away from the noise and bustle of the city. "July is such an oppressive month," the Duchess laments as the bags are packed into the car. She fixes her gaze onto Heath. "Wouldn't you agree?"

Neither she nor the Duke are particularly enthused by his insistence on staying in Manhattan, but they have no real grounds for protest when he promises to spend the time thinking seriously of his future and weighing his options. Amelia can tell that this at least partially a lie, but she hides her sniggers behind her hand before fixing a sunhat over her bobbed chestnut waves. She also suggests that Frankie might have some eligible young lady friends to introduce to Heath—only he knows that is a lie.

Heath wanders through the vast rooms of the house, listens to his footsteps echo over the floor; no other noise stirs throughout. Martha will come and go, to take care of the house while the rest of the Johnson family is in Long Island. Heath assured her that he would be more than capable of fending for himself. He relishes the idea of a brief period of freedom, out from under the scrutiny of his parents.

Art seems to be expecting him when he arrives: his eyes crinkle with his smile when Heath swings through the door to TJ and sprints toward him. Heath leaps into his arms with a cry, locks his legs around Art's waist and wraps his arms around his shoulders. Art stumbles under his weight before he gets a firm grip on the backs of his thighs.

"What's gotten into you today?" Art asks after Heath greets him with a kiss. TJ is empty so early in the afternoon, but he would have done it anyway.

"My family has left the city for a couple of weeks," Heath explains and lets Art deposit him on the bar. He kicks the heels of his shoes against the wood gently as Art finishes unloading clean glasses onto the shelves. "I feel a little giddy."

"Really?" Art gasps. "I hadn't noticed a single change in your demeanor, baby."

Heath ducks his face to hide the grin that tugs at his lips.

"Aren't you two sweet? Barely past noon and already making whoopee." Alfie comes through from the back room and puts a few fresh bottles on the shelves before he pours himself a glass of scotch. He swigs from his drink before he offers one to Heath.

Heath opens his mouth to accept but Art cuts him off. "I think it's time I expanded your horizons farther than a whiskey sour." He tut-tuts and sets down a champagne flute alongside various bottles and a shaker.

"He's a drink snob," Alfie whispers, and sits on one of the stools on the other side of the bar with his own, basic scotch on the rocks.

"I am not a snob," Art retorts. The ice clinks in the cocktail shaker. "I simply have more honed tastebuds than you do when it comes to alcohol."

Alfie mutters something incoherent to Heath but doesn't make any more comments on Art's tastes.

Heath tries to peer past Art's shoulder to see what is going into the concoction being made for him—he spies gin, which is different, but also an egg white, just as would go into his usual whiskey sour. The lid of the shaker is snapped on, and Art shakes it before pouring the cocktail into the champagne glass.

"*Et* voilà." Art hands the glass to Heath. "One White Lady for the handsome young gentleman."

"Does this handsome young gentleman get anything?" Alfie tries, suddenly more interested in Art's offerings now that his glass is empty.

"Maybe, once he finishes wiping down the tables," Art says as he leans back against the shelves and folds his arms across his chest.

Heath sniffs at the top of the glass as Alfie slouches off to do as he's told. "Lemon?" he asks. Art nods. Heath takes a small sip and licks his lips, chasing the taste. It's sharp, tangy from the lemon, and some other citrus taste comes through, the gin keeping that clear taste rather than allowing it to sweeten. He takes another sip. "It's good. Sour, but different from the whiskey sours. I like it." He grins at Art and takes another sip.

Art looks at him with fond warmth in his eyes. He chuckles and steps over to him. "You have a little—" Art's eyes flicker to Heath's lips before he kisses the light foam, created by the egg white, away.

"Whoopsie daisy," Heath murmurs, smiling against Art's lips. "I probably shouldn't be drinking on an empty stomach," he admits. He pulls back and sets the glass and its remaining contents down.

"I'd take you to a late lunch, but I have to—"

"Work," Heath interrupts him and rests his hand on Art's shoulder. "I understand." He traces the curve of Art's neck before cupping his jaw. "What about this evening? Could you take an hour or two and come have dinner with me?"

"At your house?" Heath nods. Art cocks his head around Heath's arm. "Alfie?"

"Yes, yes." Alfie sighs. "I heard. I can take charge for a couple of hours, I suppose. You two are going to owe me a very expensive thank you gift before long." He slings the rag he used to wipe the tables over one shoulder. "My birthday is in October, incidentally."

Heath taps his temple. "Noted, Alfie." He turns back to Art. "I'll see you at half past six."

"Half past six. Until then, baby."

Art's grin and the memory of his tongue curling around the word "baby" carries him all the way back to Fifth Avenue.

IT TAKES A LITTLE FIB or two to Louis, but he agrees to make a meal for two and then take the rest of the evening off. Louis seems to suspect that Heath has a girl coming over, and if he weren't so worried that it would get back to the Duchess and send her hopes spiraling, he'd have simply agreed with that theory. Heath waits to hear the door click shut behind Louis just after six o'clock before he sprints to the dining room to set the table for him and Art.

It is twenty-seven minutes of utter disaster. He burns his fingers on a match trying to light candles on the sideboard and both stubs his toe and knocks a plate to the floor when he runs full tilt into the table. He hops around the dining room, clutching his bruised toe as he checks the plate. He deems it still fully intact and carefully sets it back on the table.

The bell sounds at precisely six twenty-nine. Heath thinks he could use a lie-down after all of this, but allows himself only a moment to breathe before he goes to greet Art. He glances over his efforts. The food awaits them, tucked in the oven. The sound of the grandfather clock striking half past farther down the hallway pulls him from his thoughts and propels him toward the door.

Art is brandishing a neat bouquet of a half-dozen roses, and if Heath weren't so touched by the gesture, he might have teased him a little over it. His hair is slicked back and he's changed since the afternoon: a black bow tie is a little askew against his throat. Heath lets him in and shuts the door before he kisses him. His fingers creep up to fix the bow tie as he does so.

"I tried my best," Art mumbles against his lips before he turns them to Heath's jaw and lays another kiss there. "For you." He presses the flowers into Heath's hands and steps back; his eyes flick past Heath toward the main body of the house.

"No one's here," Heath assures him. Leading Art inside, he puts the roses into an empty vase on the sideboard in the dining room.

"If no one's here, then I am even more intrigued by that incredible smell." Art's hand fits to the small of Heath's back as he looks over the dining table with a small smile. "I didn't know you could *cook.*"

Heath titters. "Oh, gosh, no. I think Louis would run me out of the house before trusting me in the kitchen." He turns to face Art and skates his hands up over his arms. "I didn't cook, but I will serve. That, I am capable of, I'd like to think."

"Although, knowing my luck," he mutters under his breath, and pushes the door to the kitchen open with his shoulder. A dishcloth sits on the counter with a little note on it, that says, "Use me" in Louis's handwriting. In slightly smaller script he has added, "Dishes are hot!" Heath rolls his eyes and drapes the dishcloth over his hands. Some things he can figure out for himself.

He manages to get the food to the table without incident, careful of each step he takes lest he crash headfirst to the floor, taking their dinner with him. Art looks impressed, and he pulls Heath's chair out before taking his own.

"So, just how many dates before me have you enthralled with your romantic airs?" Art's tone is light, all in jest, but Heath can't help but take it seriously. He reaches for Art's hand and looks him square in the eye as he laces their fingers together.

"You'll be the first."

As they eat, Heath lets himself imagine that this could be his future: windows overlooking the park, dinner served by candlelight and someone like Art by his side—or, better still, Art himself. His own fairy tale, the man he met behind closed doors, a story he could tell his children just as his parents told him of their meeting.

Heath didn't think so far as dessert and allows Art to tease him with only a small amount of sulking.

"Don't fret." Art's thumb traces circles into the back of Heath's hand. "There's an ice cream parlor just past the end of the park. What do you say to an evening stroll? My treat."

That only causes Heath to sulk further. "That would, however, involve us having to leave the house."

"I wasn't aware you were as lazy as all that, with how often you quite happily trot from your Fifth Avenue palace to my little establishment, which is an entire ten blocks away."

Heath huffs. "That's an entirely different set of circumstances, now, isn't it? You almost make it sound as though you dislike my visits." He pulls his hand back and folds his arms across his chest haughtily. "That couldn't be the case, could it?"

Art coaxes his hand back and kisses the back of it, then turns his hand over and presses another kiss to the center of his palm. He folds Heath's fingers around it before his gaze shifts back up to Heath. "However could you think such a thing of me?"

"Well, you—"

The doorbell sounds, echoing through to the dining room. Art frowns and sets Heath's hand down on the table. "Were you expecting someone?"

Heath shakes his head and stands. "Wait here, won't you? I'll see who it is." He wonders if Amelia decided to return to the city early, perhaps with Edward, whom he knows planned to join the Johnson family at Cove Neck for at least the better part of a day. His stomach settles unpleasantly as he tries to think how he might explain the spread in the dining room, should it be his younger sister.

But when he opens the door, it is Frankie on the step, with a bulging brown paper bag tucked into the crook of his arm, feebly hidden by his suit jacket. Frankie frowns. "Don't look at me like that, I come bearing favors."

"Did we have plans for this evening?" Heath tries, but Frankie is already pushing past him into the house, as familiar acquaintances are wont to do.

"We do now. I overheard my godmother on the phone to the Duchess, making plans to visit them in Cove Neck early next week. It came out that you hadn't left with them, and I couldn't stand the thought of you all alone in this big house."

Frankie veers into the doorway of the dining room and stops short, as Heath follows behind. "Or perhaps not alone."

Art raises a hand and offers a sheepish smile. "Evening, Frankie. Good to see you again."

Frankie David is not one to show any semblance of uncertainty, but he hovers now, rocks between his heels and balls of his feet as his gaze skitters back and forth between Heath and Art.

"I'll fetch some glasses," Art suggests. "We can have a drink, the three of us."

"If you're sure I'm not interrupting." Frankie sends Heath an apologetic look, but he shrugs it off.

"Not at all. We'd finished eating." Heath regards the dishes. "I should clear the table at the very least. Frankie—set yourself up in the other room."

Frankie's usual demeanor returns and he nods. "Right. I'll make myself at home."

Heath stacks the plates into his arms and teeters toward the kitchen; Art holds the door for him. He sets the plates down and brushes his hands off on his pants, then points to the appropriate cupboard for Art to select tumblers for them. "Are you sure this is all right?" He asks and leans back against the kitchen counter. "I don't at all mind telling him to let us be, if you'd rather."

Art nudges the cupboard door closed with the back of his wrist. "Frankie's your best friend, if I recall correctly?"

Heath nods.

"Then it's important to me that I get to know him, and there's no time like the present, hm?" When Heath doesn't respond, Art puts the glasses down on the counter and pulls him in to his chest. "If I could, I would want to meet your family—properly, I mean. Be introduced formally as your beau and spend hours charming your mother into finding me utterly endearing and perfect for her only son." He tips his head down enough to rest their foreheads together. "We can't do that. But I can get to know Frankie, if no one else."

"Would you like me to introduce you formally as my beau?" Heath teases. He tugs his fingers through where Art's hair is longest, curling at the nape of his neck. "I'd rather prefer it if you didn't charm Frankie until he finds you utterly endearing, however. I'm the only one you should be charming."

"A statement I agree with entirely, my dear." Art pecks his lips. "Now, let us get back to him lest he think we're doing entirely unspeakable things in this kitchen."

Heath raises an eyebrow. "Louis might even let me cook in here if he knew *that* was an alternative."

🍸

It becomes the first of many nights spent with both Art and Frankie—most of those at TJ, if only so Art can show both his customers and Alfie that he hasn't completely abandoned them. Frankie seems to find the whole environment as liberating as Heath now does, if for entirely different reasons.

"For once, I may spend an entire night without having my attention taken by girls in summer dresses," Frankie exclaims after a few drinks have been knocked back. "I need not be charming *or* complimentary to anyone!"

Heath snorts and kicks his legs up onto an empty stool opposite him. "What a life you lead, my friend. How terribly taxing that must be," he replies drily. He decides to keep quiet as to how many of the regular club patrons have quietly asked Heath whether or not his handsome friend has someone special in his life.

Other nights, they spend at Heath's family townhouse, with the balcony doors flung open onto the night sky as they drink and talk and smoke. Heath's eyes usually droop by the time they call it a night. His head rests in Art's lap as Art combs his fingers through Heath's dark hair, and a smile touches his lips whenever he feels Art's laugh reverberate from his stomach.

Heath's parents call once. The Duchess claims concern over his well-being, but really it's to enquire as to whether he has spent time with any nice young girls in Manhattan. Heath's answers are vague. By the time they return—their stay in Cove Neck is extending beyond the original two weeks they had planned—perhaps he will have some female companion he might be able to satisfy his parents with, if only for the time being. He says as much to Art one evening and immediately feels guilty for the cloudy expression that crosses his features.

"Perhaps Frankie can show you where to meet a nice girl. I wouldn't say it's my area of expertise."

Heath promptly changes the subject.

HEATH TURNS THE TICKETS OVER in his hand with the phone propped between his ear and his shoulder. "You'll have to make other plans this evening."

"How rude of you not to include me." Frankie pauses—Heath can hear the clink of ice in a glass. "But I suppose I've intruded on many potential date nights already." He sighs melodramatically.

"Yes. You have. So tonight you make your own plans, and I'm taking Art to the theater."

Frankie snorts. "The theater? I can as much imagine Art attending the theater as I can see you at Coney Island riding the Cyclone."

Defiantly slipping the tickets for *Rio Rita* into the back pocket of his pants, Heath chooses to ignore this comment. "Always a pleasure, Frankie, see you tomorrow," he chirps and hangs up the phone before Frankie has a chance to reply.

In truth, Heath had the same concern when he bought the tickets. The Duchess has taken him and Amelia to Broadway shows a few times; the list of possibilities becomes longer every year. He adores the theater, himself, and is often as mesmerized and distracted by the architecturally beautiful theaters themselves as the performances on stage.

But Art? He comes from a wealthy, upper-class background like Heath, but Heath can't imagine Art's uncle showing him galleries or plays rather than exploring the nooks and crannies of the city as Art seems to love to do.

Heath gets a taste of Art's family background that evening before the performance, when he collects him from his apartment. It's as hot as ever, and he rolls the sleeves of his jackets to his elbows as he walks to Lexington Avenue, fanning air to his neck with his lapels while his eyes keep track of the numbers as he strolls up the eight hundreds.

It's the first time their roles have reversed—the first time he has been given Art's home address. Heath blushes: he nearly forgot that Art has a house at all, he has always thought of him as so tied in with TJ. He doesn't mention this to Art, but merely makes a promise to collect him a little before seven that evening.

Art answers the door himself, with his shirt gaping open over his collarbone and a bow tie resting over his shoulder. "Alfie broke a chair," he says. "I won't be long."

Heath snaps his gaze from the light dusting of chest hair just visible and nods. He steps into the house and closes the door as Art goes upstairs to finish getting dressed.

From the outside, the house is much like Heath's own: wide windows to let in the light, stairs that lead up to the front door and an ornate knocker, his in the shape of a golden lion. But inside, it does not seem like much of a home at all. How much—or how little—time does Art actually spend here? The furniture in the living room is covered with white sheets; the curtains are half drawn, and the room is dark. It is eerily quiet, too—he can just hear Art above, the sound of his shoes on wooden floorboards, but save for that, the house seems devoid of movement. Of life, almost.

Heath shudders and steps back into the hallway to wait for his date, who comes down the stairs not a minute later. Heath tries not to pout in disappointment at his buttoned-up appearance but fails, as Art catches it all the same.

"Wouldn't do to turn up anywhere with half my shirt off, now, would it?" Art teases, and winks as he slips his watch over his wrist. "Of course, that would depend on where we are going, should you now be willing to disclose that information…?"

"Absolutely not." Heath loops his arm through Art's and kisses his cheek. "It wouldn't be a surprise if I told you now."

Art sighs. "Never did like surprises much."

"A taste of your own medicine, baby." Heath grins smugly and pecks his cheek one last time before he lets his arm drop as they open the door.

Heath glances back toward the front door as they begin to walk, then looks over at Art. "Seems rather like a museum in there," he admits, in a gentle tone. He doesn't wish to offend.

Art simply chuckles and nods. "I suppose it does, yes. I haven't made up my mind what I want to do with the place, but I hardly spend much time there besides to sleep or occasionally eat, so it doesn't seem worth keeping it open only to be cleaned every week."

"What might you do with the place?"

"Sell it."

Heath is taken aback. "It was your uncle's, wasn't it?"

"Hence my reservations in doing so. In theory, it is my childhood home. But it stopped seeming like a home when Uncle TJ died, and I wonder if perhaps I'd be better off selling it and finding something smaller, more convenient. Perhaps in Midtown, so I'm nearer the club." Art shrugs. "As I say, I haven't decided."

"Perhaps being farther from the club is a good thing," Heath muses aloud. "You spend so much time there as it is, I can't imagine it does you any harm to get a little farther away from that environment when you do leave. Clear your mind of it all."

"You might be right." Art squeezes the curve of Heath's elbow momentarily before he drops his arm back to his side. "I'll think on it."

They pass TJ on their way down Sixth Avenue to the Ziegfeld Theater, and Heath feels Art hesitate, as though they might stop in there. "No," Heath says with a smirk, putting a hand around his bicep to tug him past Jerry's barbershop and onward down Sixth. "Not tonight, Art."

Art huffs out a laugh. "That would have been a mighty poor surprise, if TJ had been our destination."

"Have a little more faith in my surprise-planning capabilities!"

The lights from the Ziegfeld beam into the sky as they come to the corner of Fifty-fourth Street; the bulbs illuminating the sign for *Rio Rita* flash and blare, and Heath can hear music coming from within. People spill out over the sidewalk, smoking and chattering as they wait to go inside, brushing off the scalpers who try to pester people into buying forged tickets for extortionately high prices.

"This is why I hate Broadway," Art mutters into his ear as he tries to steer them past the crowds. "Can't walk two feet down here at this time of night without running into hordes of people who couldn't care less if you want use of the sidewalk."

Heath stutters, and his feet stop. The tickets burn a hole in his breast pocket. "Surprise," he manages to mumble and gestures to the theater. "Two tickets for the stalls. One of the best views in the house, or so I was told."

Art looks up at the theater and then back at Heath before a smile lifts the corner of his mouth. "Of course," he says smoothly, as though he hadn't just cursed the very people they are to be this evening. "Shall we?"

Heath hesitates. "We don't have to, if you'd rather not. I always loved the theater, I thought perhaps—"

Art cuts him off and ushers them toward the open doors. "Then we shall spend the night at the theater. It was a very thoughtful idea, Heath. Thank you."

Heath nods and follows after Art dumbly. Despite Art's reassurances, he still feels as though he has failed in his plans for the evening. Art's surprises were enough to leave Heath astounded, giddy with excitement.

Heath's, it seems, missed the mark entirely. He gives the tickets to the usher and they walk inside the gilded doors.

The inside of the theater is as luxurious as any Heath remembers, even if he hasn't visited this one. His eyes are arrested by the chandelier hanging from the ceiling, its dozens of individual bulbs lit and casting patterns across the interior of the entrance. "It's beautiful," Art murmurs as they follow the usher to the stalls, and Heath feels a little better.

When the lights dim and the orchestra begins to play, Heath feels that familiar bubble of excitement in the pit of his stomach. He has to physically restrain himself from reaching across to grab Art's hand; instead he clutches his own wrist as he leans forward in his seat. The curtain is raised, and Heath sucks in a breath and resorts to twisting the playbill in his hands as he watches the scene unfold.

He doesn't become aware of the fact that he is the only one of the two of them to enjoy the night's performance until the interval sounds, the first act closing to thunderous applause before people begin to pile toward the bar for alcohol-free libations and cigarettes. He doesn't become aware, in fact, until he sits back in his seat and turns his head to ask Art how he is enjoying it and finds him with his elbow propped up on the arm between them, head in his hand, asleep.

Heath looks around at the other patrons as they filter through the rows of seats, some lingering there for the interval. No one seems to have noticed, and the last thing Heath wants is to make a scene within the auditorium—they are more befitting the stage. He nudges Art's arm gently but he doesn't stir, only snuffles in his sleep.

It's irrational to feel hurt that Art has fallen asleep. Completely irrational. As though Heath doesn't know Art's been at work all day, and perhaps the theater wasn't a well thought-out choice of surprise. Yet if Art had taken him somewhere he might not want to go, he would have tried to make more of an effort. Art took him, reluctant, to the subway; and he had assisted Art in breaking into one a few days after that. Heath had let Art guide him, and enjoyed himself more than he thought he would. Apparently, the same courtesy does not extend from Art to him.

Heath sighs and tugs Art's wrist so that his head lolls forward, which snaps him into consciousness.

"I'm sorry, what were you saying?" Art mumbles. He blinks at Heath blearily.

Heath doesn't correct him. Rather, he stands, and says: "I think perhaps it was time we left." He slides past the empty seats to the right and turns toward the door; Art's footsteps are close behind.

"Heath. *Heath*, wait, won't you? I think there might be another act."

"There is. I won't force you to sit through it, however nice a sleeping place this might be." He quickens his pace and pushes out onto the street. It's far quieter than it was when they entered, and Heath slips through the few people out on the sidewalk easily, wrapping his suit jacket tighter around himself as he walks.

"Heath." The heels of Art's shoes click against the concrete. "Heath. Stop. Please stop running from me."

"I'm not running from you," Heath replies coolly and stops short as they come to the corner. The street teems with taxicabs and private cars. "As you can see."

Art draws up in front of him and huffs. He reaches to tuck in a strand of hair that has come loose behind his ear. "I apologize for falling asleep. But we needn't have left. We can get back to our seats, still. Come." He puts out his hand—a gesture, if not quite an invitation.

"No, I think I'd like to go home." Heath pushes Art's hand away.

"You're upset."

When Heath says nothing, Art grunts and reaches into his pocket for a cigarette and lights it. "If you'd like my honest opinion, I do think you're acting a little childish right now, Heath."

Heath's head snaps up. "Perhaps I am," he retorts. "But I *tried*, Art. I tried to organize one thing for us, one special surprise as you have done for me. I apologize if I am not at the great Arthur Houston's level of surprise-planning abilities!" He throws up his hands in exasperation and then tucks them around himself again as a cool breeze ripples down the avenue.

Art has the indecency to look amused by Heath's little outburst.

"Stop laughing at me," Heath grumbles, not at all caring if he sounds petulant or has the pout to match.

"I'm not laughing." Art takes a drag from his cigarette and blows the smoke to one side. "You organized dinner for us. That was a lovely evening."

"Yes, but it's not…" Heath trails off and gestures vaguely. "I didn't *take* you anywhere. It wasn't interesting, or a surprise, either."

"My darling." Art steps a little closer so he can talk in a whisper. "What if I say you took me to the heavens and the stars with the power of the food you so graciously carried to the table but did not cook, and with your charm alone?"

Heath snorts. "I'd say you were a big rotten liar."

Art shrugs. "Perhaps." He grins and stubs out his cigarette. "Heath, I am sorry. It's been a long day, and I've had a lot on my mind in recent weeks, and the last thing I really wanted to do was sit through some godawful theatrical display about a woman named Rita in a place where I can't take your hand should I want to."

Heath sighs before he nods. "Let's just go, shall we? No sense in standing on street corners for the rest of the night." He turns and crosses the road to start walking. He unwraps his arms to rest his hands in his pockets.

Art doesn't object and keeps in step at his side.

"You do know you could talk to me, Art."

Art looks at him with a hint of confusion flickering over his expression. "Of course."

"Only, you said you had a lot on your mind. Perhaps I could help."

Art shakes his head. "Nothing for you to worry over. I promise."

Heath frowns. He wants to protest that that wasn't what he meant. What he must worry over is in no way the same as a wish to help, if by doing nothing more than lending a listening ear. But he can tell from

Art's expression that he considers the subject dropped, and Heath has no real desire to argue with him anymore.

"Would you like to come down for a nightcap?"

Heath would far rather go home, truthfully, but nothing awaits him there save for dark, empty rooms and his own miserable thoughts. "Why not?" He forces a smile onto his face and they cross toward TJ.

It turns out to be a good thing that Heath agreed, for he finds Frankie tucked in the far corner. He nurses a half empty glass and looks rather petrified—not a normal state for his friend, least of all in the club. Heath leaves Art to check up on Alfie while he makes his way to the back and slips into the seat beside his friend.

Frankie looks up. "You're back early. I didn't expect to see you here at all tonight, in fact."

Heath ignores the obvious question in his words and addresses his friend with his own. "Why are you sitting all the way back here? Usually you sit with Alfie at the bar, or with those loons who play that ridiculous game that seems to involve throwing cards all over the floor." He steals Frankie's glass from between his hands and takes a sip.

"Those loons, as you so kindly refer to them, are not present this evening. And you ought to be nicer; their alma mater is not dissimilar to our own dear establishment."

Heath rolls his eyes—he has nothing against the group, save for their penchant for hollering and how they remind him of the crowds from Yale.

"As to why I am sitting here, Alfie would be a good guess." Frankie steals his glass back and drains the remaining contents.

"Alfie?" Heath glances toward the bar, where the man in question is serving with a dazzling wide smile on his face. Art, he notes, is nowhere to be seen. Alfie catches him looking and glances at Frankie before waggling his fingers in greeting and then turning to the next customer.

"He's rather friendly, isn't he?" Frankie's voice sounds strained.

"He's harmless," Heath assures him.

"You should have *heard* what he said to me earlier, I—"

Heath holds up a hand. "I'd rather I didn't. I have a good idea already."

Frankie still looks ruffled.

"He's only playing with you, Frankie. He knows you rather well by now, after all."

"Not well enough, if he had his way," Frankie grumbles, before he shrugs off his surly expression and fixes Heath with a pointed look. "So, the theater wasn't quite such a raving success as you'd hoped, then?"

Heath stands up. "I'll get us a round of drinks."

They stay later into the night than is sensible, tucked in the corner, and take turns to buy the next round, even if Frankie protests about having to face Alfie. Heath doesn't see Art again that night, and if he drowns all thoughts of him in the bottom of his glass, so be it.

It's only when they wander home late into the night, arms looped around each other's shoulders, that Frankie broaches the topic once more. "Sometimes it seems as though he doesn't trust me," Heath admits into the cool night air as he tilts his head up toward the stars and the moon. "As though I somehow wouldn't understand, or *couldn't*. As though I'm not entirely his equal."

At the corner of Central Park, where they will part ways, Frankie turns Heath around to face him and places his hands firmly on his shoulders. "For what it's worth, I'm quite sure that I've never seen you as happy as you are around Art." Frankie's words make Heath's insides feel warm and fuzzy, even if his breath reeks of whiskey, which causes him to wrinkle his nose in distaste. "And Alfie said the same of Art, around you. In between his ploys to unbutton my shirt."

Heath grins and hugs Frankie. "You're the best friend a simple city boy could have, Frankie David."

Frankie straightens his shirt when they pull apart with a comically slow air to his movements. "That means a lot to me, Heathcliff. I shall bid you *adieu*, lest I start weeping with joy over your poetic words."

Heath shoves at his shoulder and turns to start up Fifth Avenue. "Goodnight, Frankie."

WHEN HEATH AWAKES, IT IS to a mouthful of the pillow beneath his head. He groans and curls his tongue around the dry, stale taste of the inside of his mouth as he blinks his eyes open. Drool clings to the corner of his mouth, and he would like to stick his head under the faucet to wake himself up this morning.

He is not granted the luxury of a slow ease back into full consciousness, however, as the phone starts ringing angrily from the hallway. Content to let it ring, he stuffs his head under the pillow. But the sound persists, and he reluctantly pulls his legs free from the tangle of sheets and pads his way downstairs in just his pajamas. He takes the phone from the cradle and tucks it to his ear, letting his eyes droop closed again.

"Hello?"

"Heath! Oh, darling, it's so wonderful to hear your voice. You couldn't have called? I was starting to worry." The Duchess's bright tone is too much for this time of the morning. "How are you? Are you eating? Has Louis been coming by?"

Heath rubs at his temples with his fingers. "I'm fine, mother; you needn't worry so much. I've been busy with friends, that's all. I'm sorry I hadn't thought to call sooner."

"Friends? Francis, you mean? And what was his name now—Arthur, wasn't it?"

"Yes. Yes, them, and a few others."

The Duchess is silent, but Heath can hear her fingernails tapping on the end of the receiver. "And?"

"And the time has been very beneficial for me, I feel. To think. About everything."

The Duchess hums, but she doesn't sound entirely satisfied. "Well, I'm glad for that. You will call, won't you? At least every other day would be nice, Heath."

Heath hangs up with a promise to do just that. He sighs and pushes his fingers through his hair and back from his face. He still has time. He still has plenty of time—July is not yet over. Pushing inevitability from his back, he clings to that thought and starts toward the stairs. His eye catches on a small white envelope resting by the door.

Scooping it up, he slides a finger beneath the seal to tear it open. It has only his name on the other side, no address, so it must have been hand-delivered. The note within reads simply: *One o'clock, by the west side of the lake in Central Park.* It is unsigned, but Heath recognizes Art's handwriting. He isn't so petty that he would simply ignore it, throw it away and continue to sulk over Art's recent behavior.

Instead, Heath takes his time to bathe and dress, enjoying a slow breakfast that he puts together himself. He stands by the windows and swirls lukewarm coffee over his tongue to dispel the stale taste from his mouth. The heat is already beginning to seep into the living room. It presses against the back of his neck, and he instantly longs to get out of the house in the hope of finding fresher air.

He selects a volume from his shelf and slips it under his arm, then leaves the house though it is not quite midday. He looks for a shady spot beneath a tree to sit and read until one o'clock; the park is pleasantly quiet for a change. Many will have done as his family has and fled to Long Island and the cooler touch of the water's edge.

A squirrel darts out of the branches of a tree, scurries down the trunk and disappears in search of another resting place. Heath glances at the branches overhead before he settles back against the trunk and opens his book. It's a hefty volume, a gift from his favorite philosophy professor at Yale when he graduated.

"We never did get time to study Locke, but you might find this interesting," his professor had told him. Heath has picked through the old, hardbound volume slowly, dipping in and out and marking his progress with a faded maroon leather bookmark he received for one birthday or another. And it is interesting to Heath, even if he finds himself frowning at the pages and disagreeing with some of the things he reads.

He loses track of time. The sounds of children playing by the lake and of a dog barking seem far more distant than they actually are. Fortunately, Art spies him in the shadow of the branches and comes to pull him from his reverie. "For a moment there, I worried terribly that you might not turn up at all." Art reaches out a hand to help Heath to his feet.

Heath tucks the bookmark between the pages and securely places the book beneath his arm before accepting his hand. "Perhaps I shouldn't have," he replies coolly. The sentiment doesn't match his interior, where his heart has warmed a fraction just to be in Art's presence. "You all but vanished last night when we got to TJ."

"And I apologize for that. There've been a few," Art pauses, licking his lips, "*complications* in recent business. I'd like to tell you about it. If you want to listen." His hand touches Heath's cheek so lightly that he wonders if he imagined it. "I do trust you," Art assures him in a murmur. "I suppose I'm not used to having someone to trust. It takes a little adjusting."

Heath nods and steers him toward the lake with a hand at his elbow. "I understand. Let's not dwell on yesterday."

Art smiles and then stops still, clearing his throat. "I had organized a small surprise for you," he admits sheepishly.

Heath doesn't know whether to find this frustrating or endearing. "Of course you have." An involuntary grin curls at the corner of his mouth. "Well, come on, then. You're awfully good at these surprises; I can't be too upset over being treated to another."

The surprise, it turns out, is a boat. A small, rickety-looking rowboat.

"If you tell me you've never been rowing on this lake, I shall be appalled. Especially when you can almost see the lake from your house."

As Art steps into the boat, Heath hesitates and clutches his book to his chest. "I have been. Only I fell in, and I made sure not to do so again."

Art barks out a laugh and quickly claps a hand over his mouth. "I'm sorry." He grabs hold of the end of the small wooden jetty. "I promise to not let you fall in." He raises an eyebrow. "Don't you swim, anyway?"

Heath huffs. "There's all sorts of debris in this water," he retorts with a shudder. "And I was only seven at the time. I'd barely learned to swim, and it was too much too soon."

But Art's gaze is persuasive, and Heath supposes it's an irrational fear to hold anymore. "If my book goes overboard, then you shall be the one to go after it." Heath grunts with the rock of the boat, which is momentarily unsteady as he steps in.

"I will go in after you, if you fall overboard." Art pushes them off the dock when he sees that Heath is seated. "I cannot be forced to make the same promise for your book."

Heath gasps, but it's only banter, really. "I should never have gotten in the boat, only for you to deceive me once I'm in it."

"I didn't deceive you, my dear, you got in of your own free will." Art winks as he lifts the oars from the sides of the boat and pushes them out onto the water. "Perhaps you could read to me. Then I might agree whether the book is worth saving from the murky depths."

"It's not exactly poetry, Art." Heath rolls his eyes fondly but flips the book open all the same and skims through the pages he read in the hour before Art found him.

"Well, I know nothing of philosophy. Teach me something. What does—" He peers forward to inspect the cover. "Mr. Locke say?"

Heath props his elbow against his knee and rests his chin in his hand. "Mr. Locke says many things, some of which I'm not all too sure I agree with." He glances down at the book and skims a finger over the page. "He believes that we are born with the mind nothing more than a blank canvas, as it were. Our minds, our beliefs, then, are shaped by experience, to some extent, but predominantly by education."

Art reacts much as Heath expected, with a disgruntled grunt and curl of his upper lip. "You are not enticing me to want to save your book one bit, Heath."

"So you don't agree?" Heath teases as they row around the first curve in the expanse of the lake.

"Experience, I could believe. But education? If that were the case, every one of the men careering down Wall Street would think exactly the same, with the same education as the one before."

Heath thinks of his lunch with men of Wall Street, and how that could almost be believable, given their behavior.

"Take you," Art continues, before Heath can attest to that idea. "A Yale-educated man, and yet here you sit, with me and your precious book of philosophical theory. Not cantering down Wall Street and making eyes at girls in blind pigs in Lower Manhattan."

"You make a valid point. I don't disagree with you. But I don't know if I agree with the first part, either."

"The blank canvas?"

Heath nods. "I can't think that one could be born with nothing, or how would one ever have the ability to learn at all? To begin to talk or walk or understand the world around one?"

"Doesn't sound much as though you would care about the fate of that book, either." Art chuckles. "Toss it overboard!" he booms, and his voice echoes across the water and startles a flock of ducks that takes off in a flurry.

"I needn't agree with everything he says to find it interesting or worth my time."

Art falls quiet with a small smile. He pauses in his rowing to roll his sleeves up, which are slipping over his hands, before starting once more. The muscles in his forearms stretch taut beneath his suntanned skin as he rows, and Heath can't help but admire the older man's physique.

Heath lets him row out his frustrations in silence rather than pry straightaway into whatever it is that's bothered Art recently. He leans back in the bow and forces himself to dismiss the urge to curl up in the middle of the boat and stay very, very still. He hesitates only a moment before he lets his hand hang out of the side of the boat, skimming his fingers over the top of the lake. He shudders as they brush plant life that tickles his fingertips. They curl up and away from the water instinctively.

"I believe you met him the very first time you came to TJ," Art says finally, as he slows the pace of the boat. They have reached a quiet corner of the lake, where families walk near the water's edge but there are no other boats on the water. "Perhaps not *met*, but you certainly encountered him."

Heath rubs a hand over his chin. "The man in the suit receiving the shave." He tries to tick back through his memory to come up with a name, but it escapes him and he looks to Art to fill in the blank.

"Mr. Peters," Art offers as he docks the oars. He pops open his silver cigarette case.

Heath leans forward. "Butt me." He lets Art light his cigarette for him before he sits back. "So what has this Mr. Peters been harassing you over so persistently? Expansion? Closure?"

After lighting his own cigarette, Art shakes out the flame of the match and tosses it into the bottom of the boat. "He wants to buy me out. Says he knows a good investment when he sees one."

Heath laughs in disbelief. "It's not for sale."

"Exactly." Art sighs and runs a hand through his hair. "When I first opened the club, I had no interest in bringing in investors, let alone—" He takes a drag from his cigarette. "The investors were Alfie's idea. The more money pouring in, the more we could do, giving them the smallest return we possibly could."

"Is that why Mr. Peters is pushing? Because he thinks he's been cheated?"

"No. No, I never cheated anyone." Art gives a small shrug. "I took Alfie's advice on all but the returns. I give the four investors a perfectly fair percentage. Neither I nor Alfie desperately need the money for ourselves."

Heath has never thought to ask Alfie about his background, where he lives or what he does in the rare moments when he's not at the club. He wonders if it is really his place to ask, of Art of all people, rather than Alfie himself. "Alfie takes a salary for his work, I presume. Or has he invested, too?"

Art shakes his head. "Just the salary. His family is wealthy, but I think eyebrows would raise were he to put large sums of money into anything his father hasn't approved."

Heath hums in understanding. Alfie's home life may not be so different from his own.

"There was a moment, after I first bought the place, when I absolutely panicked. It was every last cent Uncle TJ had left me. I had nothing but the house and our few possessions and whatever bills were tucked into my pocket. But the club quickly began to pay for itself, and now I have more than I know what to do with."

"You could invest in something else. Buy some shares."

Art raises an eyebrow and regards Heath coolly as he exhales smoke into the summer's air. "There's that economics degree talking," he teases. "I could, but I don't much trust Wall Street. All that glitters is not gold."

Heath chooses not to protest; despite his reservations about going into the stocks and shares business, he certainly understands the sense behind investing one's money, as much from his education as from his father's many lectures on the subject. "So Mr. Peters wants the club. You aren't selling." Heath gestures to Art to continue; he knows that's not the last of it.

Art straightens up and finishes his cigarette. "He's taken to a new method of persuasion, now that he's come to terms with how serious I am about keeping TJ. He's threatening to expose the whole enterprise."

"Would he really do that?"

"I have no idea. They could be empty threats. After all, what does he have to gain? If anyone got wind of his investment in the place after it closed, it would knock his reputation throughout Manhattan. He's got shares in at least a handful of other speakeasies in Midtown; they'd drop him in a heartbeat if they thought he might do the same to them."

The cigarette between Heath's fingers has gone limp with the humidity, and he puts it out after one more drag. "But he might. He *could*, if he really wanted to."

Art stares at his palms, at the rough skin of his fingertips that Heath knows the press of against his neck, his collarbone, his own hands. "One phone call and he could take all of it."

"For every one that closes, another three open in its place," Heath recalls.

"Maybe. But as lucrative as TJ has been, I wouldn't have the capital to set it up a second time, not if it is seized. They'll take everything. And, we could be charged for far more than breaking the Prohibition law."

Heath swallows. He can't begin to think of what might happen. "We'll figure something out," he says. He tentatively kneels forward to touch Art's arm, doing his best not to upset the boat.

"We will." Art turns his blue gaze up to meet Heath's eyes. "Thank you, Heath."

Heath sits back in the boat and discreetly blows Art a kiss. Art's grin crinkles the corners of his eyes as he touches his fingers to his lips.

"Now." Heath nudges one of the docked oars with his toe. "Row us somewhere into the shade, won't you? I'm baking like a pie in this heat."

"Why don't you take the oars? We can switch places."

Art is up and moving carefully across the boat before Heath can protest that this sounds altogether far too dangerous. He has to start moving himself, or else their combined weights will overbalance one end. He staggers to his feet and they cross paths in the middle. Art's hands steady his waist as he helps him over the bench. Heath's hands scrabble for a hold on the seat at the other end, and he sighs in relief. His relief turns out to be premature, for when he turns his head to see that Art is settled, it's to see that his book is precariously close to being knocked out of the boat.

Heath snaps upright, letting go of the bench. "Art, the book—" Art lunges for the book, and the movement sets the boat rocking. Heath loses his balance and hits the water, spluttering as lake water floods into his mouth. The water isn't a refreshing reprieve from the heat; it's been made lukewarm by the sun. He pushes himself to the surface and emerges, shaking water and greenery from his hair.

Art is having fits of laughter as he leans over the edge of the boat; Heath can just see that his precious book, for which he'd lost his balance, is now in the bottom of the boat. He deems it safe enough to push down on the side of the boat where Art leans with just enough force to send him tipping headfirst into the lake.

Heath giggles as he grabs for the boat to pull himself out before Art emerges, but Art is faster. A hand wraps around Heath's calf and pulls him under. Heath opens his eyes underwater, where the world is a foggy, greenish shade of blue. Bubbles cloud his vision before he feels Art's lips touch his own as the grip on his leg disappears.

They're both out of breath when they resurface, plant life clinging to their hair and clothes plastered to their skin, matching smiles on their faces.

"Hey, misters!" A little boy with a scar on his left knee stands by the edge of the lake, brandishing a large stick. "Are you all right?"

Art gives him a friendly wave. "Of course! Lovely day for a swim, wouldn't you agree?"

The boy looks concerned and tears off back toward the path, exclaiming loudly to his nanny about the madmen in the lake.

Heath gets into the boat first and then helps to tug Art in. They lie back against the wooden slats on the bottom of the boat with their legs hanging over the side as they let the sun dry them from top to toe. Much to Heath's chagrin, Art uses his book to prop up his head so the cover gets damp from his hair, but Art protests that it's the book's fault he's wet in the first place.

"I'm not sure of your logic, there," Heath replies drily as he throws an arm across his forehead to shade his eyes from the sun's harsh glare.

The lake water has left their clothes discolored and dirty. They decide to return to Heath's house rather than take a turn around the park; they encounter enough looks of surprise and distaste in that short walk. The house is quiet, although Heath can tell that Martha has been in from the fresh flowers in the vase in the hallway and the smell of chocolate coming from the living room.

Heath squeaks delightedly and snags a cookie from the plate awaiting him with a note reminding him not to eat them all at once. "Chocolate and orange peel, my favorite." He picks up another and passes it to Art. "Martha always made them for me when I was sick as a child, to make me feel better."

"Clearly, Martha must have had a sixth sense that you'd be taking a nosedive into the lake today."

Art leaves his shoes and still-damp socks at the bottom of the stairs as Heath goes up to run a bath. He steals a pinch of Amelia's lavender bath salts, causing sweet-smelling steam to curl around the bathroom. It is refreshing after the dank smell of his clothes from the lake water, and he sits on the edge of the bathtub a moment, having turned off the faucet. The steam makes his hair fall loose over his forehead and his shirt stick to his skin.

Knuckles rap softly against the doorframe. "I could wait downstairs, if you'd like to bathe first." Art's shirt is untucked and open at the collar. His bare toes wriggle against the floorboards.

Heath shakes his head and beckons him in, standing to shut the door behind him and keep the steam from escaping. "There should be room for both of us." He smiles shyly at Art, who catches him and pulls him to his chest.

"You smell rotten," Heath murmurs and scrunches up his nose with a chuckle.

Art hums and brushes Heath's hair back. "I think I'm falling in love with you," he responds quietly. His thumb traces the curve of Heath's hairline before he cups his cheek.

Heath swallows and lifts his shaking fingers to Art's shirt, undoing another few buttons so he can press a kiss over where his heart beats in his chest. "I rather think so, too."

HEATH'S ESTIMATION OF HOW MANY bodies the bathtub can take turns out to be exaggerated. Even with his back tucked up against Art's chest and Art's chin hooked over his shoulder, it's a bit of a squash; their legs are tangled and their toes are pressed into the other end. Water spills over the sides every time one of them moves, and Heath gets soap in his eye often enough that it is red and irritated by the time they get out. But they both emerge smelling much better, and with skin soft and flushed. Heath wraps Art up into a towel and then takes one for himself, too.

The sun has started to set: Streaks of pink and orange stream through the front windows over the hallway and warm the floors. Water drips down the back of Heath's neck as he pads downstairs to the kitchen. Art is close behind; his hand rests on Heath's hip. The house is warm from the day's sunshine, enough so that they can comfortably lounge in robes, each with nothing more than thin undergarments beneath.

"Louis didn't come today, but I suppose there's some bread and such," Heath says as he swings open the door to the kitchen. He manages to put together a spread of bread and cheeses and cold meats and fills two tumblers with lemonade over ice. They eat in the living room, side by side on the window seats. The window is open, letting in the soft evening air and the noise of traffic from the street.

"Uncle TJ would have adored you."

Heath turns his gaze from out of the window to Art. "You think so?"

Art nods and curls his legs up under his body. Their knees knock together gently. "He would have liked the way you see the world, with your air of caution." He chuckles as Heath slaps his arm playfully in protest. "He would have found it endearing, I imagine. No doubt would have encouraged me to corrupt your moral sense as much as possible."

Heath raises an eyebrow. "I think you already achieved that. I can't say I'd ever thought of breaking into a closed subway station before you came along."

Art leans forward. "Wasn't it worth it?" His gaze dips from Heath's eyes to his lips and he steals a languid kiss. "I think it was worth it."

"All right," Heath concedes teasingly, his eyes half-lidded. "I suppose it was worth it."

Art's hand curled around his bare knee would have been enough to distract Heath from hearing the front door click open, but the way he pulls it back sharply is enough to kick him back into the present moment. Heath frowns and adjusts his robe, tightens the sash. "It's Amelia," he whispers, catching her voice and another, too. Edward, perhaps. "Wait here." He touches his lips to Art's forehead and steps into the hallway.

"Heath!" Amelia is suntanned and glowing; her hair has grown out a little, and curls toward her shoulders. She bounds to embrace him and smacks a kiss on his cheek. "Why are you in your robe at this hour? Are you sick?" She holds his face between her hands and peers at him curiously.

He pushes her off and shakes his head. "Long story involving a boat," he says vaguely. "A dinner party anecdote for another time."

He looks past Amelia's shoulder to where Edward stands, their bags in hand. "Edward. How was Cove Neck?"

"Wonderful," Amelia answers for them as she toes off her shoes and breathes a sigh. "But Mama and Papa were really starting to get on my last nerve, so we thought we'd escape to Manhattan a few days early."

She slips past him toward the living room, pausing to run her fingers over the petals of the flowers in the hallway. "Are these fresh?" she asks over her shoulder as she continues on. "They smell divine. Oh. Hello."

"Hello." Art's voice comes from the next room.

Edward raises an eyebrow and claps Heath's shoulder, having set the bags down. "I take it things are going well, then?" he whispers before he joins Amelia in the doorway and slips an arm around her shoulders.

"It's Arthur, isn't it?" Amelia says as Art steps forward to greet her properly.

He smiles. "Art is just fine. And you must be Amelia. I can only apologize that we haven't been properly introduced until now." He kisses her hand and she titters.

"Were you a part of this long story involving a boat, then, too?" Amelia tugs at the lapel of Art's robe playfully, and he quickly tightens it before it gapes further.

"I was, yes." Art grins at Heath. "Some might say perpetrator, but I beg to differ on that account."

Edward clears his throat and offers a hand to Art. "Wonderful to meet you, Art. I'm Edward."

Art's eyebrows furrow before he recovers and returns the handshake. "Pleasure." He mouths his bewilderment to Heath when Amelia is distracted, but Heath shakes his head. *Later.*

"Well." Amelia fakes a yawn into the back of her hand. "We're awfully tired from the drive, so I do think it best if we went to bed."

Heath rolls his eyes. "Goodnight, Amelia." He pecks her cheek. "Please remember that your bedroom adjoins mine," he whispers in her ear, not at all reassured when she cackles gleefully and tugs Edward toward the stairs.

"So that's Amelia's beau," Art comments when the door upstairs has clicked shut behind the couple and his hand is falling to the small of Heath's back.

"I meant to tell you earlier. Just in case something like this happened."

Art hums and skims his nose over the curve of Heath's jaw. "I'd best get dressed and take my leave."

Heath sighs and leans back on Art's chest. "Is it cruel of me to say I rather dislike my sister right now?" He takes Art's hands, laces their fingers together and wraps them around his waist to rest against his stomach.

"An understandable feeling, I think. I had meant to call at the club this evening, anyway. Fate intervenes, hm?"

"It doesn't do to put too much of one's faith in fate."

"Is that part of Heath's philosophy?"

Heath smirks. "Perhaps. Perhaps I'll write a book. Number one: endeavor to lock your little sister out of the house when you are home alone with your lover."

"That's more just a reminder for oneself, baby."

"Damn. So much for the book."

CH. 7

THE DUKE AND DUCHESS RETURN just two days later, the Duke with some threadbare excuses about work he had to do in the city that he could put off no longer and that couldn't be taken care of from Long Island. Really, the Duchess simply needed someone to fuss over, and Heath says as much to Amelia, who agrees wholeheartedly and with a hint of despair.

"We shall have to send Martha to close the house for the season," the Duchess comments once she's settled and her presence is felt throughout the many rooms of the house.

Heath pauses in thought a moment before he approaches her. "Would it be all right if you waited a little longer? I thought perhaps I would go for a weekend."

The Duchess looks up. "Well, of course you can, sweetheart. But why on earth would you choose to go *now?* You'll be all alone in that big house." She smiles innocently. "I could always accompany you."

"No!" He clears his throat, his brash response clearly having startled her somewhat. "No, I thought perhaps I could take, uh, my—my girl," he stutters. His cheeks heat up.

"Heath," his mother coos. Her eyes light up as she cradles his face in her hands, peppering kisses over his nose and forehead. He protests and tries to bat her away, but without conviction; it is something she used to do when he was a child and it tugs on fond memories. "I think that's a charming idea. Well, what's her name? Who is this lovely lady we have yet to hear anything about?"

Luckily, she doesn't give Heath a moment to respond, let alone think up more fibs, for she claps her hands together and calls for Martha. "Martha! Tell Louis to put together something special for dinner, won't you? And set an extra place at the table."

Heath panics. "I don't know if—tonight, it's very soon, perhaps—"

"Nonsense," the Duchess declares. "You shall bring her over tonight so we can meet her before you take her to Cove Neck. It's only proper, Heath."

Heath swallows and tugs at the collar of his shirt, where it is suddenly rather tight. "I shall call her right away, then." He scampers down the hallway, grabs the phone and dials Frankie's number, stretching the receiver as far as he can so he can tuck himself inside the closet containing the winter coats and shoes. He wrinkles his nose at the musty smell and waits for Frankie's godmother's housekeeper to answer, then asks for Frankie. "I need a girl," he hisses as soon as he hears his friend on the other end of the line. "Immediately. You have to help me!"

"You know, I've been under the strangest impression that girls weren't your type, Heathcliff." Frankie makes a sound as though he's just bitten a large chunk out of an apple.

Heath groans. "Don't tease right now, I haven't the time. The Duchess expects to meet my girl at dinner tonight. The girl I plan to take to Cove Neck because I'm clearly awful at fabricating excuses under pressure."

Frankie chuckles. "Couldn't you have just told her you wished to spend time with your friends there? Seems you could have saved yourself a whole load of bother."

"Frankie!"

"Fine, fine. So what you need is an… actress."

"Yes." Heath frowns. "Hold on, no. No. Frankie, I am not paying for any girl's services. I need a girl, not a flapper!"

Frankie sighs. "How dull. However, you're in luck. I think I have an idea. I'll be in touch."

The phone clicks off, and Heath lets his head fall back against the coats with a sigh. Perhaps he could just hide in this closet and never come out again.

Y

It's mid-afternoon when Frankie comes to the door with a young woman by his side. She's tall and lithe, with blindingly fair hair cut in a bob that accentuates her pale skin. Martha sees them into the living room where Heath sits reading; the Duchess has retired for her afternoon rest and the Duke is at his office. Frankie introduces her as Ginny, and they form a conspiratorial circle around the couch.

"I'm seeing a man who works on the railroad. Daddy couldn't possibly understand, and he's quite content thinking I'm going steady with some Upper East Side boy I'm not ready to introduce to the family." She grins wolfishly. "So, how did we meet?" she asks as she reaches for his hand and holds it between her own.

It takes a few hours for them to muddle through all the details. Frankie chips in with suggestions where he deems them helpful, although he is almost always rebuffed. Ginny rolls her eyes at Frankie's elaborate tale of how they met when her bracelet became caught in the cufflink on Heath's shirt, but also turns down Heath's more reasonable suggestion of having been introduced by a mutual friend at a party.

"One is too obviously a lie in its eccentricity; the other certainly believable but far too bland to hold any weight," she insists. She twists a lock of her hair around her finger and tugs on it.

The three of them compromise. Ginny rattles off her likes, her dislikes, her interests—enough that Heath can talk about her and not have his facts disproved by his date later in the evening. Ginny notes a few things Heath tells her in a small book she pulls from her purse, including the story of how Heath and Amelia were in a bike accident as children, earning Heath a broken bone and Amelia a gash on the head from which a scar could still be seen in some lights.

Heath fetches them all a round of drinks before his friends depart; Frankie accompanies him to carry the ice bucket. "You really did find me a professional," Heath murmurs out of the corner of his mouth as they walk across the living room. He nods toward Ginny, who is perched on the edge of the couch, practicing introducing herself to an invisible guest as Heath's girl.

"Oh, he's quite the catch," she says to the thin air and accompanies it with a girlish, high-pitched giggle. "Even with his penchant for having his nose buried in a book half the time!"

Frankie gives an unapologetic shrug, then snags an ice cube from the bucket, pops it into his mouth and crunches on it. "I imagine she's had quite the education in lying to parents."

GINNY AND FRANKIE TAKE THEIR leave before the Duchess rouses from her rest; Ginny promises to be there by six o'clock sharp, dressed and primed for conversation. It's only just after four, and Heath wonders if he might have time to rush to TJ to see Art, perhaps bring up his idea to take him out to Cove Neck. He pictures breakfast on the porch and dinner by the bay windows. Afternoons on the beach with their toes buried in the hot sand and swimming naked in the pool long after the sun has set.

Of course, this all rests on the premise that Art can rush away with him to Long Island. Away from Manhattan, away from TJ. And that isn't a promise that Art has made him, nor one Heath can expect him to make. Alfie overseeing the bar for a night here or there is one thing. Heath will owe Alfie rather a large gift should he, or Art, agree to his idea.

He has no chance to consider it much more that afternoon, however, for as soon as his mother awakes she is keen to know all about the girl he is to introduce them to this evening. He relays tidbits of information, considering it practice for the evening, when he will be surely be asked the same questions over again.

Ginny vowed to wear red, claiming it was her most flattering color. Heath accordingly dresses himself to match, with a vibrant crimson bow tie and matching suspenders. Ginny arrives, and they make such a sickeningly sweet couple that the Duchess coos and clutches her hands to her bosom as she takes in the sight of them.

"You must be Ginny. My dear, I've heard so many wonderful things." The Duchess embraces her tightly and sends Heath an approving smile over her shoulder.

"And I of you, Mrs. Johnson. Thank you so much for welcoming me to your home," Ginny gushes as the women exchange air kisses.

The Duchess titters, holding Ginny's hands as she looks her over, head to toe.

"She's eyeing her for a wedding dress, already," Amelia singsongs in Heath's ear. She giggles.

"Do call me Agnes."

"Not that anyone does," Amelia adds, drawing the two women's attention.

"Of course." Ginny glances at Heath before she continues. "I must say, the first time Heath mentioned the Duke and Duchess I almost took a turn! I fancied myself having found a member of the nobility in disguise."

"How did you two meet? I've yet to hear the story from Heath." The Duchess lets go of Ginny's hands so she may walk to stand by him, laying a hand on his chest in a familiar gesture.

"Utterly down to this man's incredible sense of chivalry. I was in the park with a girlfriend, and we stopped for ice cream only to discover that neither of us had taken our purses with us! We were frightfully ashamed, as I'm sure you can imagine, two ices dripping in the heat and no money to pay for them."

"That's when I appeared," Heath chimes in as he slips an arm around her waist. "I offered to pay, and in turn, they welcomed me to join them in their stroll around the park."

"Tilly was making eyes at Heath the whole way, but it was me he was fixed on." Ginny grins. "To my delight, he asked me to join him for dinner the next day." She gives a breathy sigh as they come to the climax of their tale. "The rest, as they say, is history."

Heath breathes a small sigh of relief. If he and Ginny could keep up appearances as well as this into the evening, they would be just fine.

"Come." Amelia slips her arm through Ginny's. "I simply must tell you all of Heath's most embarrassing stories from over the years." She winks at Heath and steers his date into the living room.

The Duchess greets Edward, whom Amelia had shown in not moments after Ginny, before she excuses herself to hurry her husband. Edward and Heath are left alone in the hallway; the sound of the girls' voices floats through from the other room.

"Cigarette?" Edward suggests, and they move to the dining room. They throw open the wide windows and perch there.

Heath sneaks them two of his father's superior cigarettes from the case on the sideboard, and they share a conspiratorial grin as they light them.

"I happened to be taking a drink at TJ this afternoon, so I mentioned to Art that your parents had returned. So you needn't worry about him expecting you there tonight." Edward takes a drag from his cigarette. "He says to call or stop by when you can, but he understands if you have familial obligations to attend to."

"Thank you." Heath leans back and tilts his head to the view. "I considered calling today but I hadn't the chance, in the end. I had something I wanted to discuss with him." He bites back the giddy smile that threatens to overtake his face.

Edward clears his throat, dragging Heath's attention to him before he can dip too far into his daydreams. "He seems quite fond of you. Art, that is."

A flicker of a frown tugs at Heath's eyebrows before he controls his expression. "We're very fond of one another," he replies. He doesn't like Edward's implication that the feelings are not entirely mutual.

"Yes. I thought as much." Edward taps ash from the end of his cigarette. "And Ginny? Are you quite fond of her, too?" He cocks his head, his stare cool and unflinching. "Has Art heard this wonderful story of how you two met, say?"

"Well, at least I can be glad that our lies are altogether quite convincing. In truth, we met this afternoon for the first time. A friend of mine, Frankie, was able to answer my cry for help to have a girl on my arm this evening, to appease my mother."

Heath explains the situation until Edward's firm look of disapproval softens into one of understanding. "It's not like you and Amelia. I would never do that to Art," he finishes, his tone quiet.

"I apologize for judging you." Edward squeezes Heath's elbow in a gesture of companionship. "Art is a good man, and in all the time I've spent at TJ, I've never seen him take to anyone as he's taken to you. I wouldn't want to see him hurt. You understand, I'm sure."

"Of course. And I'm glad that he has people around him who care so much." Heath glances up as he hears his parents descend, calling for the girls to come through to the dining room. The other members of the dinner party leave them to their conversation, save for the Duke teasing that he hopes that it is not one of his finer cigarettes between Heath's fingers.

"I had hoped to ask you something, this evening, Heath." Heath looks up. "It's not about Art or the club." Edward puts out his cigarette and wrings his hands. "I should like to ask Amelia to marry me, before the summer is out."

Heath nearly drops his own cigarette and narrowly avoids burning a hole in the material of his pants.

"I will ask your parents for their blessing, also. But I know how close you and Amelia are from how she speaks of you. And it did not feel right to not have yours, too."

Heath turns to look at his sister where she stands, comparing shoes with Ginny as the Duchess looks on with pride at their blooming friendship. "Do you love her?" he asks Edward, as he returns his gaze to the other man. "You told me once that you'd never met anyone like Amelia." Heath smiles wryly. "I can imagine that to be true, but that's not enough. Do you truly love her? As a man should love his wife?"

"For someone with such unconventional tastes, you certainly have a conventional view of love," Edward comments before he nods. "I do. I do not feel that I could love anyone more than I love Amelia. I swear to that."

"Then you have my blessing."

The two men move toward the dinner table, but not without Heath giving Edward a one-armed hug. "Welcome to the family," Heath whispers as Edward swings his arm up around Heath's own shoulders.

"At what point should I start to call you brother?"

"She hasn't said yes yet," Heath teases, before he slips away to pull out Ginny's chair.

The dinner goes far better than Heath could have hoped. Ginny is charming and quirky, and he can tell that his family is as infatuated with her as he pretends to be. They almost slip up when Ginny mentions the large party she is planning in a few weeks' time for her birthday. The Duchess immediately fixes her attention on Heath and reminds him that he had better have a good idea in mind for a birthday gift. Amelia giggles behind her water glass and surreptitiously waggles her ring finger at him.

Heath stumbles, for he had not thought to learn when Ginny's birthday is, so had no way to prepare for such a question. Fortunately, Ginny pulls attention from his flaming cheeks and lack of an answer by looping her arms around his neck and pulling him close.

"I think he forgot," she teases. She tickles the hair at the nape of his neck as the other dinner guests titter along with her. "Don't worry, darling, I'll forgive you," she purrs.

He touches his lips to her temple by way of a thank you and doesn't miss how his mother nearly overturns the glass in her hand in delight.

The Duke tries to coax the party into a game of charades or cards after dinner, but the Duchess claims a headache and Edward admits that he ought to be getting home.

Heath is exhausted from dinner. He feels much as though he has just sat a three-hour, intensive examination: The Life of Ginny, An Introduction. Or, perhaps: The Art of Faking It, Advanced Level. Ginny seems to feel much the same; she stifles a yawn as he walks her to the door.

"Are you sure you'll be all right getting home?" he asks, with completely genuine, unforced concern for his new friend. He touches a hand to the small of her back and gives her a soft smile. "I wouldn't be put out to walk you home."

"Phonus balonus." Ginny kisses his cheek. "I'll pick up a taxicab," she assures him. "I'd be no sort of company, anyway. I can barely keep my eyes open."

"Exactly why I should worry." Heath chuckles and wraps her up into a hug. "Thank you. I cannot begin to express my gratitude, Ginny."

She pulls back and places a hand on his cheek. "I'm rather partial to Tiffany's," she whispers and winks before she steps out into the night. "Be good!" she trills, by way of a farewell.

"She's wonderful," Amelia comments as Heath closes the door behind her and steps back into the hallway. Amelia's shoes have been toed off and lie, abandoned, at the bottom of the staircase. She sits a few steps up, head propped against the twisting, ornate rungs, a few finger curls springing free from the bobby pins stuck into her hair.

Heath slips off his own shoes at the bottom of the stairs and pads up to settle next to her. He leans to rest his head on her shoulder, though it makes his neck ache something awful. "She is," he agrees. He taps the freckles on Amelia's forearm, which have sprung up under the sun. He remembers, as a child, being put out over these mysterious dots that appeared on his sister in the warmer months and which he never received himself. His lips curl at the memory, but he only lingers on it a moment before he lifts his head up. He rubs at the back of his neck, massaging the sore muscle with his fingers.

"Will you marry her, do you think?"

Heath starts at the question. Louise was one thing; his mother must have always had some inclination that Heath was not fond of her, despite her pushing and attempts to make it so. But Ginny is another matter. Ginny he brought into the family himself; he'd introduced her to his parents and he pretended to be in love. A young man in love, he may be. But he is not in love with Ginny. How far can he take this elaborate tale? All the way to marriage? It seems unthinkable, even without considering how Ginny might feel. Her man on the railroad may let her act as someone else's girl during a dinner, should she tell him, but he doubts very much that he would allow her to marry Heath.

"I don't know," Heath answers honestly, when he realizes that he has let the silence hang too long.

Amelia yawns and raises her arms, stretching her body right down to the tips of her toes. "Whyever not?"

"I'm not sure it's quite that simple, Amelia."

She hums and stands up, smoothing down her dress as the grandfather clock in the hallway begins to chime eleven o'clock. "It can be," she replies and ducks to kiss the top of his head before she takes the stairs to her bedroom.

He watches her go with a small, if a little sad, smile on his lips. For her, it would be simple. Edward would sneak into her bedroom tonight and would have proposed before long, too. Amelia would say yes, and all would be well for her.

As for him, simple is not the word he would choose. Heath pulls himself to his feet and collects both his and his sister's shoes and deposits them tidily in the hallway between their two rooms before entering his own. He cannot think to sleep just yet, so he busies himself packing a bag for Cove Neck, for a trip he does not yet know his lover will be able to accompany him on, but which he hopes very much they will take together.

And when he does finally go to bed, it is with nothing but his love on his mind: Art's crystal blue eyes, burning the inside of his own eyelids as they flutter closed, and the memory of the taste of Art's lips, which he can no longer go without.

Y

JERRY LOOKS SURPRISED TO SEE Heath so early the following morning; he's only just hooking open the shutters of the barber's salon. "He's here," Jerry assures him before he shakes his head with an amused smile. "I don't think he made it home again last night."

Heath frowns; he hadn't realized that it was quite so common for Art to forgo returning to his apartment and spend the night in the club. He slips past Jerry and takes the stairs down into TJ, slowing his pace as he reaches the door leading into the club. It's quieter than Heath has ever known it, with one solitary light on above the bar; the rest of the club is shrouded in darkness, and thick with it.

Art is nursing a cup of coffee with a ledger open beside him. He looks weary, with bags under his eyes and his hands clasped around the cup as though it's a lifeline.

"Good morning, baby," Heath calls out softly, so as to not startle him, before he lets the door swing shut behind him.

"Aren't you a sight for sore eyes," Art murmurs, but his smile doesn't quite meet his eyes before they drop back down to the ledger. "I'd hoped you might at least call yesterday."

Heath rocks on his heels before moving closer to the bar. "Edward said—"

"He told me, yes. But a short phone call simply to tell me everything was all right wouldn't have gone amiss. That's all."

"I'm sorry." Heath slips onto one of the bar stools and slips his hands around Art's. The heat from the coffee tickles his fingertips. "I should have called, you're exactly right."

Art's shoulders drop a little. "How are things with your family?"

Heath's mind ticks back to the previous night, to Ginny. "It was fine. I managed to placate them." He decides that any further explanation of the evening's proceedings can wait until Art at least looks a touch more awake.

Heath touches his fingers to Art's jaw, rough with stubble. He almost comments on the irony of it, with Jerry right up the stairs. "Have you slept at all?"

"An hour or two." Art gestures to one of the upholstered couches near the piano. A blanket is slung over the back; a few cushions are propped up at one end. "It was nearly dawn by the time we closed up. I didn't much feel like walking back to the house at that hour. Alfie promised to be in before midday, and then perhaps I can rest before the evening."

"I have an alternative proposition for you, which involves Alfie, in a way."

Art looks up in alarm. "I didn't—I wouldn't have thought that would be something you'd be interested in," he stutters. His eyebrows shoot up nearly as far as his hairline.

Heath feels his cheeks burn. "No, *Art*. That is *not* what I was alluding to. I have absolutely no desire to share you with anyone, thank you very much."

If nothing else, this makes Art laugh, and the sound soothes Heath's worries. Art flips the ledger closed, his place marked with a cocktail napkin, and turns his full attention to Heath. "So what is this proposition, then?" he asks with a flirtatious waggle of his eyebrows.

"Come away with me," Heath breathes out. "To Cove Neck. We'll have the entire house to ourselves: the beach, the gardens. No interruptions, no work. Just us."

Art looks pained. "Heath, baby. I don't know if I can ask that of Alfie. It's one thing for me to disappear for a night or two somewhere in Manhattan, but out to Long Island?"

"We can go for as little or as long as you can spare," Heath persists. "A weekend, three days, five days. Even just a day if it's all you can manage!"

Art sighs and skims his fingers up Heath's wrist, nudging at the cuff of his sleeve. "I don't know."

"Please. You need to rest, Art, and I know you well enough to know you never will when you're only a few blocks away from the club." Heath tilts his head and beams at him. "If you won't do it for yourself, then do it for me?" He bats his eyelashes.

Art groans and leans forward to join their lips. "You're playing dirty," he protests, nibbling at Heath's lower lip before pulling back. "I'll ask Alfie, when he arrives. If—*if*—he feels comfortable being left here with TJ, and for that long, then we'll go."

Heath yells triumphantly and grabs Art's face between his hands to smack a loud kiss to his forehead.

"In the meantime, you could at least make yourself useful and clear up those tables at the back," Art suggests with a hopeful grin.

Heath is happy to help out any day, but today it really is the least he could do. "Yessir." He gives Art a two-finger salute and swipes a rag from the end of the bar.

ALFIE ARRIVES TO FIND THE club in full swing. Heath has turned on the gramophone to motivate his cleaning, and is humming along under his breath and twirling from table to table. Art protests that he is far too distracting, but makes no move to take his work to the back office; he remains by the bar, pencil tucked behind his ear.

"I'm offended; you started the party without me!" Alfie holds up a paper bag he has in his hand. "What a good thing I brought extra."

They sit down to brunch: bagels drenched in butter, and a selection of fruit. Alfie is willing to accommodate Heath's plan, unsurprisingly; Heath can read the concern in his face about Art's exhaustion and, not for the first time, he is glad that Art has people around him who care so much.

"Five days," Art concedes finally, stealing glances at Alfie, who nods enthusiastically. "Does five days seem fair?" He looks between the two of them.

"Five days seems perfect." Heath resists the urge to hustle Art straight to his feet to get home and begin packing. "Alfie?"

Alfie toasts them with his coffee cup. "Five days." He grins toothily. "I think I can manage five days."

"That smile does nothing to reassure me," Art grumbles, but gets to his feet, closes his books and stores them beneath the counter. "When do we leave?"

"Immediately?" Heath suggests. "Allow me to reintroduce you to the world that exists above ground, Art Houston."

CH. 8

HEATH COLLECTS ART FROM HIS house in the car, with the windows rolled down to let in the breeze. Fortunately for him, his father rarely makes use of his car when he is in the city, preferring to call for a driver or take a taxicab. He had handed Heath the keys with nothing from Heath but a promise to enjoy his time away. And to watch the paint.

"Door-to-door service." Art whistles as he jogs down the steps, bag in hand. He pops the trunk and sets his bag next to Heath's before he swings into the passenger seat. "This is quite some vehicle." He runs his hand over the dashboard with an admiring eye. "However did you get your father to let you have the car for nearly a week? A car like *this?*"

Heath starts the engine and pulls out into the heavy stream of traffic, driving south toward the bridges. "By telling him I was taking my sweetheart, and everything had to be perfect."

Art raises an eyebrow.

"Of course, he thinks my sweetheart is a sprightly young blonde named Ginny," he concedes. He shares the details of the dinner party, down to the agreement he and Ginny made and his conversation with Edward.

Art listens in silence. If it weren't for his fingers tapping irregular patterns on the side of the car, Heath may have believed he'd fallen asleep.

"I know it's not ideal, but you should have seen how happy my mother was," Heath says quietly. The bridges come into view, the towering structures that will allow him to cross into Brooklyn and onto Long Island. "It's a harmless fib, and it keeps everyone satisfied."

"I'm not upset with you over it," Art assures him and exhales. "I suppose I don't much like the idea of anyone else claiming to be your sweetheart, but I understand."

Heath smiles and reaches one hand from the wheel to rest on Art's knee. "You're my only sweetheart, no matter what I tell my parents."

Art joins their hands as the car rumbles onto the bridge. Heath squints as the sun hits his eyes, but before he can reach for the sunglasses on top of his head, Art tips them down for him and pushes them into place. "I got you, baby," Art murmurs, and then leans back into his seat, closing his own eyes.

"Sleep," Heath encourages him. "I'll wake you when we get there."

Art sighs. "Just a few minutes. I want to take in the view." His hand is already a little looser in Heath's. "Just a few minutes," he repeats, his voice little more than a mumble.

Heath glances at him and grins as Art's jaw goes slack, sleep fast overtaking him. He turns his gaze back to the road and catches the disappearing skyline of Manhattan through the rearview mirror as they speed toward Long Island.

Y

LOOKING SKEPTICAL OF HEATH'S PLAN to handle the house and kitchen himself, the Duchess had tried to suggest he take Martha. She relented eventually, but not without reminding him that Mrs. Banford, Ginny's maternal aunt, who will accompany them as a chaperone, is to be treated as a guest and not as a housemaid. She clearly hopes that under Mrs. Banford's watchful eye, Ginny will return with a ring upon her finger, although she didn't say as much. Heath just nodded until she let the subject drop and packed him off with some sandwiches for the road.

Art sleeps the whole way to Cove Neck and wakes up a little put out when he realizes they're pulling up by the beach, where the water is blue and glitters under the late afternoon sun. The sandwiches form their dinner that evening; they eat on the beach and try not to get sand in the filling. They watch the sun set over the horizon; their bodies are bathed in orange and pink hues.

Heath can feel Art droop again, his head propped on Heath's shoulder, his breathing heavy. "Let's get you to bed," Heath whispers as he combs his fingers through Art's long brown locks.

"But it's beautiful out here."

"How would you know? Your eyes are practically closed." Heath chuckles. "The view isn't going anywhere, baby. The sun will rise again in the morning and set come evening. We have time."

"All right." Art allows himself to be helped to his feet. Their bare soles sink into the sand as they stumble back up the beach.

Heath guides him up to his bedroom. It is still decorated with childish trinkets from his younger years, down to a stuffed bear on the bookshelf, which Heath still thinks of fondly as Teddy. Though he feels a little silly as he shows Art into the room, he knows it would feel odder still to take the master bedroom.

Art is clearly too tired to notice the furnishings, although he does give the rocking horse by the door an affectionate pat on his way past. Heath tucks him in and promises he'll join him soon. Art's eyes are closed before he can kiss him goodnight.

Heath unloads the car and opens the shutters in the lower rooms to let some air through the house, though it hasn't been long since his family left. He considers taking the car to buy food for tomorrow, but he doesn't want Art to wake and find him gone. It can wait until morning.

Although it is dark outside and the house is quiet, sleep doesn't tug at him the way it has at Art. However, he knows how much Art needs the rest, away from the constant pressures he has in the city. For something bred from Art's passions, TJ takes a lot out of him—although Heath gets the impression Art doesn't want to admit as much.

He decides to call Frankie, lest he call at the house in Manhattan looking for him, not realizing he already left for Long Island. He isn't at home, but his godparents' soft-voiced housekeeper suggests that he might find Frankie out with friends, should he know better than her where that might be.

Heath assures her he may well know and dials through to the private number Art gave him for TJ. Alfie answers. He sounds a little flustered at already being checked on.

"It's only been a few hours; everything's under control." His tone is terse. Heath is sure this is the first time Art has put this much trust in Alfie, and it shows in both of them.

"I'm not calling for Art, he's asleep and—I hope—dreaming of everything that *isn't* the club." Alfie chuckles, sounding infinitely more relaxed. "Is Frankie there tonight?"

"Yeah, came in about an hour ago. Hold on."

Alfie bellows Frankie's name across the club, and Heath hears the rustle of the receiver being passed to another hand.

"Heathcliff, however did you find me?"

"Gut instinct. And Dottie told me you were out. Listen, Alfie may have told you, but I'm at Cove Neck with Art."

"All going according to plan, then. Good, good."

"Right. So I won't be at the house for a few days, just remember that, won't you?"

"Of course. How fortunate I have other friends when you have abandoned me so." A pause. "Julian's here," Frankie adds.

"Send him my best, then."

"I shall. See you back in the city next week."

"See you."

Alfie apparently steals the phone back before Heath can hang up. "Heath?"

"Everything all right?"

"Don't tell Art. I wouldn't want to worry him. He needs time to relax."

Heath grimaces. He resents the idea of keeping things from Art, particularly if they are to do with TJ, but he agrees that Art needs the time. "What is it?"

"Mr. Peters is here again. I told him Art is on vacation and that he couldn't contact him. He said he knew Art's answer anyway and that all he wanted was to enjoy a drink."

"That's good, isn't it?"

"I don't know. I don't trust him."

"No. I wouldn't, either." Heath sighs. "I suppose there's not much we can do. Try to keep on his good side, and hopefully he'll give up his pursuit soon."

"I'll do what I can. Have a nice time away. Take care of him, won't you?"

Heath smiles. "I promise."

THE OTHER SIDE OF THE bed is cool and empty when Heath awakes. The brush of the breeze from the water filters in through the open window. The curtains billow with it, white and wild. Art slips back in not a minute later, his voice thick with sleep when he greets Heath. He slides under the blankets; his toes are cold against Heath's ankles.

"How did you sleep?" Heath asks. His eyelids droop again as he buries himself deeper in his cocoon of blankets.

"Like the dead." Art's nose nudges his own and he sighs a warm breath against Heath's lips. "Thank you. For getting me away from Manhattan a little while. For forcing me to rest. I needed it."

"I won't argue there."

Heath yawns widely. He arches his back and loosens his joints, stiff from sleep. His stomach growls; the sandwiches are not going to sustain them. "We need to go to the store," he mumbles, remaining stationary.

"Thought so." Art's hand skims up underneath Heath's nightshirt and tickles his ribs. "That means it's time to get up, Heath, not time to go back to sleep."

Art's laugh is a low rumble as Heath bats at him until he has his head firmly pillowed on his chest.

"Not yet." Heath wraps an arm around Art's waist and presses closer to his chest, listening to the gentle thud of his heartbeat. "In a little bit." His stomach growls again, and Heath groans.

"What was that you were saying, baby?"

Heath grunts and reluctantly drags his eyes open. "Fine. I'm awake."

Art jabs a finger between his ribs, and Heath jerks. "Get some clothes on."

Heath props his chin up on Art's chest and looks at him, eyes narrowed. "I could say the same for you." He tugs at Art's shirt, crumpled from being slept in, and smiles widely. "Or don't." He squawks as he is tipped backward onto the bed, his legs flailing.

Art walks over to the bags that Heath had quietly brought upstairs. A pair of pants and a shirt hit Heath in the face. "Get a wiggle on."

Υ

THE STORE IS QUIET WHEN they get there, and Heath's senses are immediately overwhelmed. He doesn't know the first thing about cooking, but faced with the freedom ahead of him, he has half a mind to buy one of everything. It's fortunate, then, that Art seems less nonplussed by the contents of the grocery store; he simply grabs a small cart and starts to fill it. Heath trails after him and occasionally sneaks things into the cart when Art's not paying attention.

The lobsters are Art's idea. Heath has eaten lobster before, but frankly, he's a little terrified by the clawed beasts that Art has packed in ice. He taps his knuckles on a shell. "Anybody home?" he mumbles, sure that at any moment the creature will snap one of his fingers off. Or perhaps his nose.

"Do you know how to cook a lobster?" Heath asks, for the fifth time, as they traipse back to the car. Heath munches on strawberries from a paper bag, which he delves into the moment they've paid for their food.

"Have a little faith. I *can* cook. At least a little."

"Lobster seems quite complicated for someone who can cook *a little*," Heath counters, sucking red juice from his fingertips.

Art sighs and pops the trunk to put the bags inside. "Quite the shame I can't shut you up as I usually would."

Heath grins and pinches one last strawberry before the trunk is closed. "Now you're just encouraging me to keep going."

The lobsters turn out not to be quite the unmitigated disaster that Heath predicted. He keeps well out of the way of the cooking process and nominates himself in charge of drinks instead. Art seems displeased and adamantly refuses to drink a scotch on the rocks simply because it's the only thing Heath knows how to make.

"It's not the only thing," Heath protests meekly as he rummages through the Duke's liquor cabinet, which he discovered the summer of his sixteenth birthday. "I could probably fumble my way through a mint julep, too. It's the Duchess's favorite. I've seen Martha do it a hundred times."

Art makes a pained nose as he dunks one of the lobsters into a pot of boiling water. "Please," he sighs. "Baby. Just tell me what you have. I'll tell you what to mix."

Heath does as he's told and comes to the conclusion that the kitchen is not the place where he is likely to excel.

Meticulously mixed Bijous go down well with the lobster, which they tear from the shell with their hands, their bare feet entwined beneath the table they've dragged closer to the windows. They can see the water and hear the whistle of the wind past the house. Heath promptly declares the Bijou to be his new favorite drink.

"I shall have to mix you a Hanky Panky when we return to the city," Art comments, and Heath gives him a soft kick until he relents and laughs. "All right, you've got me. The only kind of Hanky Panky worth preparing for you can be done here just as well."

Art persists with the cocktail anecdotes, and if it weren't so endearing, Heath would be utterly irritated. He teaches him, too, plucks bottles from the depths of the cupboard, so old and unused that dust clings to them. Heath doesn't worry in the slightest that his father might notice—by the time he returns next summer, he is unlikely to remember what was in there.

Heath isn't the best of students: he finds himself too easily distracted by watching Art measure various liquids into a tumbler and carefully lock two tumblers together in lieu of a shaker to mix the drink. He's enamored by the frown of concentration that etches the space between Art's eyebrows; his eyes follow the trail every time a drop flies free and slides down Art's wrist and forearm.

He suspects that Art knows a lost cause when he sees one, but he persists anyway, all but holding the bottle up to Heath's face to try to capture his attention at each stage before he moves on. Heath is far more interested in testing Art's concoctions—old favorites of Manhattan and beyond, as well as creations of his own invention—and kissing the taste of gin from Art's lips when they're finished.

Y

Heath cannot remember ever having felt quite so relaxed. He can see it in Art too, which pleases him. His shoulders don't seem so tense when Heath drapes himself over them to kiss his temple. His laugh is lighter, and his eyes sparkle when he smiles.

He hasn't quite left it all behind, though. Heath can read that much from the way his gaze lingers on the telephone in the hallway, as though perhaps willing Alfie to call from TJ or wondering whether he should call himself. Fortunately, Heath finds ways to distract him from his staring contest with the telephone. He shows him the rocking chair on the porch that Heath fell off as a child, and tells Art how he had only been placated when he had his feet dangled in the pool and a hard candy to suck on, sticky between his fingers. He shows him the marks Heath and Amelia carved out on the back of the house: their initials and a cross for every summer spent at Cove Neck. He tugs him along to find their own spot on the house, to start a new set of crosses, for every day they spend here together.

"And next summer, we can add more," Heath murmurs, his mouth pressed to Art's cheek. "And the summer after that, and the summer after that."

"If the club keeps doing as well as it is, we could buy our own house." Art casts his gaze over the water and points across the bay. "One of the sheltered ones. Our own little haven."

They drive to the other side of the bay one evening, once the sun has set and dusk has fallen. Heath pulls the car up as close to the houses as he dares. Some have people within; light streams through open shutters.

"What do you think of that one?" Art points to the house nearest them. It is a grand affair, with a large white porch that seems to wrap all the way around the house. The upstairs has a balcony, too, perhaps opening off the master bedroom, with a view over the water. One could probably see all the way to their side of the bay on a good day.

"It's beautiful," Heath murmurs. He sighs under the touch of Art's hands as they slip over his shoulders and massage the muscle there. "We could watch the sunrise in just our bedclothes up on that balcony. Take breakfast on the porch and entertain in the gardens at night."

Art's thumbs dig into the junctures between his neck and shoulders, and Heath's eyes slip closed. "Swim before midday and have a picnic lunch on the sand. Read in the living room in the afternoon," Heath continues, a giddy grin tugging at his lips.

"You'd fall asleep," Art teases. "Sun-kissed and sleepy, you'd doze right off with the book going unread on your stomach."

"And you'd love me in spite of it."

Art's lips touch the shell of his ear ever so softly. "I'd love you *because* of it, baby."

They are startled from their daydreams by the sound of voices from the house, and giggle like children as Heath fumbles to get the engine started.

"Did you see headlights, Pansy?" they hear someone cry from the beach. Heath puts his foot down harder on the gas.

OTHER EVENINGS THEY PASS ON their own side of the water where it is quiet, desolate almost. The Thornes' house is closed up for the summer already; the shutters are closed, the garden furniture stacked under a small wooden shelter. Heath thinks he spies the next closest neighbors as he goes to pick flowers from the edge of their property one morning; their voices float nearby, but even they are some distance away.

It adds to their sanctuary, the privacy. The world and its reality are but a phone call away, but out here they feel so much farther away. Heath remembers the first afternoon he visited TJ and his resentment of the freedom he saw in the men there, how much it cut into his understanding of his life and his future.

He tells Art as much one evening as he digs his toes into the sand. His pants are rolled up to his calves; the water laps over his ankles and sends a shiver down his spine despite its warmth.

"Do you still resent them?" Art asks from behind him where he remains on dry land, his excuse being that he's wearing his only pair of pants that haven't been dirtied around the ankles from wading.

Heath glances back at him and flicks a few drops of water at Art with his toes. Art huffs and takes a step back, tripping over the cascading sand. He crosses his arms over his chest, awaiting an answer.

"No." Heath turns back to the horizon. He spreads his arms wide and lets the light breeze billow his untucked shirt away from his skin. "No, I think I've found my freedom." He closes his eyes to the setting sun with the warmth touching his cheekbones. His skin has bronzed in the sun, but it's nothing compared to the beauty of Art's skin, sun-kissed as it is, with freckles appearing over his forearms.

Heath hears movement behind him but doesn't react, not until he feels Art's arms winding around his waist and his thumbs digging into the hollows of his hipbones. He chuckles and tries to tug at Art's pants, but finds that he has shucked them completely. The pants lie discarded on the sand. Art is in nothing but his underpants, with a few buttons open at the top of his shirt. Heath runs his palm flat up Art's exposed chest before he loops his hand around the back of his neck and drags him down for a kiss.

Art's lips don't stray far from Heath's, even as the kiss comes to a natural break. "We can't stay here forever."

Heath sighs and rubs his thumb down the column of Art's neck. "I know. But perhaps if I can find freedom here, I shall figure out some way to find it there, too?" His voice rises in question, as if he hopes that Art might hold the answers, or be able to predict his future.

"Perhaps." Art tilts his head and presses his lips to Heath's cheek. Heath can feel Art's lips curl into a smile. "What are you going to tell your father about—"

Heath cuts him off with another kiss, more heated this time. His fingers tangle in his hair as he clings to him. "Please," Heath begs in a soft voice. "Please, for a few more days, at least. Can we leave my father, my family, all of it—can we leave it behind?"

Before Art can reply, Heath starts to walk backward into the water. The force of it pulls him in deeper quickly. Art stutters but doesn't get a word out before Heath pulls him down, clothes and all, into the water. It's sandy and murky in the shallows, and Heath's once-white pants are quickly turning a disgusting shade of brown. He has to spit water from his mouth as he laughs, still with a fierce hold on the front of Art's soaked shirt.

Art grunts and shakes his wet hair out so it smacks back over his head at a comical angle. "All right, you. Enough of that." He scrambles to his feet and nearly careers face-forward into the water because of the shifting sand. Heath continues to giggle, situated quite comfortably half in the water and soaked to the skin.

Or he is until Art hikes him up over his shoulder. Heath wriggles and shrieks in feeble protest. Strands of wet hair fall into his eyes as he is carried back up to the house.

"Arthur Houston, you dreadful man! Put me down!" Heath cries. But there isn't much heat behind it.

Art carries him straight around the house—Heath quietly thankful that he won't have to clean wet sand from the house later—to the swimming pool at the back. It's circular in shape, with a seated rim within for the Duchess, who prefers to sit with her shoulders exposed to the sun and her body cool beneath the water for hours on end, rather than swim.

Heath is set down onto his feet but remains limp as a rag doll as Art undresses him and tosses his clothes into a sodden pile by the deck chairs.

"Into the pool with you," Art says with a crooked grin before he sheds his own clothes and hops into the water with a splash that sends jets spilling out over the surrounding tiles.

The water is cool compared to the muggy heat that lingers into the evening, and Heath feels goosebumps as he submerges himself. He sucks in a breath and ducks below the surface to push his hair back from his face, carding his fingers through the dark locks.

He resurfaces not a minute later and rubs his eyes as he blinks Art back into view. Art has moved to lie flat on his back on the surface of the water with his head turned up to the pink of the sky.

"Adonis," Heath murmurs as Art propels himself back onto his feet and clears the water from his ears.

"Hmm?"

"Adonis. God of beauty and desire. The archetype of handsome young men." Heath doesn't shy from letting his eyes linger on the breadth of Art's chest, or the way the drops of water catch on his toned, tanned biceps.

Art wades toward Heath so he can wrap his arms around his smaller frame and pull him to his chest. "Whom would that make you, then? I can't say I have much knowledge of Greek mythology."

Heath kisses the hollow of Art's throat. "Aphrodite, I suppose. If mythology is to be believed." His lips linger over Art's collarbone. "Goddess of sexual love and beauty, also."

Art's smile could blind. "How apt," he whispers. He directs Heath's lips from his skin to his mouth.

Y

HEATH HAS LOST TRACK OF the days when Frankie telephones from Manhattan. He pretends to a social call, but there's a strain in his voice and Heath senses something amiss as he babbles nonsense. Babbling is unusual for Frankie, and enough to set Heath on edge.

"I swear, Heath! I tell you, it was her—Clara Bow in the flesh. And she is quite lovely, incredible, truly. Now I wanted to speak to her, of course, but it was as though I was frozen on the spot. Starstruck! Heath, I believe I was starstruck by the wonderful Miss Clara Bow, and—"

"Frankie." Heath tries not to let exasperation seep into his tone as he tucks the receiver closer to his ear and sits on the floor. "Whatever it is you're stalling over. Do just tell me."

Frankie is silent. Heath doesn't know whether that is better or worse than the chattering. "You and Art, you're having such a marvelous time out there though, aren't you?"

"Frankie," Heath insists.

"It's only—it's only, I saw the Duke yesterday. Quite by accident; I happened to be having lunch near the water and I suppose he had decided to take his lunch there, too. And of course I didn't think to be anything but polite and say hello when he spotted me."

"And? You weren't jazzed, were you?"

"Heath, it was barely one o'clock!"

"It would hardly be the first time."

"I take offense; I am perfectly capable of holding my liquor, and what's more—"

"Frankie, my father? What happened with my father?"

"Well, you see. You see, I had a companion with me for lunch. A friend I'd happened to cross paths with in the morning and whom I'd thought it would be nice to invite with me. Ginny."

Heath doesn't need any more details to be able to picture the scene: the Duke's gaze falling from Frankie to Ginny. The young lady he'd last seen on the arm of his son; the young lady supposedly summering with him at his house in Cove Neck. A young lady he probably hoped would return with an engagement diamond upon her hand, or at least the promise of one within a few weeks.

"I'm so sorry, Heath. I didn't think to have her hide until it was too late. Much too late."

Heath looks up as Art comes down the stairs, bare-chested, hair still rumpled from sleep. He smiles tightly in the hopes that he won't worry Art.

"Did he say anything?" he asks Frankie, and stares at the hardwood floor. He scratches at a mark with his fingernail.

"He seemed confused, at first. As though he might ask—but, no, not really. He greeted Ginny and me cordially and asked if I'd heard from you. I said I hadn't but was sure you were having a wonderful break from the city."

Heath closes his eyes and presses his head against the wall. "He hasn't called," he says quietly. "I suppose he's waiting until I get back."

"Heath, don't jump to the worst assumptions straight away. I couldn't tell you what he believes. He might simply think things didn't go quite so well with Ginny as expected, that she returned early while you stayed on. Or perhaps that her aunt had to return to the city for a day or two and wouldn't allow Ginny to stay behind alone! I'm sure he wouldn't guess, simply from this—"

"One can hope." Heath's throat feels dry, tight. He often wondered what might happen should his parents discover the truth about him. He hoped that it would be his mother, rather than his father. The Duchess would be disappointed in him, he imagined, but her love seemed unconditional in a way that the Duke never expressed.

To the Duke, what was he besides a legacy? Someone to continue the Johnson family name, through Yale and on to Wall Street? Was he nothing more? Anything but the pristine image that the Duke expected of him? Heath couldn't conceive any response to that but anger and outrage.

"Heath, listen. I don't know how much longer you planned to stay there, but perhaps it's time you came back. Both of you. You can't hide there forever."

"We're not hiding, Frankie," Heath whispers. He squeezes his eyes so tightly closed that it makes his head throb. "This is the one place where we needn't hide."

"You know what I mean. I was merely suggesting that you return to Manhattan. Sooner rather than later. Put together a good story to spin to your father; have Ginny join you for dinner—she's more than happy to do that, she said as much to me—and everything can return to normal."

Heath thanks Frankie for calling him and leaves the receiver dangling off the table until Art crosses the room from where he's been hovering by the window and returns it to the cradle. Heath shuts his eyes and tries to dull the pain that pierces his temples.

The breeze comes in through the open window, and the gentle sound of rainfall begins outside. Art's hands curl over his knees.

"Should I pack our things?" Art asks, his face close when Heath wrenches his eyes open.

Heath tilts his head and looks outside. Thick stormclouds are gathering over the water. "Perhaps I'll say no. Lie and act as though nothing has changed. That we still have our sanctuary."

Art looks concerned, but he is not given a chance to reply before the telephone begins to trill again, rattling against the cradle. They both look at it, neither moving. Heath is sure he's had quite enough bad news for one day—and it's not noon yet. "You'd best answer, Heath. Should it be your father, or anyone in your family, it wouldn't help matters to have to explain why a strange man is answering your phone."

Heath sighs and reaches for the receiver. He sits up on his knees as he tucks it to his ear. "Johnson residence at Cove Neck. Heath speaking."

"Heath, Julian here. Is Art there with you?"

Heath looks up at Art. "Yes. Yes, he's here." He hands the receiver to Art. "It's Julian. For you."

Art raises an eyebrow but takes the receiver while Heath resettles himself on the floor. Art's spare hand remains on his knee and he stiffens visibly as he listens to whatever it is Julian has to say.

Heath tries to catch Art's attention but fails; he sits in the dark as the color drains from Art's face and his teeth dig into his lower lip.

"All of it?" Art says after what seems an infinity. His voice is hoarse. "The back entrance, is it—?" He falls silent again and nods, his head drooping. "What of the boys, the regulars? Jack and his friends?" He lets out a shuddering breath. "Alfie? Is Alfie all right?"

"Art," Heath hisses. He wraps his hand over Art's on his knee and digs his fingers between his. "What is it? What's happened?"

Art shakes him off almost violently; his actions match his harsher tone. "What do you mean you don't *know?*" He laughs bitterly. Art is shaking, but Heath is almost too scared to touch him, for fear that he'll be pushed away, again.

"I'll be there within a few hours," Art says in a clipped tone. "I don't *care* if there's nothing to be done, I won't sit here while—" He sighs. "Yes. Yes, thank you, Julian. I'd appreciate that. I'll see you soon."

Art gets to his feet and slams the receiver back into the cradle. "Pack your things; we're leaving." He's already halfway to the stairs.

"Art." Heath scrambles after him. "*Art.* Baby, talk to me." He catches Art's arm and locks his fingers around Art's wrist. "Please. Tell me what's happened."

Art shakes his head and looks down at him. He is a fragment of the man Heath has come to love, the man he's come to know so well. "It's gone," he rasps. "TJ. It's been busted. It's over."

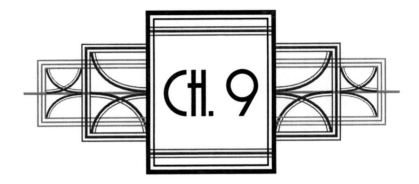

CH. 9

HEATH IS NOT UNUSED TO silence where Art is concerned. Art can adopt a quietly pensive manner, when his mind seems to be a million miles away. Heath can draw him back with little more than a touch to the back of his wrist, enough to have Art turn to him with a smile in his eyes and an apology on his lips that Heath would never ask him to give for simply wanting a moment with his thoughts.

But this, this Heath doesn't know. Art is stoic as they pack their things: shirts retrieved from where they were tossed over chairs and dressers; pants from the staircase railing where they were left to dry after Heath's attempts to wash the dirt from the ankles. Art's face is impassive and unreadable, and Heath winces at every noise he makes, sure it will be enough to further upset or anger Art.

It doesn't come. No yell of frustration or cursing or, heaven forbid, tears shed over the news received from Manhattan. Any of those things Heath might have expected and understood implicitly. The silence is what scares him.

"I'll pack the leftover food for you to take back with you," Heath says in an undertone as he curls a hand around Art's shoulder.

Art glances at him before he turns back to his bag, forcing the buckle shut. The bag bulges from clothes thrown in haphazardly, with none of the sense of order that Art seems to portray in all aspects of his life. He doesn't knock Heath's hand away, but he doesn't reply, either, and Heath draws back of his own accord and takes his bag downstairs with him.

He has no need to linger. Grace, who lives in Cove Neck and tends the house during the winter months, will come shortly to place white sheets over the furniture as dust covers and to wash the floors, leaving them smooth and polished until summer comes around again. Heath simply clears the last of their things and ensures that all the windows and doors are fastened shut before he goes outside.

The rain lashes down hard and fast now, blurring his vision as it drips coldly down his forehead and into his eyes. Art has already put his own bag into the trunk, but he has not gotten inside. He stands halfway down the driveway, looking away from the house. A cigarette is between his fingers, but any attempt to light it has clearly been abandoned; the stick has turned limp and soggy. His shirt is plastered to his skin, and his wet hair curls at the nape of his neck.

Heath fills the trunk before he goes to him and pulls him toward the car. "Come on now," he urges, nearly shouting as thunder rumbles overhead. "You'll catch a chill standing out here like this. Come."

Art lets Heath guide him to the car, his feet unsteady, as though he were drunk. He shivers in the passenger seat when Heath gets in alongside him but makes no effort to acknowledge Heath's offer of a blanket. Heath has half a mind to refuse to drive anywhere until Art says at least a word. He might do it, too, if he didn't understand just how badly Art needs to be back in the city right now.

"I feel it, too," Heath says finally, when they're on the road and the house is a receding point behind them. "I know how upset you are. I can *feel* it, Art." He takes a breath. "I love you."

Art says nothing. His eyes are fixed straight ahead; his hands are clasped in his lap. It's as though he is paralyzed to his core.

Heath doesn't mean to push, he only means to help. He talks enough for both of them, thinking he might be able to bring Art out of his stupor if only he keeps talking. He means to talk of anything but TJ, but meets many a roadblock; everything in their entwined lives comes back to Art's corner of Manhattan that no longer exists for them. Or at all.

So he changes track and chooses to talk of TJ. He recounts his first visit there. His laugh is too bright, too loud in the tiny space of the car when he regales Art with his first meetings with Alfie, below ground, and Jerry, above. Heath talks of the many propositions Frankie has received given the frequency of his evenings spent there; he talks faster and faster until he is nearly breathless and catches himself clutching the wheel with manic intensity.

Art says nothing, and if it weren't for the sound of his harsh breathing as he shivers through his soaked shirt, Heath would pull the car over to ensure he is still alive.

Heath's own teeth chatter from his short stint in the rain, and when he catches his reflection in the rearview mirror, it's to see that his hair is drying in an eccentric mess. He laughs, then, almost a bark, as he points to his hair and looks at Art, begging for some reaction.

"What weather this is!" he exclaims and scrubs a hand over his scalp before he returns his hand to the wheel. He shoots Art glances continually, whenever he can afford to take his eyes off the road, which is slick with water and dark from the thunderclouds. "To think, of all the wonderful days we have had this summer and today! Today it rains, it thunders!"

He catches Art's wince, and hope flares up in his chest. It is the first response of any kind that Heath has gotten from him since he hung up the telephone. "Rain, rain, go away! Come again another day!"

"Heath, for Christ's sake," Art growls. His hand slaps down tight around Heath's on the wheel. "Quit your jabbering and focus on the goddamn road before you get us both killed."

Heath swallows and mumbles an apology, settling both hands tighter on the wheel as he stares down the road. They're nearly at the bridge; the arches are coming into view through the hazy sheen of the storm. The tops of the buildings of Manhattan are obscured, as though the cloud bank had chosen to perch over the city itself.

Heath wonders if that is all he will get from Art, now that he's sat back and resumed his stony silence. The wheels of the car groan over the ridge of the bridge and they join the light traffic that's moving onto the island, and then Art speaks again.

"It's all my fault."

Heath's foot nearly slams on the brake. "What?" He frowns but keeps his eyes on the road. Despite his reckless driving earlier, he has no real wish to send them spiraling into the depths of the now-visible Hudson River. "Art, you can't truly think that. Mr. Peters must have—"

"No, Heath." Art laughs bitterly. He has a hand pressed to his forehead and his fingers digging into his scalp. "I don't doubt he was involved in bringing TJ down, but Mr. Peters wouldn't have done anything if I hadn't been distracted. If I'd been taking care of the club the same way I always have."

"Distracted," Heath echoes, his voice hollow. "By me. So, in truth, what you're saying is that it's *my* fault."

"That's not what I said," Art snaps.

"It's what you meant," Heath mumbles. They roll off the bridge, and Heath swings the car to take them uptown. "Isn't it?"

Art sighs. "I meant that I've taken too much time away from TJ recently. I expected Alfie to be able to handle everything while I spent my summer frolicking with you, and that's not fair to anyone." His tone becomes softer, less accusatory. "Julian didn't know who was there when it was busted."

Heath opens his mouth to ask what he means, but realization hits him like a steam train: TJ is more than just another juice joint; it always was. And if they rounded up anyone in the raid, Art would have a lot more to answer for than illegal liquor purchase and consumption.

"Alfie? Edward, Jack, the other—"

"I don't *know*," Art hisses. "He couldn't tell me. There was no sign of Jerry; he went down to find the place boarded up. An envelope was tacked to the padlock with my name on it."

Heath drives up Seventh Avenue, and Art hollers at him to stop when they reach the corner of Fifty-seventh. The rain has slowed enough that Heath can make out the individual drops hitting the windscreen.

On the corner of Fifty-seventh and Seventh stands Julian, a large black umbrella held above his head and a cigarette burning between his fingers. Art is already reaching for the door, and Heath hasn't come to a complete stop yet.

"I'll take the car home and then come—"

"No." Art won't meet his gaze. "Go home, Heath. Go home and stay there."

"But—"

"Go."

Art steps out of the car and slams the door shut. He walks around to the trunk and pops it open to shoulder his bag.

Heath risks getting pinched if any coppers come past and find him parked on the street like this—one taxicab has already hooted at him as it rushed past toward the park—but he can't let Art walk away from him like this. He scrambles out of the car, scraping his hair back from his face as he hops onto the sidewalk.

Art's back is to him as he converses in hushed tones with Julian beneath the umbrella, but Julian sees him coming and nudges Art to turn.

"What do you want, Heath?" Art spits out.

It's a contrast to everything Heath has become used to in thinking of Art. Art, *his* Art, is gentle and kind. He's playful and soft, and even when he's rougher, he's never this. Never to Heath.

"What are you going to do?" Heath pleads. He reaches for him, but Art recoils and Heath has to bite back the bile that rises in his throat. "Please, Art. Be sensible. Don't be doing something rash." He steps closer and takes solace in the fact that Art at least doesn't move from him again. Julian is doing his best to give them a moment of privacy. He stares at a point across the street and seemingly tries not to listen in.

"It's mine—it *was* mine. If anyone's going to take responsibility for the business, it'll be me. I won't let anyone else be hauled away while I stand on this sidewalk like any other man going about his day." Art controls his angry expression, returns to his marmoreal determination. "It was all I had. If it's gone, then I have nothing."

Heath rises onto his toes and cups Art's face tightly between his two hands. "That's not true," he replies fiercely. "You have me. TJ might be gone, but that doesn't mean it all ends here."

Art sighs and pinches Heath's wrists between his thumbs and forefingers and pulls them from his face. "I wouldn't expect you to understand. You've never fought for anything a day in your life."

Heath shudders. It's getting harder and harder to force back the tears that threaten at the corners of his eyes and to push down the urge to collapse at Art's feet and beg him to think of something other than TJ and what's been lost. "I'm fighting now. I'm fighting for us." He searches Art's expression for some flicker of the man who had been there just that morning, sleep-rumpled and smiling. Where did he go? "Doesn't that count for something?"

Art turns his face away. "It's not enough, Heath." He steps away from Heath. "Go home," he repeats.

Heath shakes his head, stubborn to a fault. "No, I shan't. I'm not going anywhere without you. Not when you're like this."

"Art, maybe—" Julian tries in a gentle tone, but Art cuts him off with a sharp look.

"Fine," Art snarls in Heath's direction. "By all means, do whatever you want. Perhaps for once you might figure out what that is." He turns back to Julian. "I'm going downstairs to take a look."

"There's not much to see," Julian mumbles and pulls an envelope from his pocket and hands it to Art. "I pinched it before anyone else could."

Art stuffs it into his pocket and marches into the barbershop without another glance in Heath's direction.

Julian opens his mouth and promptly snaps it shut again. Raindrops slide off the edge of his umbrella and drip onto Heath's forehead. Heath reaches up to wipe them from where they've run down the bridge of his nose.

"I'll go," Heath says. He doesn't expect Julian to try to stop him, but he does expect that he might ask to be driven home. There was always a certain animosity between Julian and Art, which Heath can't believe has completely disappeared even if Julian was the one to call them at Cove Neck.

Julian nods and slips his free hand into the pocket of his pants. "I think that would be best." He nods toward the dark windows of the barbershop. "I could keep an eye on him, if you'd like me to."

Heath shrugs. "I'd say don't let him do anything stupid, but he's stubborn as hell when he's set his mind on something." He sighs and scrubs his hands over his face. He feels weary, and it's barely afternoon. "I'll see you around, Julian."

"Heath." Julian catches his arm. "He still cares for you. That doesn't just disappear like that—" He snaps his fingers to emphasize the point, and Heath takes the opportunity to wind his arms around himself. "Or with a few harsh words. He's just upset."

Something about having Julian, *his* friend, tell him how to handle the man he's in love with irks Heath. "Maybe all it took was for him to get upset to tell me how he really feels about me," he snaps back, before his shoulders droop. "That I'm a distraction." Heath takes a few steps back.

Julian calls after him but Heath doesn't allow him the opportunity to stop him, just keeps walking until the car door is safely shut behind him. He pulls away from the curb and narrowly misses hitting a taxicab.

The driver hurls obscenities at him through the window, and he flicks his gaze away. He focuses not on the cabbie, or on Julian—a single, receding figure out in the rain, dark next to the vibrant red of the barbershop—but rather on getting back to the house without a traffic accident.

The dampness is setting into his skin by the time he hauls his bag to the front steps. He feels the chill right down to his bones. His teeth chatter and his hands are stiff where they're wrapped tightly around the bag handles. He tosses the remaining food he packed for Art straight into the garbage can that sits beside the steps.

Martha looks alarmed to find him on the doorstep when she answers his three raps of the knocker. "Goodness!" she exclaims, and ushers him inside. "What are you doing wandering around in this storm? Are you mad?"

Heath doesn't have the energy to fight off her clucking, so he simply sets his bags down at the foot of the stairs and allows Martha to bring two large towels to the living room. She puts one down for him to sit on, and save the upholstery, and tucks it around his legs before he wraps the other around his shoulders.

She clicks her tongue three times in rapid succession and squeezes her hands to Heath's pink cheeks. "I'll make you some tea to warm you up. Let's endeavor to stop these shivers before your mother comes home, at least!"

Heath nods and closes his eyes. He leans back against the couch carefully and clasps the towel around him. But it's no good, for all he can see against the backs of his eyelids is Art. His beautiful, sweet Art turning into the viper-tongued man, almost a stranger, that he saw today. Art had suffered a loss, and all Heath hoped to do was to provide some assistance, some comfort. If he had been allowed to do so...

He opens his eyes, but the dialogue keeps playing through his head, even as he stares at the window smattered with raindrops. On the horizon, the sun pushes through the dark clouds; streaks of light illuminate the tops of buildings here and there across the city.

Art didn't want him there any longer. Art didn't *need* him anymore. Perhaps he never did. Heath hasn't the energy to cry; he just feels numb to his core. He hears footsteps behind him, court shoes tapping over the hardwood. They pause, and then there's a squeak that can only be Amelia.

"Heath! I hadn't realized you were coming back already! The Duchess said next week." Her head pops above the back of the couch and she tucks her chin over his shoulder. "You chose a bad day for it," she observes, as she looks him up and down. "Couldn't you have waited out the worst of the storm there, rather than start driving through it? The roads could have been dangerous." She frowns as she moves around the couch to perch next to him and pushes wet strands of hair back from his forehead. "How was Cove Neck?"

"It was wonderful." *Until it wasn't.* He marvels that he is able to get the words out without his voice shaking.

Martha brings the tea and he takes the cup between his cold palms eagerly, holding it close to his face to let the steam tickle his nose.

"Mama is going to have a fit if she sees you in this state," Amelia whispers. "Perhaps you should bathe and change into some dry clothes before she returns, hm?"

Heath sighs; it creates a ripple over the surface of his tea. "I suppose I'd better." He hazards a sip and winces as the hot liquid burns the tip of his tongue. "Where is she, anyhow?"

"She and Papa are having lunch with Edward's parents." She waggles her eyebrows and wraps a hand tight around his elbow. "You know something? I do think he might propose soon!" She giggles and holds out her hand, tilting it this way and that. "I'm hoping for diamonds."

Heath's heart clenches, and the cup wobbles in his hand. "About time," he teases, careful not to allude to having known about Edward's intentions for some time. Retaining a smile makes him feel a little nauseated, but it's worth it for the expression of pure joy on his sister's face; dimples are etched into her cheeks from the stretch of her grin.

"And what of your romantic vacation?" she probes, and tries to tickle his ribs through the towel. He swats her hand away but nearly upends the teacup in the process.

He sets it down on the table for safekeeping and wrings his hands into the towel. He can deduce, then, that his father hasn't shared his news of seeing Frankie out with Ginny over lunch—at least, not with Amelia. The Duchess could be a different story entirely.

"What of it? I told you, it was wonderful."

"*Heath*," Amelia protests in a whine. "Did you propose? Mama was quite sure you would; I overheard her gossiping about it with her friends one evening after dinner. She was practically bragging about how both her children would be engaged to marry by the end of the summer. And summer's nearly over—so if you didn't, you really ought to get a move on."

Heath shakes his head. When Edward does indeed propose, it will provide a welcome distraction from the scrutiny over his own love life. The Duchess may well be so taken with wedding details that she mightn't notice should he and Ginny's "romance" fizzle out as summer turns to fall.

Although, he supposes, he no longer has another romantic entanglement to conceal. And that hits like a fresh bucket of ice down the back of his neck. He need no longer sneak out of the house under the pretense of seeing Frankie, or some other friend; need no longer give vague and misleading explanations as to where he has been seeing these friends. He need no longer hide in the closet in the hallway with the phone cord stretched under the closet door to whisper a "Goodnight" and "I love you" as the sounds of TJ busy and thriving filter through from the other end of the line.

"Heath," Amelia prompts and pinches his thigh. "Well? Did you?"

Heath stammers and rubs a hand over the back of his neck. "No. No, of course not, Amelia. It's a little soon for that, I think."

"You took her to Cove Neck. You must love her, don't you?"

Heath blinks a few times and swallows around the lump that's formed in his throat. The image of Art's eyes, cold and piercing, before he turned from him into the barbershop burns persistently in front of him. "Yes. Yes, I do."

Amelia raises an eyebrow. "So…?"

Heath stares back at her blankly.

Amelia makes a noise of irritation. "Honestly. *Men.*"

They both start at the sound of the front door opening. "Heath? Heath, darling, are you here?" The Duchess calls out, clearly having spied his bags in the hallway.

Amelia quickly gets to her feet. "Don't say I didn't warn you," she whispers and tugs on Heath's towel before she slips into the hallway, greeting her parents on the way.

Heath groans under his breath but there's little he can do anymore—it's not as though he can go upstairs unnoticed now. He fixes his hair as best as he can and pats at the front of his pants with the towel.

The Duchess stops short in the doorway of the living room. She looks aghast at his appearance. "Heath Maximilian Johnson! What have you been doing, and was it really necessary to do whatever it was in your best pair of pants?"

Heath winces and stands up to greet his mother with a kiss to the cheek. "Hello, Mama."

The Duchess wrinkles her nose. "Please, darling. Go and bathe, you're dripping all over the carpet."

Y

HE GETS SICK—EXACTLY AS HIS luck would have predicted. The Duchess insists on quarantining him in his room while he sweats out the worst of the fever and to keep his boisterous sneezes from offending her delicate ears. Martha is the one who tends to him, which is familiar, at least. He thinks back on days spent suffering from colds as a child, wrapped up in blankets as he sat on the floor before the fire, until Martha came in to check his temperature and haul him back into bed. There would be a few stern words about how bed was the place to rest, not the floor, but there was always hot soup, too.

No need for a crackling fire now, his room is much too hot already. The storm has cleared and it's bright and hot outside again, if a little less humid since the thunder has chased it away. Martha leaves the window cracked open an inch to let in some fresh air, although it makes Heath shiver when the breeze touches his toes where they poke out of the blankets.

The sickness brings both blessing and curse, in the form of his solitude. It allows him the opportunity to wallow in private, to not be forced to plaster a smile onto his face and play himself off as a young man in love, with the world at his feet, when he feels as though he has aged a hundred years in a day and is now a weary man, exhausted with the prospect of envisioning a future for himself.

Best of all, he has not yet had to come face to face with the Duke. He knows he cannot stay in bed forever, that his body is slowly starting to recover and then he will be expected to look his father in the eye and find some way to either tell him a truth—or some version of it—or twist deeper into his tangle of lies and elaborate tales.

The solitude brings an ache, however, that he wasn't prepared for. It is unlike anything he has ever felt, the throb beneath his ribcage that is already present when he awakes in the morning and lingers long into the night. He misses Art in more ways than he knew it was possible to miss anyone—different from how he missed Amelia while he was away at Yale, far more than he missed Frankie when he spent summers in the South with nothing but a few letters exchanged during the long months.

Amelia comes to read to him for a little while every day that he is confined to his bedroom. She drags a chair from the desk and sits a foot from the bed, delicately resting one ankle behind the other.

She has a book tucked under her arm this afternoon, too, but she puts it on the nightstand. "Mama had me practicing my French verbs all morning." Amelia rolls her eyes. "She says I mustn't allow myself to become uneducated or dimwitted just because I've got a man on my arm."

Heath smiles a little and rasps a cough into the back of his hand. He pushes himself up into a sitting position, propped up against the headboard, and winds the blankets around his body tightly. "Teach me something?" He suffered through the mandatory Latin at his preparatory school, but never studied French as Amelia did.

Amelia hums and props her elbows on her knees, resting her chin on her hands. "*Tu me manques*," she enunciates carefully. "Meaning, I miss you. When the French talk of missing someone, they talk of that person as being missing to them. It's somehow more poetic, wouldn't you say? More poignant."

"*Tu me manques*," Heath echoes in a murmur and he feels it, too. Art is missing to him, and it weighs heavily on him as a stone slab borne on his back. "I like that."

"I do too." Amelia sits back and reaches for the book. "Shall we return to the French Revolution in the meantime?" she asks, and plucks through the pages of Dickens's *A Tale of Two Cities* to find where they left off the day before.

Heath nods and sinks lower in the blankets, closing his eyes. "Yes. Let's."

Y

THE TREES HAVE TURNED GOLDEN in his absence from the outside world; leaves are crisp and falling on the sidewalk. Was he really sick so long, for the seasons outside to shift and take away the last of the summer? It seems that way; the air feels cooler, too, where it pinches at his forearms, which are exposed with his shirtsleeves rolled up to the elbows.

What strikes Heath most is how quiet it is. No shouts of exaltation come from the park, no figures stroll the avenue with hands crooked through lovers' arms. Not a single taxicab or car is on the street, though judging by the height of the sun in the sky, it must be the middle of the day.

Then he sees him, shrouded in shadows around one of the entrances to the park—undeniably the broad shape of Art's shoulders, his familiar stance, his hair, being displaced by the light breeze.

"Art!" Heath cries and darts across the empty street.

The figure turns, and Heath catches a glimpse of blue eyes before he's gone, moving into the depths of the park.

"Art, wait, please!" Heath breaks into a run as he enters the park. He lets out a bewildered cry as he slams into an elderly woman and nearly sends her tumbling to the ground. "I'm sorry, I'm so dreadfully sorry—"

She scowls and pushes away from him, continuing on the now-crowded pathway. The park teems with people now, though Heath is sure that a moment earlier he didn't see a soul on the grounds except for Art.

"Art," Heath murmurs and takes off. He pushes as gently as he can past families and couples and children, through the winding pathways, with no real sense of rhyme or reason as to where he's going.

He sees him, then, and nearly falls in his haste to get to him. He doesn't register the tears that stream down his cheeks until he pauses to take a breath, and frantically rubs them from his cheeks. He cannot explain why, but he has the sickening sensation in his gut that if he doesn't reach Art in time, something awful may happen.

Heath runs again, but this time he doesn't have to go much farther, for Art has stopped. He stands by the side of the lake and looks out over the water with his hands tucked in his pockets. Art's head turns when Heath's feet pad over the soft grass toward him. Heath stops still, not sure how close he can get; Art is an untouchable mirage before him.

Heath glances back the way he came. The park is deserted once more, and the trees are bare. The ground is hard and dark with frost.

When he looks toward the lake once more, a thin sheet of ice coats the surface.

He feels unsteady on his feet all of a sudden, sick to his stomach and lightheaded. "This isn't real," Heath whispers, and he squeezes his eyes shut as if to rid himself of the images around him. But when he opens them again, all is as it was before.

Art stares at him, unmoving. "You weren't worth all that I lost," he seethes, venom in his eyes as he starts to walk toward Heath, each footfall echoing sharp and heavy around him.

Heath can't breathe: He sucks air into his lungs but none of the oxygen reaches his bloodstream; his vision blurs; his brain is unfocused.

Art's figure looms over him, and Heath blacks out.

HE AWAKES TO FRANKIE SHAKING his shoulder and calling his name. He's panting; his sleep shirt is stuck to his back with sweat. He blinks rapidly to clear the spots marring his vision and falls back limp against the bed as Frankie hovers over him.

"Nightmare," Heath explains in a cracked voice. He rubs his eyes with the heels of his palms. "Just a nightmare, that's all. I'm fine."

Frankie sighs in relief and perches on the edge of Heath's bed. "I thought you were having a fit, tossing and turning the way you were." He pauses. "You were crying, too," he says gently. He rubs a thumb over Heath's cheekbone and wipes away the tear tracks.

Heath says nothing, but he doesn't turn his face away from Frankie's touch, either. It's such a simple gesture, but it makes emotion well up in his chest and he has to stuff his face into the pillow lest he start bawling like a child all over again. He's missed physical contact, something that he became accustomed to when waking up next to Art, day in and day out, at Cove Neck.

"That's why I came," Frankie says, talking louder to be heard over Heath's muffled snuffles. "Julian called me when he couldn't get a hold of you directly. He hoped you might have heard from Art. He would have stopped by himself, but he wasn't sure he was entirely welcome at this time."

Heath swallows roughly before he turns his face around and shakes his head. "No. No, I haven't heard from him. I didn't much expect to." He sighs. "And Julian is always welcome, I hadn't meant to make him feel that way."

Frankie frowns and drums his fingers on his thigh. "Are you sure? Are you positive Art hasn't tried to visit or phone while you've been sick?"

Heath nods. "I'm sure. I told Martha should he call that she was to tell me immediately, no matter whether I was awake or asleep."

When Frankie doesn't reply, Heath feels a worry wrap around his ribs. Julian mustn't have heard from him, and he wouldn't have contacted Frankie, anyway.

"No one's heard from him? Since... that day?"

Frankie hesitates and then shakes his head. "Not that we know of. Julian has tried to talk to Alfie but to no avail."

"How so?"

Frankie pulls a crumpled slip of paper from his pocket. "We managed to locate a phone number and an address—it would appear he lives with his parents on the West Side. But every time either Julian or I tried to call, we were told he didn't wish to be disturbed. We thought perhaps you could go there—once you're feeling better, of course. Only, he might respond better to you than to us."

Heath chews on his lower lip, worrying at the dry skin with his teeth. "He's all right, then? Alfie. He must be. He's not been—" Heath snaps his mouth shut. "He's all right?" He repeats.

"I suppose so. Unless his family is lying to protect their name, but the impression we got was that he was purposely avoiding the calls from us alone. For what reason, we can't fathom."

"I'll go to him," Heath promises, taking the slip of paper and placing it under his pillow for safekeeping. "Just as soon as they let me free of this prison, I will. I swear."

"I know, Heath. You needn't make any promises to me. There's not a single person in this world who would care more about making sure Art is all right than you."

Heath smiles stiffly. "Maybe. It's all I can do. It's all he'd let me do, anymore; if he'd allow me to do that. Besides, I'd like to see for myself that Alfie is safe and sound." For all his eccentricities, he has come to mean a lot to Heath.

Frankie nods before he slips off his jacket and slings it onto the chair that Amelia left behind the day before. He toes off his shoes, helps Heath to shove up to a sitting position and moves next to him so their shoulders are pressed together.

Heath leans close to the warmth of Frankie's body and rests his head on his shoulder. It harks back to nights at Yale when the sun was beginning to rise on the horizon and the effect of liquor consumed was gradually wearing off. They used to swap secrets then more than ever—silly secrets of childhood and of future plans. Of tricks Frankie used to play on his parents and of places in the house Heath used to hide when he snuck things from the kitchen to have a secret picnic.

"I asked Art about family once. About his uncle, TJ." Frankie's voice is gentle and soothing as a lullaby. "I've never understood family in that way, mine being how it is. And you are close to Amelia, the Duchess too, but not so far as to tell them everything about yourself. But from all that I've heard, Art and his uncle were impossibly close.

"He told me that when his uncle died, he thought he'd lost all his family for good. But in setting up TJ, he gained a family so much bigger and more spirited than he ever could have imagined having."

Heath closes his eyes. "It wasn't just the club that meant so much to him," Heath agrees. "It was every person in it. I think that's what scared him most, that morning when Julian called. The fear that something might destroy the lives of the people he cared about most, when that family had already been taken from all of us."

"Exactly," Frankie murmurs. He falls silent; Heath's head shifts with the gentle rise and fall of Frankie's breathing. "Julian wouldn't tell me exactly what happened when you and Art returned to Manhattan, but I gather it wasn't the most pleasant of situations."

"I'm all right, Frankie," Heath replies, though it's a lie of gigantic proportions and they both know it. "I only worry for him, that's all. I worry he might do something impulsive. I worry he already has. He thinks he has nothing left to lose with TJ gone."

"But what about you—"

Heath shakes his head and slowly opens his eyes to look up at Frankie. "No, Frankie. No, I wasn't enough. I never asked him to love me more than the club. But he blames me for taking his attention from it, all the same."

"He doesn't," Frankie breathes, his face twisting in anger as his tone rises. "He couldn't. This was no more your fault than it was his. It was no one's fault, nothing but poor luck and that shady investor who was always hiding in the shadows with his ledgers and his sneering face. You told me of the deal he pitched to Art, but I think he knew Art wouldn't take it and thought to twist him more as part of his wicked plan. He's a foul man, and if Art isn't already plotting how to have *him* thrown behind bars, then I'll do it myself."

An uncontrollable trill of laughter bursts from Heath and he latches his arms around Frankie, hugging him tight. "Oh, Frankie David. There aren't enough men like you in the world."

Frankie chuckles and hugs him back. "I've been saying as much for years, Heathcliff. How glad I am that you've finally come around to my way of thinking!"

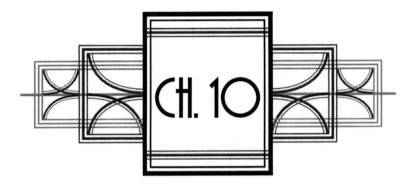

CH. 10

FRANKIE MAKES IT HIS PRIORITY to hunt out Mr. Peters, telling Heath to focus on getting better so he can call on Alfie and then find his way back to Art. The worst of Heath's sickness dissipates after a few days, and Martha allows him out of his bedroom to join the family for mealtimes, satisfied that he is well enough to be on his feet once more.

He's anxious to see Alfie, but he knows he cannot draw any suspicion to himself—especially when the Duke fixes him with a tight look every time he speaks at the dinner table. He has yet to mention Ginny or Cove Neck to Heath, but Heath doesn't fool himself into believing that that means he won't. The Duke's look speaks volumes of how much he knows for sure; how much he has deduced for himself, Heath cannot bear to think.

It's well into the week by the time Heath manages to slip from the house, saying he is going to stroll through the park and take in some fresh air and sunshine. It's mid-afternoon, hot but not with such baking intensity as earlier in the summer. Fall is well and truly on its way; the end of summer is calling on the edge of the breeze.

Despite all that has happened, Heath hasn't forgotten the decisions he has looming. He is no closer to clarity on what he wants from his future—except for Art. Art was his one certainty, the one thing he knew he wanted for every day of his life. But his constant has been ripped away. He doesn't know if he's permitted to fight for it, but he'll be damned if he doesn't at least try.

The walk to the address Frankie gave him takes him through the park, and while usually he'd dawdle to take in his surroundings—no matter how many times he's seen them before—he doesn't today. He's all but out of breath by the time he reaches Central Park West and is back into thick of the city, with the bustle of the taxicabs filling the avenue.

Heath smooths back his hair and tucks the paper into his pocket before he raps on the door with the knocker. The housekeeper answers with the same kind of fond air that he is used to from Martha.

"Can I help you, sir?"

"I certainly hope so." He smiles his most charming smile, even if it doesn't quite reach his eyes as it once might have. "Heath Johnson. I was hoping to talk to Alfie. Is he here?"

"Of course, yes. He's in the living room taking lemonade with his mother. Charles is visiting for a few days, you see, so she'll barely let the two of them out of her sight for a second! You'll know of Charles, I'm sure?" She ushers him into the house.

Heath nods dumbly. "Of course," he lies and lets her take his hat before he is shown to the living room.

"A Mr. Johnson to see you," the housekeeper announces and then takes her leave.

Heath nearly starts as two men turn to him. One is Alfie; he recognizes the birthmark on the length of his neck. The other could be an identical copy save for their slightly different clothing and the absence of a birthmark.

"Heath," Alfie says finally, his eyes wide as saucers as he stares up at him. "What are you doing here?"

"Alfred! Really, that's no way to greet a guest," Alfie's mother—Heath presumes—chastises and rises to her feet to introduce herself. "Mrs. Miller, it's lovely to meet you—Heath, was it?"

Heath nods and takes her hand politely.

"Clearly you know the ruder of my two boys." She gestures to Alfie's twin brother. "Charles. He's visiting from Chicago; such a rarity these days. I'm sure you'll understand if perhaps you haven't been able to get hold of Alfred."

"Of course," Heath says quickly. "I'm so sorry for the intrusion."

Mrs. Miller smiles. "Nonsense. Now that you're here, you must sit with us. I'll have Kathy fetch another glass." She squeezes his arm and urges him to take a seat.

Charles holds out a hand. "A friend of Alfie's from Columbia, then?"

"I—" Heath glances at Alfie, who looks at him imploringly. "Yes. Pleasure to meet you. I've heard so much." Heath wonders just when he got quite so adept at lying. He sits, having shaken Charles's hand, and thinks how lucky he is that his Yale ring sat abandoned on his dresser while he was sick and that he didn't think to recover it before he left.

"What brings you by?" Charles leans back and crosses his leg over the opposite knee. He takes a sip of his lemonade, ice cubes clinking against the glass. It's striking, how similar he and Alfie are in look, in mannerisms, too. He exudes the same confidence and charisma that Heath is used to seeing in Alfie—characteristics currently lacking in Alfie now: His shoulders are hunched, his face is pale, his fingers are wrapped tightly around his lemonade glass.

Alfie coughs into the back of his hand and flashes Heath a warning look. As if he would be foolish enough to explain why he is really here in front of Alfie's family. He understands secrets; he has plenty of them himself.

"Some of the other boys and I tried calling, hoping to steal Alfie here away for a night. Of course, if we knew you were visiting, we wouldn't have bothered you." Heath throws Alfie a winning smile. "Only we were concerned when we couldn't get a hold of him."

Charles clasps an arm around Alfie's shoulders. "Good friends you've got there, Alfie. I'm glad for it. Always were too quiet in our school days."

Heath tries not to let the surprise show. Quiet is not a word he would have chosen to describe Alfie. Alfie, whose rendition of "Blue Skies" was known to every man who frequented TJ, and had usually been performed atop one of the tables or, when Art wasn't looking, the bar. Alfie, whose typical greeting to those entering the club was one that included a salacious offer. Alfie, whose back Heath once had to rub as he leaned his head against the cold wall, sure that he was going to throw up from laughing too hard.

"I couldn't imagine my life without Alfie in it," Heath replies, for it is the truth. Even if the man sitting before him could be a stranger, judging by how he acts.

Charles looks pleased. "Well, I'll let you two catch up without me eavesdropping." He shakes Heath's hand again and stands to leave.

Heath sits beside Alfie as his friend sighs in relief and sinks into the cushions.

"And, technically, I'm older than him. Would you believe it? He treats me like a child, sometimes," Alfie grumbles and rubs his eyes with his fingers. He looks exhausted, now that Heath is up close. His eyes are a little red and have deep circles beneath them. It's more than just physical tiredness, which Heath has seen plenty of times, when Alfie was propped up behind the bar with his eyelids well on their way to closing. He looks positively drained of all energy.

"By how many minutes?" Heath teases with a small smile, hoping to bring back at least a little of the light he is used to seeing in Alfie.

Alfie huffs out a laugh, and Heath considers it a success. "Five and a half. But that's a very important five minutes, thirty seconds. Makes a world of difference." He grins for a moment, a fraction of the Alfie Heath knows, and then it slips. "You shouldn't be here, Heath. It isn't fair to just turn up. My family can't—they can't know. About any of it."

"I know," Heath soothes him, resting a hand on the crook of his elbow. "I understand. I do. It's exactly the same with my own family." He pauses and withdraws his hand. "But I had to do *something*. Frankie said he tried to call and he was told you weren't here; we were worried you might have been…" Heath trails off and swallows around the lump in his throat.

Alfie shakes his head. "No, I'm fine. Everyone was fine. The night that it happened."

"Everyone?"

"Everyone," Alfie promises. "Jerry ran down to warn us—it didn't give us much time, a minute or two at most. But it was enough that I could get everyone out the back entrance. I saw him come down—Mr. Peters. I saw him come in, and the *look* on his face—he was so goddamn smug when he came through that door. I think he hoped to get more than just the club, he hoped to take us with it. But even without that, he knew he'd won.

"I couldn't stay to watch him board over the entrance," Alfie finishes in a murmur. "Not when I felt so… so guilty. For letting it happen."

"You didn't, Alfie. You can't blame yourself," Heath insists. "There was nothing you could have done—not without risking being caught and taken in. Art wouldn't have wanted that. He'd have wanted you safe."

Alfie lets out a shuddery breath. "I know. He said as much. But I also know how much that club meant to him. I've never seen him so beaten down."

Heath wants to weep; whether from joy or misery, he isn't sure. "You've seen him. When? Where? Is he all right? He hasn't done anything foolish, has he?"

Alfie looks a little pained by the onslaught of questions. "He came by a few days ago, to check on me. Just as you have." Alfie gives him a look, as if telling him that he's aware Heath came to pry for information as much as to check on Alfie himself. "He was erratic when he got here. Wouldn't stop moving, pacing around as if he had ants in his pants. I thought he was going to work himself into a fit. But I told him just what I've told you, and he relaxed some, knowing that no one had been taken in or wrongly held accountable for TJ."

"He's all right," Heath murmurs, to himself more than to Alfie. "He's all right."

"He's all right. I think all he needs is some time to make sense of where he can go from here."

"Of course." Heath nods. He taps his fingers on his thighs. "I could go to him, see if I can be of any help. Perhaps—"

"I'm not sure that would be for the best."

Heath blinks wordlessly, his jaw slack and gaping like a fish. "But I only mean to help," Heath protests weakly. His stomach churns. "I'm his friend, too. Just as much as you are."

"You were so much more than his friend, and that's exactly why I think you're best to let him be. Let him come to you, when he's ready to do so," Alfie pleads.

"I don't understand," Heath whispers. His head feels as though it's been stuffed full of cotton candy, clogging his ears so he can't hear more than muffled sounds, least of all make sense of anything.

Alfie groans and tugs at his hair. "I hadn't wanted to tell you this, I didn't want to make this any harder on you. Art is like a brother to me—more so than my own brother, in some ways—but I do care about you, too."

Heath prepares himself for the worst and straightens his spine as he looks Alfie dead in the eye. "Tell me what, precisely?"

"When I asked after you, and your time in Long Island, he clammed right up. He said…" Alfie grimaces but Heath doesn't back down, so he continues. "He said he doesn't wish to see you."

All the fight that drove Heath to Alfie's door seeps out of him until he feels weak. "I see." Heath licks his lips. "That's all he said? That's it?"

"I'm sorry, Heath. That was it. He was very clear. I don't know what else to tell you."

Heath can't be angry with Alfie no matter how much he may want to be; it isn't Alfie's doing that Art now cannot stand to see his face. "It's not your fault," Heath mumbles, and rises to his feet as steadily as he can manage. "I should be going."

Alfie opens his mouth as if to say something, but Heath cuts him off. "Home. I'll be going home. You needn't worry—I've received the message loud and clear. I won't be going to Art's anytime soon."

"For what it's worth, I've never seen Art so happy, in all the time I've known him, than he has been this past summer with you. I thought it no bad thing that he had something else to focus his intensive passion on besides just the club."

A week ago, those words would have made Heath beam from the inside out. Now, they are like pins embedding themselves deeply in his body. "Good day, Alfie. Take care of yourself, won't you? Don't forget yourself, being stuck under this roof."

Alfie stands, too, and draws Heath into a hug. "I'll try my best, if you promise to do the same," he whispers into his ear.

Heath nods and takes his leave, hindered only by Mrs. Miller, who catches him in the hallway.

"Leaving so soon? We hoped you might join us for lunch. It's so lovely to finally meet some of Alfred's friends. Perhaps you know Arthur? He called just a few days ago. Handsome young man," she gushes and titters as she smiles at Heath fondly.

"I do, yes." Heath smiles tightly. "But I shan't impose on your hospitality a moment longer, as my own mother is expecting me back for lunch. It doesn't do to disappoint one's mother."

Mrs. Miller coos. "Well, I hope to be seeing you again, Heath. You're welcome to call anytime."

Heath thanks her once more and slips out of the door onto the sidewalk. His mother indeed expects him back for lunch, and he hasn't much time to linger. But he can't help the pull of curiosity that leads him toward TJ—or what remains of it.

He doesn't go to Jerry's, but rather works his way around the block to the alleyway that runs between the buildings. He knows of the back entrance, but he can't say he's ever used it, so it becomes a game of guesswork as he moves down the alley in search of the correct door.

A heavy black door leans crooked and slightly out of place against the bricks. It's propped open a fraction by a heavy stone, and Heath uses the gap as leverage to slide his fingers around the wood and drag it open so far that he can slip inside.

With nothing but a small stream of light from the door flickering inside, he has to blink a few times so that his eyes can adjust. He takes the crumbling stone staircase one foot at a time, testing each step with his toes before he puts his weight down, descending until he reaches what he figures is the storeroom.

He picks his way through the dark room, hissing as he bumps into a heavy wooden crate here, an overturned chair there. He pats the length of the wall at the far side of the storeroom until he finds the master switches for the electric lights within the club. He flicks them on and continues inside.

Walking into TJ, Heath isn't entirely sure what he expected to find. Perhaps he expected to find the place in disarray, chairs and tables scattered, broken to pieces and discarded over the floor. Perhaps to find the piano torn up and glasses and bottles smashed. Perhaps he thought he might find Art here, one lonely figure at a table, nursing a Gin Rickey in one hand with a cigarette burning between the fingers of the other.

Instead, the interior of the club looks as though it has been frozen in time, save for the absence of people. It could be a scene from a museum: every table and chair exactly as it must have been left; sheet music still on the piano, a tumbler of whiskey with a finger's width left in the bottom of the glass. The only difference is that the shelves, once stacked high with bottles, are barren; only empty glasses are left behind.

Heath curls his upper lip and snorts, for of course Mr. Peters would have had the liquor cleared out, to be sold to the next bar over for an extortionate price before he turns around and plays the same nasty trick on them. He remembers Art telling him that as much of the liquor he purchased came from secondhand trade after another speakeasy was raided as it did from underground producers. Heath wonders if Mr. Peters discovered the concealed basement within the storeroom, or whether there is still a goldmine of illicit liquor beneath the floorboards.

He picks his way across the room, and his eye catches a piece of paper discarded beneath one of the tables. He collects it from where it is gathering dust, brushing it off on his pants.

On the paper is written, in large, strong letters:

The Rules of TJ:

1. In Art we trust.

fin.

Heath traces the letters of Art's name before he folds the paper neatly and tucks it into his pocket. To serve as his one souvenir of a place that came to mean so much to him and of the person—the *people*—he met there. He has no other keepsakes of his time with Art, besides his memories.

He starts as he hears the rattle of the chains on the boards that now bar the space where the door had been, before it was pulled right off its hinges.

"Hello? Is there someone down there?"

"Jerry!" Heath cries and springs over to the boards, peering through them. The boards are wound tight with a thick chain; a padlock is attached to them and fastened closed.

"Heath! Best be careful down there, kid." Jerry's face presses up to one of the gaps. His white mustache quirks as he smiles. "It's good to see you."

"You too." Heath laughs, perhaps the first true laugh that's fallen from his lips in a week. "Hold tight, I'll come round to the barbershop." Heath makes quick work of shutting off the lights and takes the stairs to street level, leaving the door to the back entrance not entirely closed just as he had found it. He jogs to the corner of Fifty-seventh and Seventh.

The barbershop looks almost entirely the same, save for how quiet it seems with the knowledge that TJ is empty and abandoned downstairs.

"I asked after you when Art came round, but all I could get from him was a grunt." Jerry raises an eyebrow. "I won't ask, because it's none of my business, but it sure is good to see you round here again." He sighs. "Business is slow without you boys and a lot less interesting, besides."

"I didn't think you'd still be here," Heath admits. He trails his fingers over the countertop before he slings himself down into the barber's chair.

"Mr. Peters didn't seem the least bit interested in whether or not I kept my business, except to warn me against harboring any secret activities in the basement in the future." Jerry chuckles and reaches for his brushes. "If you don't mind me saying so, you look as though you could use a shave."

Heath scrubs a hand over his jaw. "I suppose I could. Not as though I have much to do. No harm in me sitting here with you a little longer."

Jerry whistles as he lathers the shaving cream before he ties a towel around Heath's neck. He has Heath tip his head back, and Heath closes his eyes as he relaxes under the touch of the lathered brush to his jaw.

"I'll tell you what I told Art when I saw him," Jerry says as he sharpens the razor blade and applies it to the underside of Heath's chin. "You shouldn't worry yourself too much. Just when the world seems to have screwed you over worst—that's when things have a funny way of working themselves out."

HEATH FINDS HIMSELF LULLED INTO a state of calm by the time he walks home. It is a welcome reprieve from the cycling stages of panic, misery and worry in which he has been stuck since his sudden return from Cove Neck. He doesn't fool himself into believing it will last; not when his father still awaits him for a long overdue conversation. Even if he were so lucky that the Duke might not question him about Ginny, there's his future to think of. Heath isn't so sure he has a choice, although he enjoyed the illusion that he might.

The sun's out, and he'd love nothing more than to dawdle through Central Park, perhaps go to the water's edge to watch the ducks paddle about. He remembers days gone by, visiting the ducks in Central Park with Amelia, scattering breadcrumbs over the surface of the water and watching with avid fascination as the birds fought over the morsels with their feathers fluffing up this way and that. Amelia liked it best when two or more of the birds would truly get into a fight, nipping at each other with their sharp beaks—but Heath would be scared then and tuck himself behind Martha's skirts so he didn't have to watch.

However, it is likely that he is already late for lunch. The Duchess doesn't take well to tardiness, and he has no good excuse for his absence. He scrubs a hand over his smooth jaw. If nothing else, she'll be pleased to hear he stopped for a shave.

Heath is correct: she clasps her hands to his cheeks when he steps through the door and tells him how much better he looks now that he's had a shave—and a barber's professional one at that. She and Amelia are just sitting for lunch when Martha ushers him in, so he isn't so late as to irritate his mother, but late enough that the ice in his glass of lemonade has started to melt.

"What do you think of this dress, Mama?" Amelia asks as she spears a slice of tomato with her fork. It's light green in color, nipped in at the waist and flared down to her knees. "I'm to have tea with Edward and his parents this afternoon near Broadway," she tells Heath as an aside before looking back to the Duchess. "Is it suitable?"

Heath disguises his chuckle as a cough into his napkin. Amelia is usually too fiercely independent to ask for their mother's advice or opinion on such things as her clothing choices. But he knows that Amelia's impending engagement has brought the two of them closer together and broken down some of the tension that develops between a mother and her teenaged daughter. He suspects the Duchess hopes that he would have a similar relationship with his father by now, but that has not yet happened.

The Duchess nods her approval with a fond smile on her lips as she looks at her younger child. "You look wonderful, my dear. Entirely befitting a young bride-to-be." She winks.

Amelia beams and turns to him. "And what do you think, Heath? From a man's perspective, since Papa isn't here."

"Beautiful," Heath assures her and reaches to clasp her hand. "Edward is the luckiest man in all of Manhattan, I'm certain of it."

Amelia looks giddy. Heath wonders if today is the day, since Amelia is worrying so much over this afternoon's meeting. It is not the first time she will meet Edward's parents. Or perhaps she simply hopes today might be the day, that the perfect dress and a flutter of her long eyelashes might prod him into action so she may become Mrs. Edward Stone that much sooner.

"Now now, Amelia. Be sure not to overexcite yourself before you leave this afternoon," the Duchess says, but there is little heat behind her words as she rises from the table. "Heath, you'll keep an eye on her, won't you? I'm going to retire for a short while."

Heath stands, too, and kisses his mother's cheek. "Of course, Mama. I have no plans for this afternoon, so I shall sit with her until the Stones call to collect her."

"And you shall be here this evening, too?" she asks. "Where have all these mysterious friends you were stealing off to see earlier in the summer got to?"

Heath shrugs and wills his voice not to falter. "Oh, busy with this and that. I shall be here, I promise." He takes a deep breath. "I should probably speak with father about a few things."

The Duchess nods. "Yes, he's been waiting to take you aside. He only wants the best for you, as do I. Remember that, please, sweetheart."

"I will."

The Duchess walks toward her bedroom, and Amelia is at his side, flinging her arm around his shoulders, in the next moment. "Do you think I ought to wear a hat?" she asks, tilting her head at him.

Heath rolls his eyes and leads her toward the stairs with a hand on the middle of her back. "I'll help you pin your hair the way you like, all fancy. I think that would be better than a hat."

Amelia hums and rests her cheek against his shoulder. "Brother knows best." She grins.

THE HOUSE IS QUIET ONCE Amelia clatters down the front steps with a small bag, which dangles from her hand and glitters in the afternoon sunshine. The Duchess is still resting, and Heath doesn't wish to disturb her, so he chooses a book from his room and sits by the window to read. But he can't focus on the words before him, as his mind dashes a hundred thousand different places at once.

He considers calling Frankie, if only to have someone talk his ear off and distract him from the tangled mess that weaves into every crevice of his head. Or Julian, for he owes him an apology; but Julian is bound to bring up TJ, or Art, and he doesn't much feel like discussing either subject, least of all with the accompanying lilt of Julian's pitying, sympathetic tone.

Heath finds himself picking through the contents of his desk drawer, something he can't say he's delved into in at least a year. He doesn't find much of note: a few movie ticket stubs and matchbooks for restaurants, and a journal he kept during his first year at Yale, which he pushes aside with a grimace, not wanting to read his silly, adolescent thoughts from a few years ago. Near the bottom is nestled a small sketchbook, with a set of pencils neatly in their box atop it. He'd taken up sketching during summers in Cove Neck in his later teenage years. Somewhere in the pull of college and newfound interests and friends, it had fallen to the wayside.

He picks out the sketchbook now and takes it to the window. Flicking through the pages, he lingers on a few images here and there: the outlines of his parents standing on the shore and watching the sun go down; Amelia lying on the porch swing with her legs kicked up over the arm; the birds that used to twitter on his window in the early hours, hoping he would set out a little handful of seeds as he did from time to time.

Heath twirls a pencil for some time before he decides what to draw. It's hardly surprising that Art appears: the slope of his shoulder into his back; his tousled hair as he faced away from him, sitting on the edge of the bed in the morning and looking out the window toward the water; a memory ingrained in Heath's mind, taking form and shape on the page.

Sketching proves to be therapeutic. His mind stays in the calm, cool ease he felt when he left Jerry's with the smell of cologne wafting from the underside of his jaw. The afternoon passes with his tongue tucked behind his front teeth and the pencil tight in his hand, even when he hears the door open below to signal his father's return from work.

His peace is broken when Amelia returns. He hears the door slam and then an almighty shriek goes up, a noise he recognizes as coming from the Duchess. The Duke is guffawing loudly when Heath skids down the polished wood in his stockinged feet to the hallway, where his family is gathered.

On Amelia's ring finger is a diamond the size of the moon. It shines brightly as she holds out her hand, fingers outstretched, for the Duchess to inspect.

"Goodness, it's extravagant! Would you look at that, William?" The Duchess's cheeks are pink with glee; Amelia looks much the same.

The Duke snorts. "Best be careful, Amelia. You could have someone's eye out with that thing!"

"Oh, hush." The Duchess sighs and slips her hand through her husband's.

Heath joins the small circle; his eyes widen at the ring as he sees it up close. "Not entirely a surprise, but congratulations all the same," he tells Amelia and kisses her rosy cheek. "How did he propose?"

"It was ever so romantic," she gushes. "We left his parents after tea and he took me through Bryant Park. I thought for certain he would ask then, but we kept walking up to the library. And he took me up the steps and got down on one knee, in front of all the scholars and passersby and everything! Loudly declared how much he loved me, for all the world to hear—it was like something out of a moving picture." She waves her hands wildly.

Heath ducks out of the way just in time to avoid having his eye taken out, just as the Duke warned. "And you said yes, I presume?" he teases.

"Of course I did, you goon!" Amelia giggles and claps her hands together. "Champagne! We must have champagne! Have we any?" she asks of Martha, who stands politely to one side, her eyes glistening with silent tears.

The Duke presses a hand to Heath's shoulder and leans forward to whisper in his ear. "Perhaps we'll let the women gossip before dinner while you and I have a talk in my study."

Heath nods and follows his father to his private study. It is a room he is rarely allowed into. In fact, he's sure the last time he was in it was when his father called him in to announce that he had been offered a place in Yale's class of 1927, some four years ago.

The Duke pours himself a glass of whiskey and offers one to Heath, which he declines with a polite shake of his head. The Duke pulls up a chair and sits, gesturing for Heath to occupy the one opposite.

For a long minute, the Duke says nothing at all. He swirls the whiskey in his glass and sniffs at it, his mustache twitching beneath his nose. He takes a long swig and sets the glass down on a small table, then folds his hands over his knee. "I had the distinct pleasure of happening across your friend Francis a week or two ago, while you were in Cove Neck," he says finally.

Heath feels his ribcage clench but forces himself to breathe normally. "So he told me, sir."

"He wasn't alone." The Duke's gaze is unfaltering.

Heath swallows. "I'm aware that that was the case, yes."

"Would you care to tell me just why the girl you were supposedly with in Cove Neck was having lunch with your best friend in Manhattan? Modern women are many impossible things—but capable of being in two places at once? I don't understand that to be a quality they possess."

Heath has thought of how he might answer this question since Frankie told him what happened, and he is no closer to a sensible response now than he was then. He cannot tell the truth and he has no idea how to lie his way out of it, either. Not with anything that sounds remotely believable, anyway. "I don't know what to tell you, sir," Heath replies quietly.

The room is very still as the Duke watches him. "I see." He takes another sip from his glass. "A man is entitled to his secrets, Heath. But you have only just graduated and you have yet to decide where your future lies, so I am not sure you are yet a man. These boyish games of yours need to come to a stop."

Heath opens his mouth to respond, but the Duke cuts him off with a hand held up. "Don't try to protest." Heath has no intention of doing any such thing; he knows better than to argue against his father. "Do you think me a fool, Heath?" He raises an eyebrow as he awaits an answer.

"No, sir."

"I know exactly where you've been sneaking off to this summer, where you and your friends choose to spend your time. It's my role as your father to know where you, and Amelia, are at all times, so that I may keep you safe and protect this family's reputation.

"I also know that your little establishment of preference has come to a bitter end. I may have turned a blind eye for the summer, but I hope you understand that from here on out, that courtesy ends. It's time for you to act your age.

"Now, Ginny is a lovely girl, and I think you ought to give her a call and have her to dinner tomorrow. Edward and his parents will be here, too, to celebrate his engagement to Amelia, before the public announcement and party in a few weeks. How does that sound?"

Heath feels dizzy, nauseated, as he tries to wrap his head around the fact that his father knows. Knew this entire summer—if not before, which would not surprise him. He realizes quickly how fortunate he is that the Duke is affording him this chance to redeem himself and he nods quickly. "I think that sounds fair, sir."

"Excellent." The Duke smiles. "You always were a good boy, Heath, and I believe you have the potential to be a great young man, if you put your focus in the correct places."

"Of course," Heath whispers. He straightens up in his seat. "If the offer is still extended, I should like to come work for you. To continue the Johnson name appropriately."

The Duke's grin becomes toothy and wide. "I am very pleased to hear that. I knew you'd make the right choice." He moves to his desk, where he opens one of the drawers and retrieves a small black box. "This was my mother's. She very much wanted for you to have it, when the time came."

Heath opens it to reveal an engagement ring with three small, blue stones set into the band—nothing as garish as the one now adorning Amelia's hand, but beautiful in its simplicity. He cannot imagine it on Ginny's dainty hand—much less being placed there by him. "Thank you," he says politely. He closes the box and tucks it into his fist.

"You were young when she passed away, but she could always see what a big heart you have. She told me that when you found the person whom you truly loved, you should be in possession of that ring in order to express that love."

"I'll keep it safe," Heath assures his father, and makes no mention of Ginny or how soon that time may come. He promises to take her to dinner; he can't propose marriage now, even if the Duke has plainly laid it out as inevitability rather than possibility.

Heath always avoids the path of conflict or complication, allows himself to be guided by his parents and their expectations and is suggestible to a fault. Art was the first choice he ever made for himself, and it ended in dreams cracked down the middle and empty promises.

Fall is fast approaching, and with it Heath may find it time to say goodbye to the free spirit of the summer months.

CH. 11

If Ginny is surprised to hear from him, she doesn't say so. Heath can feel the weight of his father's gaze on his back as he stands in the hallway with the receiver tucked close to his ear.

"I wanted to extend an invitation to join us for dinner tomorrow. Amelia and Edward wish to celebrate their engagement with family first." Heath pauses. "I had hoped you would accompany me, as my date."

"Their engagement? How wonderful! If you'd like me there, I'd be honored to be part of such a celebration."

While her enthusiasm sounds genuine, something in her voice is too shrill to be natural. Perhaps her own father or mother is eavesdropping.

"Good. The Duchess will be so pleased. She's been asking after you relentlessly." Heath chuckles. Behind him, his father's footsteps recede, but that does little to ease the tension between his shoulders.

"You shall have to help me pick out an engagement gift for them."

Heath frowns. "Do engagements require gifts?"

"Heath! She's your sister; you really needn't have an excuse to buy her a gift."

"She always complains that my gifts are pitiful!"

"What did you give her for her last birthday, as an example?"

Heath hesitates. "A paperweight."

Ginny is silent. "I can see her point," she says finally.

Heath laughs and tips his head back against the wall.

"We'll choose something together—how about that? It can be from the both of us."

Heath smiles. "That sounds like a lovely idea."

For a moment, he lets himself believe it. Their conversation, to anyone else, could sound like that of any pair of young lovers—playful and teasing. Heath allows himself to imagine what it would be like if they *were* just another pair of young lovers, to pretend as though the feelings of fondness he holds for Ginny are anywhere close to the intense love he still holds for Art, despite everything.

"Could we meet tomorrow at Saks? Early afternoon? That would allow me plenty of time to return home and dress for dinner."

"I look forward to it."

Ginny's tone falls to a whisper. "And I just wanted to apologize for what happened. I never meant for—I hadn't considered that something like that might happen."

"It's not your fault—I couldn't have anticipated it, either."

"And your father?"

Heath closes his eyes. "We've reached an understanding."

HEATH TRIES NOT TO ALLOW himself too much resentment about the deal he and the Duke have struck, for he appreciates it as fair. But he cannot help but anticipate his first day of work with dread. If it weren't for his date with Ginny to choose a gift, he'd probably have spent all of his last day of freedom in bed, forlornly clinging to the blankets wrapped around his frame.

He should have foreseen that it wasn't to last—him and Art, and the careless way in which they went about their summer, as if there were nothing or no one else in the world but the two of them. But he'd allowed himself to live in the present moment, to appreciate it for what it was and not worry about what might lie beyond. Now, more than ever, he is thankful for that; for, if nothing else, he knows he did not waste the precious time he had with Art.

Ginny doesn't pry when they meet that afternoon. Heath kisses her cheek politely before they go into the department store. She briefly speaks of her own lover with a giggle over their secret rendezvous a few nights ago, but otherwise they are the very picture of a young Manhattanite couple as they peruse the aisles. Ginny keeps her hand tucked through the crook of Heath's elbow and pulls him this way and that to suggest gifts for Amelia and Edward.

They settle, eventually, on a set of crystal champagne glasses that Ginny considers a suitable partnership of elegance and practicality— even if she does tease that it will be all too obvious it was not Heath's idea, if his past gift-giving efforts are anything to go by. If anything, Heath thinks it'll only make Amelia happier to know they were a gift from him and his girl, rather than just him, never mind the quality of the gift.

"Will you miss her, do you think?" Ginny asks, as they take tea with their purchases safely tucked in a bag by their feet. She fans her skirt around her knees as the hot air presses in through the open windows; it's a glorious August afternoon.

"Amelia? I hadn't thought, really." He knows Edward has an apartment, and, of course, Amelia will live with him after the wedding.

"I suppose I might, although we've become accustomed to living apart, from my semesters spent at Yale. She might prefer not to have me around all the time," Heath jokes and takes a sip of his tea. It's surprisingly refreshing, even in the heat. "It's not as though I won't see her. She'll be in the city, only a short cab ride or walk away."

Ginny hums and taps her fingernails on the side of her cup. "Of course you'll see her. But she'll be *married*, Heath. It will change the entirety of your relationship with her, for those times you do see one another."

Heath frowns and stares down into his cup. "Yes. Yes, I suppose you're right," he mumbles. Amelia is many things to him: a sister, a friend, an ally. A constant. He never really thought of a time when Amelia wouldn't be a constant.

"Well." Ginny clears her throat and takes his hand, holding it firmly in her own. "As you say. She'll still be in the city. She'll always be your sister."

Ginny's words stick with him until later in the evening. For if Amelia loves Edward the way he loves Art—and he would guess she does from the way she looks at him, eyes bright and smile blinding—he knows. Heath knows love like that is distracting and all-consuming, and Heath will be just her brother, next to Edward, her husband.

Edward glows too. He looks happier than Heath has ever seen him when he arrives at the house. Amelia all but dives into his arms; her feet leave the floor as he spins her around. It is entirely the kind of behavior Heath would expect the Duchess to tut-tut over, but instead she looks on watery-eyed with her hands wrapped around her husband's.

Heath feels starkly alone where he stands on the perimeters of these two happy couples. The knocker sounds to announce Ginny's presence, and Heath breathes a sigh of relief. At least, with Ginny by his side, it is far easier to pretend he is capable of patching over the gaping hole in his chest.

And Ginny is charming and delightful, entirely capable of keeping up conversation when Heath shrinks into himself and falls silent. They move to the day room for drinks before dinner is served and Ginny takes Amelia by the arm to ask her all about the proposal, the engagement, the *wedding*.

"Best keep an eye on your girl, Heath," the Duke chortles. "She might be getting all sorts of ideas talking to Amelia about weddings and the like." He shoots Heath a wink, and Heath does his best to smile back.

Edward pours them both a much-needed drink and clinks their glasses together. "If you'd rather we don't talk about it, we won't talk about it," Edward says tactfully and puts down his glass to light a cigarette.

Heath rests his weight on the sideboard. "Little to talk about at this point, I think." He shrugs. "Have you heard from anyone, since—?"

Edward shakes his head. "Not really. Not Art, or Alfie, anyway. Some of the other boys—Jack, Henry. But they were old friends from school, anyway. I wasn't there that night; I was with Amelia. But I hear everyone was all right, aside from being a little shook up, of course."

"Yes, as far as I know, everyone's just fine. I went back to have a look around. It's untouched, eerie, in a way."

Edward shudders. "I'll bet." He watches Heath for a moment. "Do you think he might start over? It's not uncommon for owners who have been put out of business to set up someplace new."

"I don't know," Heath answers honestly. "I think perhaps not. Not unless he knows someone who will give him a start without having the capital to his name. I didn't stop to look, but I think the storeroom may not have been found; there could be enough liquor down there to raise something, but—"

"Heath." Edward cuts him off. Concern knits his eyebrows. "Perhaps you better leave it well alone. At least until the dust settles."

Heath swallows. "No, I know. I can't, anyway." He glances across the room to where the Duke watches the women chatter with a bemused expression. "I can't risk it."

Edward sneaks a look over his shoulder, following Heath's line of vision before he looks back to him. "I see." He pauses. "Are you all right?"

"I'm fine, I'm fine. He wouldn't do anything rash; nothing that might hurt the Johnson family name." Heath feels his upper lip curl in distaste and swallows back the expression with a large gulp from his glass. "But I'd best play by his rules from here on out. It's the best thing for everyone."

"Easiest, perhaps. But that doesn't mean it's the best thing for *you*." Edward holds up a hand when Heath opens his mouth to protest. "I shan't argue with you. I know how complicated family dynamics can be." He sets down his glass and hugs him. "I hope you can be happy with whatever path your life takes. After all, we're family now, aren't we?"

Amelia skips over to them and curls into Edward's side. "Dinner's to be served in a moment," she tells them and smirks at Heath. "And do stop stealing my fiancé. He's insured."

Heath laughs and rolls his eyes. "I can assure you, he's not my type."

Edward's eyes twinkle. "Indeed I am not, I can vouch for that."

Amelia chuckles, completely unaware of the joke to which she is not privy, as Heath drains the remaining contents of his glass.

DINNER IS A LOUD AFFAIR; it allows Heath the opportunity to speak little and merely observe the scene around him. If this is to be his future, it is by no means a bad one. Art is tied up in want and desire and a promise of things he never truly dared to hope to have. This, before him, is a reality that is available to him and for which he is grateful. If nothing else.

If nothing else.

He repeats the words to himself as he sits through course after course and drink after drink. His mind is pleasantly warm and sated by the time they take to the other room, their stomachs full to bursting.

Ginny winds to his side and touches her lips to his cheek. "This truly has been lovely, Heath," she whispers into his ear. "Do you think, perhaps, you could have dinner with my family sometime soon?"

He tilts his head around to her hopeful gaze and agrees without a second's thought. He can see how happy having him here, with Ginny by his side, makes his parents. He wouldn't deny that to Ginny's family; let alone deny *Ginny* after all she has done for him.

"The pleasure would be all mine," he murmurs, and she squeezes his hand.

Ginny presents Amelia and Edward with their gift; Amelia is appropriately pleased by what she finds within the box.

"I haven't had to fake my joy, so I can only imagine that Ginny chose these," Amelia teases and chuckles at the look of indignation that crosses Heath's face. "You'd best hold onto her, Heath. We might all receive some decent gifts for a change!"

The Duke stands and clears his throat, clinking the metal of his Yale ring against the side of his glass. "Now I shan't say too much in this moment, for I must save my best material for this blasted engagement party."

The Duchess hushes him playfully as Amelia gives Heath a pained look. Their father is not much known for his eloquence.

The Duke frowns around at them to regain their attention. "So I will say merely this," he declares, raising his glass to the air. "Life is nonsensical and brief, and so shall I be. But love is a sweet relief that may fill us all with glee. Now drink to the couple, and make it a double, for soon that couple make three!"

Heath is the first to laugh; his poor attempt to disguise his snort as a sneeze causes the rest of their party to join in. Amelia looks amused and mortified; her cheeks are highlighted with pink circles. The Duke looks rather put out until the Duchess urges him to sit down and shakes her head at him fondly.

"I never claimed to be a poet," the Duke mumbles.

"And all the better for Wall Street, I'm sure." Edward raises his glass to his soon-to-be father-in-law.

The Duke perks up. "Speaking of Wall Street, now would be as good a time as any for Heath to make his own announcement—not that it will come as a surprise to any in this room, I'm sure."

Heath shifts in his seat as the eyes of those around him fall on him. "As you say, everyone knows already, so I would imagine I needn't really—"

"Please, Heath. This is an important moment. I would like to hear you say it. How excited you are." The Duke fixes him with a cool gaze from the opposite side of the room.

"Of course," Heath says in a small voice before he clears his throat and straightens up. "As of tomorrow, I will be joining my father on Wall Street, beginning as a junior broker at his firm." He smiles stiffly. "I couldn't be more thrilled. It's the beginning of a wonderful future for me."

The party raises their glasses to him as Ginny squeezes his arm. "You were very convincing, don't worry," she whispers and clinks their glasses together.

Perhaps the only person Heath has left to convince is himself. But then, what does he know about Wall Street? It could be a barrel of fun, for all he knows.

Y

WALL STREET IS DECIDEDLY *NOT* a barrel of fun. Wall Street is early mornings akin to his classes at Yale, when he had to leave his campus housing before the morning chill had disappeared; Wall Street is loud and busy and overwhelming; Wall Street is demanding and scary.

On his first day, Heath hides out in the men's restroom with his forehead pressed against the cool glass of the mirror as he fights off the waves of panic that crash through his system. It's the noise. The noise—it's all noise, everywhere. Even tucked away in here, it pounds through from the next room. A hundred men with practiced, fast-paced tongues and their phones tucked tightly against their ears.

Heath loathes the environment; loathes that he spends his lunch breaks in the restroom. He feigns wanting to work hard during his first week, just so he doesn't have to take lunch with his father or his colleagues at any number of the dark clubs that have the power to make him both wildly uncomfortable and ache for the familiar sanctuary that TJ once was.

It gets easier, day by day, if only because he begins to adjust to the atmosphere around him. He learns how to move with the crush, rather than feel as though he is trapped in the rush of the flow.

He misses Art. Art, who could calm him with little more than a few words or a touch of his arm. He longs for the comfort that he can't find anywhere else, that he can't get from Ginny, as sweet and gentle as she is with him when she introduces him to her family, with him apologizing profusely for being so tired at their first meeting.

They adore Heath, Mr. and Mrs. Malt. They think him handsome and a gentleman, and all but encourage him throughout the course of the dinner to propose to Ginny any time he thinks it's right. He comes away shell-shocked and even more tired.

September trots past, each day of the week the same. Come the weekend, he is fraught with exhaustion and spends his days resting or reading and his evenings with Ginny, with her family or his own.

He makes a friend in the office—a chance encounter with Jack, whose father ushered him into the job much as Heath's father had. They take their lunch together somewhere above ground level, where the fall sunshine warms their skin as they exchange stories from school days or TJ—anything that isn't Wall Street.

But Jack has more of a natural feel for it and doesn't dislike his work, even if he abhors having to go into the same business as his father out of principle. Heath watches him with a certain awe as he makes a sale in the minutes before they're due to go out for lunch.

"I've heard whispers," Jack tells him over lunch one day as he stabs at his food. Jack can barely sit still when he eats; he says it's all the pent-up adrenalin that comes from a morning's good business. "That Art might be thinking of going to Chicago, setting up there." He points his fork at Heath. Jack never did have much tact.

"I wouldn't know, I haven't heard a thing from him in close to a month," Heath replies tersely. "But I wouldn't think—" He frowns. "Art's quite attached to New York. I can't imagine him leaving, not for Chicago. Not even now."

Jack shrugs. "Whispers, is all," he mumbles through a mouthful. "Just thought you might like to know."

Y

THE ENGAGEMENT PARTY IS PLANNED for the end of the month; the wedding itself is tentatively scheduled for the beginning of the New Year. Not that the house hasn't already been overtaken by Amelia's plans for the day, although Heath has secretly wondered more than once if the excessive mess concentrated in the day room is just her way to irritate the Duchess.

Heath's meeting with Frankie is long overdue, but his friend is understanding and claims to have been just as busy when Heath calls to invite him to the engagement party. With what, he won't divulge to Heath over the phone, but he sets aside one of his precious Saturdays and they meet for lunch.

Heath doesn't realize how much he's missed him until he's standing there before him. Amelia isn't the only constant in his life; Frankie has been there, too, a confidant for the past four years.

"It's so good to see you," Heath says in a rush when they've parted from a bone-crushing hug and take their seats at the table.

Frankie sets down an envelope. "Before I forget. Mr. Peters shouldn't be a bother anymore."

Heath touches the envelope; a part of him is scared to open it. "What did you do?"

Frankie guffaws. "Don't look so concerned; I haven't had the man killed. I may have spent a few evenings going from club to club around the city and loudly talking with anyone who would listen about what a snake in the grass he is." He points to the envelope. "Those are the names of all the clubs and their owners who've scratched him as an investor or possible one."

"You didn't have to do this," Heath says. He hopes his gratitude is obvious as he slips the envelope into his jacket pocket to peruse later.

"Consider it a parting gift. I've mailed a copy to Art, too," he adds, but Heath barely hears him.

Heath looks at him, unblinking. "A parting gift? I—I don't understand." He chuckles, but the sound is hollow. "A parting gift. Where are you going?"

Frankie heaves a sigh before he spreads his hands wide. "Where am I not going? I'm doing it, Heath. I'm doing it all. My ship to Europe sails tonight and from there, we'll see. I have a vague plan, but I may well just take it as it comes."

Another constant slipping from his fingers. Heath had thought Frankie planned to stay on the East Coast, maybe in New York, but perhaps Philadelphia, or Chicago at a push. Not Europe. Not a new country every week, with no sure way to contact him and only letters from time to time.

"I won't apologize," Frankie says with a firm edge to his voice. "I care about you, Heath, but I also care about following my own path. I did ask you to come with me, though I knew you never would. I *hoped* you might choose a future with Art, rather than—"

"I didn't get to make that choice. *Art* made that choice," Heath says sharply, as he sinks back in his seat. "And I didn't ask you to apologize. I'm not angry. I'll miss you, that's all. Aren't I allowed to miss you?"

"Of course you're allowed to miss me. I'll miss you just as much." Frankie shakes his head sadly. "But don't talk as though you made a real choice. Art slipped away, and you let your father make the choice because you thought you didn't have one anymore."

Heath blinks at his friend. "You don't understand. He knew; my father knew about it all. I had no choice to begin with, not really—but least of all when I found that out."

"You always have a choice. He's your father, yes, but you are your own man. You decided you didn't have a choice. You decided not to fight for a choice. And I'm not saying this to upset you, truly. I'm only sorry that you let this happen."

Heath wants nothing more than to push away from the table and run from the restaurant. His stomach is in knots and he's sure he couldn't eat a bite. "It could be worse," Heath murmurs, eventually. "Ginny is a lovely girl. The job is challenging and rewarding. It's something. It's a life."

"But it's not the life you want."

"The only thing I've ever truly wanted to fight for was Art, and a life with him. But he didn't let me, Frankie. He wouldn't let me." Heath's voice cracks, and he swallows roughly around the lump in his throat.

"I know. I saw how passionate you were with Art. You took chances, you were spontaneous, you were so happy. That's all I want for you. And I worry that this path won't ever give you that happiness. That's all, Heath. That's all. I don't wish to fight with you right before I leave."

Heath nods in agreement. "I don't, either. And I appreciate your caring for me."

"Just promise me you won't tie your happiness to one man who slipped away. You could still find that happiness, even without Art."

And in this, Frankie speaks more truth than Heath ever would have admitted to himself. For the summer months had brought a sparkle into his life that illuminated him from the inside out—but it wasn't Art. Or, it wasn't *just* Art. It was Art, but it was also how he challenged Heath to step out of what he knew and where he felt comfortable. It was Heath, himself: he had changed, for a time, into a man that he should strive to be always, not just for the summer.

They part in the middle of the park, for Heath admits that if he walks with Frankie to his godparents' house, he will surely be far too upset about saying goodbye to his friend.

"When will you be back?" Heath asks. He looks up at Frankie as the sunlight filters through the trees.

"Nine months, a year? Perhaps a little longer. It's not forever." Frankie looks up at the sky and squints against the sun. "I think I might settle in New York, once I return. It's a wonderful city."

Heath grins. "The best. All the better with Frankie David in it."

Frankie wraps his arms tightly around him. "Take care of yourself. Don't get into trouble."

Heath snorts. "Speak for yourself. Try not to leave a path of broken hearts in your wake. I shan't help you in the slightest if there are dozens of women arriving in New York lamenting their brief affairs with you. That'll be entirely your responsibility."

"Duly noted." Frankie takes a step back. "Farewell, Heathcliff. My heart yearns for you already."

Heath stays in that spot until Frankie's figure disappears. He may have stayed longer still if it weren't for the evening's festivities.

THE HOUSE IS ALIGHT FOR the coming evening. Every corner has been cleaned, adorned; the chandeliers sparkle. Trays of food are prepared; a stack of champagne glasses waits in the center of the living room, ready to be filled when the guests arrive. Heath has never seen anything like it.

The Duchess has worked herself into a tizzy while Heath has been out. She careers from room to room in her silk robe with her hair up in a bird's nest of pins as it dries. She doesn't appear to have noticed that she's got one earring in, and the other lobe is bare.

"Mama," Heath chuckles as he runs after her. "Mama, please. You'll make yourself ill with all this frantic rushing around. Go upstairs and finish getting dressed. I'm sure Martha has everything under control."

The Duchess laughs; her cheeks are pink as she cups Heath's face in her hands. "I'm so excited, I can't contain it," she gushes, her eyes bright. "We're putting on the ritz tonight, darling!" She presses a kiss to his forehead. "I'm so proud of you—both of you."

Heath smiles after her sadly as she goes upstairs. Then he finds Martha to ensure that everything is, indeed, taken care of, and that he may go dress. He knocks on Amelia's door when he gets upstairs, however, and waits until she calls that he may enter.

She's wearing a full-length silver dress that shimmers as she moves, the material swirling around her ankles. Her cheeks are dewy. Pins are stuck between her lips as she fixes her hair back with a headband the same color as her dress.

Heath leans his temple against the door. "You look beautiful," he tells her. "Not quite as beautiful as the house but beautiful nonetheless."

Amelia huffs and turns back to her reflection as she finishes fixing her hair. She doesn't say anything, merely picks up some lip color from her dressing table and dabs it on her lips, puckering them as she does so.

Heath turns to go, thinking he should leave her to her preparations. Edward should arrive shortly, too, before the invited guests start to arrive.

"Heath?" Amelia calls him back, although she has not turned from her reflection. "I'm scared, I think. Only a little, but there are all these butterflies in the pit of my stomach." She places a hand over her stomach. "They won't stop." Her voice is fragile; she sounds so young.

Heath walks into the room and stands behind her. He places his hands on her shoulders and smiles at her image in the mirror. "The butterflies are a good thing," he assures her and kisses the top of her head. "But you have nothing to be scared of, I promise." He quirks an eyebrow. "I've already had to deal with the Duchess flying around; don't you start," he teases.

Amelia groans. "And this is only the *engagement*. Think how she'll be the day of the wedding."

"I shudder to think." Heath squeezes her shoulders. "I should go and dress. I wouldn't want to be late."

"You wouldn't dare be late to your only sister's engagement party," Amelia retorts before she brushes his hands off and shoos him out of the room.

Heath has butterflies, too. They grow as he dresses, fluttering up through his abdomen until his heart patters faster than usual. He smooths the lapels of his suit jacket and takes a deep breath. He has no reason to be nervous, himself. All that is expected of him tonight is to stand by Ginny's side and act the doting suitor to her and the caring big brother to Amelia.

He is not late, but he is the last of his family downstairs, where Edward and his parents have already arrived and are taking champagne with the Duke and Duchess in the living room. He greets them cordially but manages no more than a brief smile in Edward's direction before Ginny arrives. Edward tries to catch his attention, but Heath shakes his head.

"Perhaps later?" Heath mouths before he slips his hand through Ginny's and kisses her cheeks.

The first floods of guests arrive, bringing with them bustle and noise and exhilaration. Heath can place few faces amongst the crowds: friends of Edward's family that he wouldn't know; some of his own parents' friends that he can't remember although he has undoubtedly met them before; a few men from the office with their wives, who greet Heath with an air of disinterest before they move along to receive a drink.

"I can see why you're always so thrilled to get to work," Ginny comments drily. She sips from her champagne glass and winks at him.

Mr. and Mrs. Thorne arrive with apologies for Julian's absence, explaining that he had a prior commitment. "He was so sorry not to see you," Mrs. Thorne tells Heath with a sincere squeeze of his arm. "He said he'd be in touch soon—perhaps steal you for lunch one day?"

"That would be wonderful." Heath owes him a long overdue apology and makes a note to himself to call Monday.

Despite the liveliness of the occasion, Heath is bone-tired. Ginny takes no offense at the occasional yawns that slip out of his mouth, and they find a quiet spot on an ottoman in the hallway to sit, the two of them, without obligation to entertain guests as Amelia and his parents must.

Someone knocks on the door and Heath nearly snorts into his drink. The house seems packed tight already; he cannot imagine so much as one more body fitting in. He turns to say so to Ginny and interrupts her singing along under her breath to the music that's playing and tapping out the rhythm on Heath's forearm.

The words die on Heath's tongue; his body goes stock-still as, farther down the hallway, Martha shuts the door behind Art. He's clean-shaven, his hair slicked back from his forehead, and he's dressed in a fitted three piece suit that hugs the breadth of his chest and the thickness of his thighs. He looks immaculate, in no way reminiscent of the broken-down Art that Heath had last seen.

"Heath?" Ginny notices the abrupt change in his demeanor. "Heath, what's wrong, darling? You've turned awfully pale all of a sudden."

His tongue feels stuck to the roof of his mouth; all he can do is shake his head with his eyes still fixed on the doorway. Art accepts a drink and shakes hands with Edward's parents in a way that seems familiar.

Ginny squeezes his hand. "Heath, is that him?" she asks quietly.

Heath glances at her. She has followed his gaze to where Art stands, his head thrown back with laughter. He sees Edward step through the crowd, too, to greet his friend. "Yes. Yes, that's Art." He drains the dregs of his drink. "He's a friend of Edward's."

Ginny scoffs. "Friend of Edward's or not, it seems rather tactless for him to come."

"That's one word for it," Heath mutters. The butterflies return in full force—so much so that he feels sick.

Art turns his head and sees Heath at the end of the hallway. The corner of his mouth turns up in a smile, and that's all it takes for Heath to snap his gaze away.

"If you'll excuse me, Ginny, I need to be by myself a moment," Heath murmurs and kisses her cheek. "Is that all right?"

"Of course. Take all the time you need. I'm famished—I'm going to go perch next to the canapés." She grins and sashays toward the living room as Heath makes for the stairs.

Edward waits at the bottom step, a one-man barricade.

Heath sighs. "Excuse me, Edward, I'd just like to—"

"I'm sorry, just let me say that I wanted to warn you, but I hadn't the chance before the party started and then I forgot. I wasn't entirely sure he would come, given everything that happened between the two of you."

"Believe me, I am as surprised to see his face in this house as you are." Heath tries again to press past, but Edward stops him.

"Just listen a moment, will you? He'd like to talk to you. He came here to see you as much as for the party. He feels awful, Heath," Edward insists.

"I don't much want to hear what he has to say," Heath mumbles as he shakes his head. "I don't want to give him the opportunity to hurt me again." He doesn't let Edward stop him this time. He pushes roughly past his grip and takes the stairs two at a time. He throws open his bedroom door and rushes inside, shutting it firmly behind him. He rests his head against it, eyes closed, as he catches his breath.

"You look so handsome, you took my breath away when I walked through the door tonight."

Heath snaps his head around to find Art staring back at him from where he sits on the window seat. The window is slightly open: a soft breeze filters in and ruffles the curtains. The room is dark, save for the dim light from the bedside reading lamp that Art must have turned on.

Art runs a hand through his hair. "I don't know where to start with all the things I ought to say to you, but I think I'd best begin with an apology. I'm sorry, Heath. I'm so sorry for how I acted. I was awful, truly terrible. You didn't deserve that."

Heath folds his arms across his chest; his body trembles. "Did you come here just to tell me the things you *ought* to say, the things *I* wish to hear, or because you wanted to actually say them to me?"

"Heath." Art crosses the room to him. He stops a few paces away.

Heath presses his back against the door. Even hearing Art say his name has an indescribable effect on him; goosebumps flare on his forearms.

"I'm sorry. I panicked. I thought I'd lost everything that was important to me. But when I did lose everything that was important to me, it was entirely through my own brutish actions." Art tentatively takes a step closer, and another, until he can wrap his hands around Heath's biceps. "There's more to life than clubs and investors and concocting new ways to hustle liquor into a barbershop. You taught me that. And I'm sorry that I let myself forget it when things got tough."

Heath wants to be resolute; he's almost angry with himself for melting a little under Art's touch, for letting his heart feel a little warmer from his words. He shouldn't forgive so fast, not after all the hurt Art caused him, but the only thing more powerful than the hurt is the love that he stills feels.

"I shouldn't have let you," Heath says finally. "I should have fought harder, pounded on your door until you had to let me in. Anything so you couldn't have pushed me away."

Art chuckles and pulls Heath against his chest. "I'm afraid it mightn't have done much good. I'm terribly stubborn when I want to be."

Heath sighs and tucks his face into the crook of Art's neck. "I'm well aware." He presses a kiss to the skin there and closes his eyes as he savors the familiar scent of Art's cologne and the smoothness of his skin.

Art's hand cups the back of his neck. "After Uncle TJ died, everything that became dear or precious to me was all under one roof. The club, yes; but also the people in it. And then you came along."

Heath smiles and rubs his thumb over the side of Art's neck.

"With your little bashful smile and your affinity for the dullest of drinks—"

Heath's noise of protest is ignored.

"And a wide-eyed wonder that I'd seen before but never found so endearing. And you were in the club, but you took me out of it, too. You reminded me of the world outside of the club. One I knew existed but seemed to have forgotten how to be a part of. I realized this a long time ago, but it took me far longer to realize that losing the club didn't mean losing you. That it *shouldn't*. I shouldn't let it."

Art's hand cups Heath's jaw and tilts his face up to him. His eyes are warm even in the dim light, and his eyelashes flutter as he bends his head. Art's lips are cool and taste of champagne and send fire racing through Heath's bloodstream.

"I'm sorry, Heath," Art murmurs. "For not realizing sooner that the best thing that ever happened to me wasn't a basement in Midtown but a living, breathing person whose feelings I hurt."

They rest their foreheads together. The room is quiet save for the sound of their breathing and the muted noises of the party below.

"You shouldn't be here," Heath says finally and pulls back a little. "I can't let my father see you."

Art frowns but doesn't push the topic; he just nods as he slides his hands down Heath's sides and rests them on his waist. "I know you can't leave yet, but will you come to my house? When you can slip away?"

Heath presses a fierce kiss to Art's lips in a promise. "I will. An hour or two, at most. I can tell them I'm taking Ginny home."

Art cocks his head in confusion and the expression is knitted into the frown lines in his forehead.

"I'll explain later." Heath fixes Art's bow tie before he removes his hands from him entirely. "Say goodbye to Edward, but try not to pass my father if you can help it."

With a nod, Art reaches for his hand and kisses the back of it. "I'll see you in a couple of hours, baby. Don't keep me waiting too long," he teases, before he slips out of the room.

Heath waits a few minutes before he follows downstairs. Edward and Amelia are near the door, no doubt having just said goodbye to Art. Heath catches Edward's gaze and feels his cheeks turn a little red.

"I'd hate to say I told you so, but…" Edward whispers as he passes by to find Ginny.

Heath pinches his arm in retaliation. He half expects to find Ginny completely jazzed on too many glasses of champagne, but instead she is sitting, just as she'd said, next to the food, flirting shamelessly with one of the extra kitchen hands hired for the evening.

"Darling," Heath says with mock outrage as he finds her and rests a hand over the middle of her back. "Have you tired of me so quickly?"

Ginny giggles and waves the kitchen hand away. "Your mood has improved," she comments with a raised eyebrow. "Am I to take it that you and your beau have, perhaps, had a reconciliation?"

Heath cannot stop the grin that stretches over his lips before he settles into a seat next to her with a sigh. "I'm not being a fool, am I?

To forgive so easily?" He had confessed the whole messy situation to Ginny one evening over mint juleps and cigarettes.

She props her chin in her hand. "Aren't we all fools when it comes to love? It is no bad thing, I think." She swipes two more glasses of champagne as a server comes past. "So, am I to claim a migraine in an hour's time so you may slip off to see your lover?"

Heath bats his eyelashes. "If you would be so kind," he purrs. They turn from their conversation to listen to the Duke give a speech.

The room toasts the soon-to-be happy couple. Heath and Ginny toast to love.

Y

ART'S HOUSE IS ALMOST UNRECOGNIZABLE when Heath arrives there later that night. Where before all the furniture had been covered and the inside of the house was dismal and uninhabited, it is now alive. There's even a mark left in the cushion on the armchair where Art must have been sitting.

Art looks around with a bashful smile. "As I said, you taught me that there are more things to care about in this life. It was high time I stopped living as though in a mausoleum. I haven't hired a housekeeper yet, but I thought Martha might be able to suggest someone."

Heath slips off his jacket and hangs it by the door before toeing off his shoes. "I'll ask her tomorrow," he promises.

"Oh?" Art's arms slip around his waist from behind and his lips find the side of his neck. "Tomorrow, hmm? How presumptuous of you, to invite yourself for the night."

"You bring me over here late at night and I should have to think how to get home, still?" Heath teases and tilts his head to one side to allow Art more room to trail his lips over the curve of his neck down to the juncture with his shoulder. "Besides, we have a lot to talk about, I think."

They do talk, though Heath thinks he could quite happily put the talking out of his mind while he reacquaints himself with the taste of Art's lips and the feel of his hands. Heath tells him of all that happened with his father, of the deal he seems to have struck with him, right up to his meeting with Frankie earlier in the day and the uncertainty it seeded in his consciousness.

Art doesn't express his own opinion, or talk much at all until much later into the night, when they lie in bed together. Heath's head is pillowed against Art's chest; their hands are entwined over his heart. A thin sheet is thrown over them, but Heath's toes poke out of the end. Shivers run down his spine when the breeze from the open window tickles them.

"Have you thought about what you might like to do next?" Heath asks. His breath skitters out warmly over Art's bare chest.

"Well." Art runs his fingers down the curve of Heath's spine with the arm he has wrapped around him. "I had thought perhaps I might go into stocks and shares."

Heath snorts and sniggers into Art's chest. "Be serious," he chastises when he recovers from his laughter.

"I don't know. Ideally, I would set up someplace new, but I don't have the capital since everything from TJ was seized. There may still be some liquor hidden that I could recover, but even if I sold it, it wouldn't be enough."

"I do," Heath says quietly, before he tilts his head up to him. "I have the capital. I could fund it. We could set up together."

Art frowns. "Wouldn't your parents notice if you were to suddenly make use of that much money? With no explanation as to where it is going?"

Heath swallows, playing over an idea that had formed shakily in his head after he saw Frankie, since Art walked through that door and possibly longer without him being fully conscious of it. "Maybe it's time I was honest. Tell them that I don't want to marry Ginny or work with my father. Let the pieces fall where they may."

"You would do that?"

"If it meant being with you, I would do anything." Heath sits up and the sheets fall to pool around his waist. "I know what I want, now. And it's you and whatever a future with you brings."

Y

THE REALITY IS FAR MORE terrifying than it seemed when it was just words, spoken under the cover of darkness, between Heath and Art. Art accompanies him, because Heath is not sure he won't buckle if he doesn't have him by his side. Heath can tell Art is scared, too.

Heath steps in first, though; he leaves Art to hover in the hallway as he walks into the dining room where his family is eating breakfast.

"There you are!" the Duchess exclaims. "We were terribly worried, Heath. You couldn't have called from Ginny's house to tell us you were spending the night? Not that it's entirely proper, but I suppose they have a guest bedroom." She motions for him to sit down.

Heath swallows around the lump in his throat and turns to Amelia, keen to speak to her in case he is thrown from the house when this is through. "Amelia, I'm so sorry for leaving early. I trust you had a good evening?"

Amelia stifles a yawn and nods. She looks tired but content as she swirls coffee in a cup. The ring on her finger sparkles in the morning sun. "I did, thank you. And you needn't apologize, I would hardly have noticed you were gone, what with all the hullabaloo, if Mama hadn't been fussing about it before she went to bed."

"In future, Heath, a phone call would be advisable, if you make spontaneous decisions such as that," the Duke adds, although he looks somewhat pleased to be chastising him for staying out all night with his girl, rather than for something else.

It would be so easy for Heath to sit down with them. To gesture for Art to leave and to act as though nothing had changed. To continue in a charade he plays so well it is second nature. But that wouldn't be fair to Art and it wouldn't be fair to him, either.

"Actually, I wasn't with Ginny." Heath braces his hands on the back of the chair to give him some support as he addresses his family. "I escorted her home, of course, as it was late. But then I spent the night with someone rather more important to me."

He feels Art step in behind him and offer a murmured greeting. The Duchess's spoon hits her bowl with a clink. Three sets of eyes are fixed on the two of them. His mother and sister look confused; the Duke is livid.

"Arthur, isn't it?" The Duchess recovers herself and sets her spoon down more neatly. "You may spend the night at a friend's house; we only ask that you tell us so we needn't worry about you."

Whether the Duchess is deliberately being naive or not, Heath isn't sure. He can tell from Amelia's silence, however, and the way she looks at them, that she has filled in the gaps that Heath has thus far left open.

"He's a little more than a friend, I suppose." Heath manages to keep his voice steady as he slips his hand through Art's. "I'm in love with him. I understand that I will have to hide it from most of the world for our safety, but I won't hide it from you any longer. No matter what you may feel about me, you are my family and I care about you dearly."

Art squeezes his hand. The room is silent, just the dull tick-tock of the grandfather clock in the hallway floats through.

Finally, the Duke sighs and puts down his napkin on the table with a thud of his fist. "I gave you a chance. A fine job, a fresh start from your summer of foolishness and playing around with…" He trails off as he gestures at them. "Whatever *this* is. I won't give you another. Either he leaves and we forget all about this, or you both do. Now."

The Duchess looks pale as she glances between her husband and Heath. "You knew about this?" She murmurs.

The Duke sniffs. "I thought it had been taken care of." He stares at Heath. "Well? What is your decision? Think very carefully about this, Heath."

Tears pool in the corner of Heath's eyes, and he blinks them back. He knew this was the likely outcome, and that it would probably be the last time he would be allowed in this house. But even that knowledge couldn't have prepared him for the sting that he feels. "I shall pack a few things and be gone."

The Duchess sobs as Heath walks toward the stairs.

"Wait outside," he whispers to Art, who nods and slips out the front door. He can hear the raised voice of the Duke as he hastily stuffs some clothes and a few books into his travel bag. It isn't everything, but it's enough, and he takes the stairs two at a time down to the hallway.

He hesitates before he glances into the living room. The room is silent: The Duchess weeps quietly as she stares at the Duke, who has returned to his breakfast as though nothing out of the ordinary has occurred.

Heath steps into the room, hoping that he may at least bid his mother and sister a proper farewell, but the Duke doesn't let him get that far.

"I asked you to leave."

"*William.* He's still our son," the Duchess begs, but Heath knows better than to push his father's temper any further today.

He turns toward the door. Each footstep sounds deafening to his ears as he walks toward the door.

"Heath!" Amelia comes flying after him, and he turns just in time to catch her in a fierce hug. "I don't care what Father thinks, you'll always be my big brother. Nothing you do could change that or make me care for you any less," she whispers as she squeezes him.

Her tears soak the shoulder of his shirt, and he buries a kiss in her hair. "Edward will know where to find me. Don't be a stranger."

Amelia smiles as she pulls back; her eyes are wet as she kisses his cheek. "Be safe," she tells him before she moves forward to open the door for him. She looks down to where Art stands at the bottom of the steps. "As for you—be good to him."

Art offers a hand to Heath as he comes down the steps. "I will. I promise."

Heath looks back at the house with his hand tucked into Art's.

"Come," Art murmurs. "Let's go home."

EPILOGUE

Three Months Later

Heath likes the sounds of the early morning. He likes the way the stairs creak beneath his feet as he makes his way down and the sound of the paperboy doing his rounds on Lexington. He likes that a snippet of whatever song was playing the night before comes to his mind. Most of all, he likes the sound of Art's voice from the dining room, coaxing him in for breakfast.

"Good morning," Betsy greets Heath brightly as she emerges from the dining room with a stack of folded laundry in her arms. "There's coffee on the table." She's little older than he is, Martha's niece: a sweet and understanding girl who bakes the best pies he's ever tasted.

"Thank you," Heath murmurs with a smile, in a voice still thick with sleep. He pads into the dining room, dressed in light-colored pants and an undershirt with a sweater pulled on to fight the morning chill. He'll dress properly before they leave for the day and he'll smarten his hair, too, where it currently resembles a crow's nest on top of his head.

He kisses Art's temple as he walks past to sit by his side. "You woke early again," he comments, pouring himself some coffee. "Is everything all right?"

Art kisses his mouth. "Now it is." He grins. "A letter came for you. From Italy this time, or so says the postmark."

Heath takes the envelope and tears into it as Art drags his chair closer to read over his shoulder.

Heathcliff—

I have little news to add from my last report—a letter had arrived from the south of France not five days ago—*but as I sit in this fine hotel I thought it only appropriate to write to you once again.*

I am thrilled to report that it is raining once again. How much of my travels seem to be taken with rain—perhaps going somewhere in the Southern Hemisphere would have been a far better use of my time. But, no, I mustn't complain so. It is still beautiful here (and the women even more so, not that I suppose you care much about all that).

The Italians have many a fine drink—you should speak to your mister about concocting a few Italian-inspired drinks for your new establishment, once it's up and running. I did see if I could send a bottle or two of their fine Amaretto as a gift but I fear it will not make the journey without someone pinching it. I shall attempt to collect some on my way back to America next year—and not drink it all on my travels—so that you may try it.

The Italians sport fine mustaches, too—I have taken to growing one myself.

Heath grimaces and rubs a hand over his own smooth jaw.

I think it looks rather fetching, if I do say so myself.

My best regards to Art in the meantime; and to Julian and Alfie, also. How funny that those two have ended up as close as they have, but I'm sure the additional help in putting the place together has been useful.

Don't lose hope over your family. I don't doubt Amelia's powers of persuasion—if she says she will have them visit you before the wedding, I think she may well do just that. Or God help them.

All the best,

Frankie.

Heath folds the letter closed and slips it back into the envelope.

"He's right, you know." Art's tone is soft but the brush of his breath against Heath's ear still makes him shiver. "About your family."

Heath nods and sets the envelope down. "I know." A vase on the table is filled with peach-toned carnations. Every year on the Duchess's birthday, Heath and Amelia would walk to the florist on Fifty-eighth and Sixth Avenue to buy a bouquet of carnations, from the time they were children and the Duke came with them to supervise and shuffle the money from his wallet to Heath's hand to the cashier, and right up until last year.

He touches the delicate petals before he puts the envelope down by the vase. Art's arm is strong and grounding around his back, and Heath turns to him, thanking him with the press of his lips.

"Don't be minding me." Betsy bustles in with the morning newspaper for Art and some fresh toast for Heath. Her cheeks are a little pink, but it is out of a fondness for the two of them more than anything else.

Art straightens and stands. "We should be going. Work to be done."

Heath looks forlornly at his breakfast, snags a piece of toast and then makes for the stairs again.

"IF I HAD KNOWN THE amount of manual labor this little enterprise was going to entail, I'm not sure I would have volunteered so willingly." Heath huffs and wipes a hand over his brow as he hauls the last of the wooden panels in place to make up the bar.

Art walks through the door shouldering three of the dozen chairs they'd managed to salvage from TJ without drawing any attention. "As I recall, I did *offer* to do all the heavy lifting, and your response was to tell me that you are just as capable of carrying a few things around as I am. Even if you don't have the—what was it? Ah, yes—the *physique* to prove it."

Heath narrows his eyes and plonks himself down onto his knees to beginning nailing the last slat down. "Well, I am, aren't I? Point proven. And now perhaps I can go back to doing something less taxing... like the accounts." He lines up the nail and barely misses swinging the hammer right onto his thumb.

"Careful, baby," Art murmurs and leans down to kiss the top of his head. "Come now. Take a break from all that, I can finish the bar in just a moment."

Heath looks up as Art studies the clock on the wall. "I wouldn't worry; you know Alfie has no sense of time. I'm sure he's on his way."

Art sighs. Alfie is due to bring around the remaining liquor from TJ this afternoon, with Julian's assistance. Heath and Art didn't want to arouse suspicion by going back too many times. "He had a sense of time, once. Before Julian."

Heath smiles wryly. "Oh, let them be," he chastises playfully. He smooths the curve of Art's broad shoulders and moves his hands around to his front. Through Art's thin shirt, Heath can feel the bump of his grandmother's silver ring, which hangs on a simple chain around Art's neck.

Art presses his hand over Heath's and laces their fingers together. "You don't suppose we could—"

His thought is cut off at the sound of footsteps tip-tapping toward the door. Amelia's head rounds the corner.

"Amelia!" Heath exclaims, going to greet her.

"Heath, I have wonderful news," she gushes, her cheeks aglow.

Heath raises an eyebrow. "Are you...?" He glances at her stomach.

"No! Heath, honestly! That would be wildly inappropriate, we're not married yet," she giggles and bats at him.

Before she can explain her wonderful news, however, a second body appears behind her. The Duchess surveys the space with her bag clutched tightly to her chest before she sighs heavily. "Honestly, Heath, there's a fine layer of dust coating this entire place. I'd suggest a broom."

Heath holds back the choking sob that threatens to overtake him as he leaps forward to hug his mother, whom he hasn't seen since the day he left the house. "Mama. It's so lovely to see you."

The Duchess smiles into his cheek and presses a kiss there. "And you, my darling. I am only sorry it took me so long."

Heath doesn't want to let her go, but he allows her to pull back from the embrace a moment later. She holds his face in her hands and studies his appearance. Her eyes shine softly. "You look well, darling. You look so happy."

He takes her hands. "I am. I truly am." He squeezes her hands. "And you're well?" He hesitates. "And Father?"

She nods. "We are." She touches her hands to his chest. "He knows I'm here, but he wouldn't—"

Heath shakes his head. "It's not your fault," he assures her and kisses her cheek.

She turns from him to Art. "I suppose a drink is out of the question, bartender?"

Heath blushes. "Mama, he's not just a bartender."

"Not just a bartender. You're too handsome to be just a bartender."

Heath tries his best to hide his flaming cheeks in his hands.

More footsteps and Alfie clatters in, heaving a crate in his arms. Julian, behind him, has a second crate in his arms.

"Did someone call for a drink?" Alfie grins and rattles the crate.

"Mrs. Johnson!" Julian exclaims, his eyes widening.

The Duchess waves an arm and settles herself delicately on one of the chairs, as though it may fall apart under her at any moment. "You needn't look at me like that; I won't tell your mother a thing."

Julian visibly relaxes and goes to help Alfie fix a round of drinks.

"So, does this little establishment of yours have a name?" The Duchess asks.

"No, Mrs. Johnson, not yet." Art sets a glass down in front of her as the other drinks are handed out.

Heath slips a hand into his pants pocket, where the piece of paper he took from TJ has been stored for the past couple of days. *The Rules of TJ.* "I had an idea about that, actually," he announces. He removes the paper and unfolds it over his thigh, smoothing out the creases.

A murmur of assent goes around the party as everyone reads the words on the page to themselves in hushed voices. Art says nothing, but a smile twitches at the corners of his mouth.

"What do you think?" Heath asks him.

"I have no objections. My ego certainly doesn't, either." Art's eyes crinkle at the corners as he laughs.

"Well, then, it's settled." Heath raises his glass and the others do the same. "In Art We Trust."

The group echoes. "In Art We Trust."

GLOSSARY

applesauce—nonsense

balled up—confused, messed up

bank's closed—no kissing or making out

bent, blind—drunk

bootleg—illegal liquor

butt me—to ask for a cigarette

cake-eater—a lady's man

cash—a kiss

cash or check?—shall we kiss now or later?

check—kiss me later

coffin varnish—poor quality illegal liquor, often poisonous

drugstore cowboy—well-dressed man who loiters in public areas trying to pick up women

drum—speakeasy

egg—someone who lives the big life

fire extinguisher—a chaperone

get a wiggle on—get a move on

giggle water—alcohol

goofy—in love

handcuff—engagement ring

hoary-eyed—drunk

Indian hop—marijuana

insured—engaged

juice joint—speakeasy

manacle—wedding ring

moonshine—homemade whiskey

munitions—face powder

Oliver Twist—a skilled dancer

ossified—drunk

phonus balonus—nonsense

pinched—to be arrested

putting on the ritz—doing something in high style

speakeasy—a bar selling illegal liquor during the prohibition

three-letter man—homosexual

to go see a man about a dog—to leave to buy liquor

vamp—a flirtatious woman, seducer of men

zozzled—drunk

ACKNOWLEDGMENTS

THIS BOOK SPRUNG FROM TWO completely unrelated things: a need to romanticize New York City in the Jazz Age and Jack Falahee, who became Heath before I'd even really figured out who Heath was. It's grown legs, feet and a bit of an attitude since then but it wouldn't feel right to start by thanking anything else.

Thanks to the entire team at Interlude Press—Annie, Candy, CB and Lex—for the faith you've had in me and all the things I've learned from you in the past year and a half. To Colin Moore for the beautiful cover art. I definitely lucked out in becoming a part of this family.

To my mother, for being both my harshest critic and my most loyal fan. To my father, for teaching me the phrase "let me just finish this sentence" which I use almost as much as he does now. To my brothers, for sparking a lifelong love for cocktails and teaching me that mojitos are delicious and vodka martinis really aren't. To the little ones, whose boundless energy keeps me going. And to all the rest of my ever-growing family, of which there are far too many of you to name.

To my Edinburgh girls—Hannah, Kirsten, Faith, Emily, Rosie, Kay and Emma—who keep me grounded and fuel my brunch-and-takeout addiction. To the internet contingent—Janine, Isabelle, Ellie, Alice, McCall and Valerie—for your encouragement, support, and the fact that you express excitement in capital letters interlaced with random punctuation. I truly adore you all.

To Sebastian Stan for having one of those faces I always want to write a character for—hit me up and let's talk about making a movie. To the baristas at my local Starbucks for keeping me caffeinated and always asking what I'm writing. To Zayn Malik, for providing me with more than enough emotional turmoil throughout the course of 2015 to help me write the painful scenes in this book. To Chuck, my old laptop, that well and truly gave up halfway through writing the first draft.

Last, but certainly not least, to that Amaretto Sour on a summer's evening.

About The Author

Suzey Ingold is a writer, linguist and coffee addict, currently based in Edinburgh, Scotland. Brought up in a household where children's books are quoted over the dinner table, literature has always had a strong influence on her life. She enjoys traveling, scented candles and brunch. Her short story, "The Willow Weeps for Us," was included in *Summer Love: An LGBTQ Collection*, published by Duet, an imprint of Interlude Press (2015).

*For a reader's guide to Speakeasy and book club prompts,
please visit interludepress.com*

interlude press
you may also like...

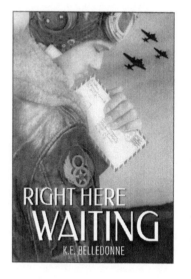

Right Here Waiting
by K.E. Belledonne

In 1942, Ben Williams had it all—a fulfilling job, adoring friends and the love of his life, Pete Montgomery. But World War II looms over them. When Pete follows his conscience and joins the Army Air Force as a bomber pilot, Ben must find the strength to stay behind without his lover, the dedication to stay true and the courage he never knew he'd need to discover his own place in the war effort.

ISBN 978-1-941530-22-1

Something Like a Love Song
by Becca Burton

trauma, the young lovers turn to a network of family and friends as they attempt to rebuild their lives. Can their one constant—their love—survive the changes both undergo on the road to recovery?

ISBN 978-1-941530-49-8

interlude ✦ press
now available...

Lodestones by Naomi MacKenzie

On the eve of a new school year, several groups of college students cross paths as they seek out a secret end-of-summer lake party—including Robin and Charlie, two inseparable friends who discover of the course of the twenty-four hours that their relationship is something much deeper than simple friendship.

ISBN 978-1-941530-37-5

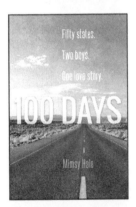

100 Days by Mimsy Hale

Jake and Aiden have been friends since childhood. Now 22-year-old college grads, they take a road trip across the United States, visiting all fifty states. A love story about two boys, an RV and a country full of highways, 100 Days crisscrosses America as Jake and Aiden learn that their futures aren't as carefully mapped as they once thought, and that the road has a funny way of changing course.

ISBN 978-1-941530-23-8

Sotto Voce by Erin Finnegan

Wine critic Thomas Baldwin can make or break careers with his column for Taste Magazine. But when his publisher orders him to spend a year profiling rising stars of California's wine country and organizing a competition between the big name wineries of Napa and the smaller artisan wineries of Sonoma, his world gets turned upside-down by an enigmatic young winemaker who puts art before business.

ISBN 978-1-941530-15-3

interlude press

One **story**

can change

everything.

interlude**press**.com

CPSIA information can be obtained
at www.ICGtesting.com
Printed in the USA
LVOW12s0956150516

488338LV00002B/358/P